GRID DOWN

PERCEPTIONS OF REALITY
VOLUME 2 PART 2

WITHDRAWN

BRUCE
BUCKSHOT HEMMING

D0169871

This is a work of fiction. Names, characters, places, and incidents are products of the author's imagination or are used fictitiously and are not to be construed as real. Any resemblance to actual events, locales, organizations, or persons, living or dead, is entirely coincidental.

This is a fictional book. No tactics or technique are recommended without proper safety training from a qualified expert. Do not attempt anything in this book, as it may result in personal injury or harm. The authors or publisher assume no liability for your actions.

2

Grid Down – Perceptions of Reality

Volume 2 Part 2

By

Bruce "Buckshot" Hemming

3

This book was finished with the help of several people and I would like to take the time to thank everyone.

Huge thank you to Doctor Terence Young for his professional help in writing the wound treatment chapter.

Albert Hall Co-editor whose attention to detail and hard work makes this a great book to read.

The final editor for the finishing polish.

Dawn Smith for another outstanding cover.
http://www.darkdawncreations.com

The Backwoodsman magazine for helping with chicken manure gunpowder recipe.

http://www.backwoodsmanmag.com/

And of course everyone else that help with their tips on survival.

The reader bears all responsibility associated with the use of the information contained in this book, including those risks associated with reliance of the accuracy, thoroughness or appropriateness of the information for any situation represented.

The authors and publishers specifically disclaim all responsibility from any prosecution or proceedings brought or instituted against any person or body for any liability, loss, or risk, personal or otherwise, which is incurred as a consequence of the use or misuse and application of any of the contents of this book.

Other books from the author:

Grid Down Reality Bites

Gird Down Perceptions of Reality Part 1

The Rabid Mind

Table of Contents

Grid Down Volume 2 Part 2 - Perceptions of Reality

America once a thriving and prosperous nation, now an empty decaying wasteland—everything changed in the blink of an eye. In Grid Down Reality Bites, a high-altitude nuclear blast causing an EMP (electrical magnetic pulse) destroys the power grid, catapulting life as they knew it, back to the 1800's. The saga continues in Grid Down Perceptions of Reality (volume 2, part 2), A small band of survivors desperately struggle to survive the chaos that ensues. Now a post-apocalyptic world, they must rely on their primal instincts to escape destruction, disease and death. In this book, the story of **Grid Down** continues, following Clint and Junior with their small band of survivors.

When we last left Clint and Junior, both suffering gunshot wounds while trying to escape after an attack on a group of Rainbow Warriors (Grid Down Reality Bites, Chapter 37).

Chapter 1

The Long Way Home

Junior became aware that he was cold and shivering. His left shoulder ached like nothing he'd ever felt before. He could feel a soft, chilly breeze caressing his face, like fingers of ice. He must be outside. He automatically reached out with his good arm for the sleeping bag to block the wind and warm himself up. He had slept outdoors so much that it seemed perfectly natural for him to be sleeping on the ground like this. His hand groped around, trying to find the top to the sleeping bag.

It took a few moments of fruitless searching before he became aware that he was lying on the ground with his backpack still on. Something inside it was digging painfully into his lower back, and a few other places as well. Maybe that was why his shoulder was aching so much. Was something inside the backpack sticking him in the shoulder? Did he fall down somehow, or trip over something? He slowly opened his eyes and saw it was pitch black, wherever he looked. There was no moon or stars in the sky. It must be a very cloudy night then. He tried to remember what he was doing outside as he shifted his body a little to ease the pain in his shoulder. Red-hot pain shot through him, radiating out from his left shoulder and making him stop all movement abruptly. It hurt so much he could only take slow, shallow, panting breaths as the darkness came for him again.

Junior slowly became conscious again. He was still lying on the ground. He was acutely aware of the pain in his left shoulder. He was shivering and each movement caused an unbelievable amount of pain to shoot out from his shoulder. He felt hot and cold at the same time. He licked his dry, parched lips and could taste the blood that welled up in the cracks. He was very thirsty. His throat was completely dry. He tried to swallow, to wash the taste of blood off his tongue, but it stuck in his throat, causing him to cough a little. That sent more pain radiating out from his shoulder, making him moan loudly in his misery. He was afraid that he would pass out again. He opened his eyes and remembered waking up like this before. It was still pitch black. He looked around, trying to make sense of the inky shadows of darkness. He tried to remember what had happened. Why was his shoulder hurting so much? Where was Clint?

He slowly remembered bits and pieces of the battle, trying to make sense out of those strange nightmarish scenes running through his mind. In the next instant, he remembered everything. He had been shot. That was why his shoulder hurt so much. He cautiously probed his left shoulder with his right hand, trying to see if he could feel how bad the wound was. He had a thick battle dressing on. He thought he could feel a bandage on his back, too. That would be a good thing. Hopefully the bullet passed completely through. He slowly moved an inch at a time and tried to sit up. Moving made his head very dizzy and he really hoped he didn't pass out again.

It took him several minutes, but he was able to get into a half sitting position. He scooted over to lean his good side against a tree trunk so he could rest for a minute and clear his head. He panted hard, like he had just run twenty miles as he tried to get the pain in his shoulder under control. He kept saying over and over again, like a nineteen sixties hippie mantra, 'Mind over matter.' When the pain had eased a little, he groped around with his good hand, found the nipple for his Camelbak water container and sucked down a long drink. God that tasted so good. His head was clearing up a little and he could finally think more clearly.

When he had his breathing under control and wasn't panting like a dog anymore, he slowly reached into his pocket and pulled out a small blue LED light. He couldn't see far with it, but maybe he could get some idea where he was. He didn't recognize anything. The best thing he could do was wait for daybreak. Maybe Clint would be back then. He leaned his head back and closed his eyes.

Daybreak came slowly, but Clint still hadn't returned. That meant that Clint had to be dead or injured. Junior slowly ate a power bar and drank a lot of water, thinking about his next move. There were creeks and streams all around here in the woods. He just had to find one and follow it north and it would lead him towards the house.

He used the tree to help him stand up. Scanning the area, he spotted Clint's rifle sticking out over by a log. The foremost thought in his mind was that Clint needed him to do this and he was determined to not let him down. He crawled over to the log and peered over. Clint was lying in an awkward heap on the ground. He slowly turned Clint over and checked if he was still breathing. He was and Junior let out the breath he had been holding in a relieved whoosh of sound. There was hope. Now he had to find help.

He looked around for a branch to help him walk and saw one a few feet away that just might work. He grabbed the branch and tested it out. As soon as he could, he started walking, concentrating on putting one foot in front of the other.

* * * * * *

Katlin was walking aimlessly in the woods, not far from the road. She had taken to doing this daily to just get away for a short while. She needed to feel her own pain and grief without anyone else around. She was armed with her 9mm carbine and a nice sharp hunting knife, in case any of the enemy was still around. They had better not run into her. The way she felt right now was not very merciful or caring. They had taken the second man she had loved, just as the first man had been taken from her. Was she cursed to live her life alone? It sure felt that way right now. If she was cursed, was she responsible for what had happened? Was her presence enough to bring this on them?

She couldn't stand to think that she had caused Clint any harm. She had loved him deeply and fiercely, almost from the very first time she had seen him. It had hit her very fast and hard, like an arrow straight to her heart. It had felt like it was meant to be, almost like she had been waiting for him or something corny like that. She sighed and tears welled up in her eyes again, blurring her vision. She had already cried so many tears and probably would cry over this lost love for the rest of her life.

Robbie had taken all of this in a very strange way and a lot harder than she thought. Just this morning he had yelled at her to stop saying they were dead and to go out and look for them. They probably needed her help and she was just staying there and letting them die for real. She had lost it when he said that and had grabbed her coat and rifle and run outside, trying to get away from his hateful and accusing words.

What would make him say something like that to her? She didn't understand his determination that they were out there somewhere, needing her help. Oh, she understood the psychology of his reaction, but Robbie had always been such an intelligent, caring child. For him to blame her totally confused and bewildered her. How did she deal with that kind of thing? How did she make him understand that she was not to blame for them dying? She wiped the tears off her cheeks and took a deep breath, letting it out slowly. She needed to get some sort of control of her emotions so she could figure out a way to help Robbie. Crying wasn't going to give her the answers she needed. She prayed for guidance and strength so she could help her troubled, grief filled son.

She walked and thought for a long time before she realized she had strayed into unfamiliar territory. She stopped and looked around, wondering where she was. She had lost sight of the road. She had never come this way or this far before and had to look up at the sun to get her bearings. She turned around to go back before she got lost, but hadn't gone far when a feeling overcame her that she had to turn around and go farther yet, that she hadn't found what she was looking for. She shook her head, trying to get control of her emotions. What on earth had put that kind of a thought in her mind? Was Robbie's obsession rubbing off on her, too? She had to get control of herself right now. Was this what it was like to lose her mind?

No matter what she told herself, she couldn't quite convince herself to go on back to the house. Well, she reasoned, even if she were losing her mind, what would it hurt to go a little further? Then she would know for sure and hopefully find out why she had these feelings and fanciful thoughts. She sighed and realized she was probably delusional from grief, but what the hell. She could go on a little further and prove to herself that she was just chasing rainbows or whatever. This was totally not like her at all. She had always prided herself on being reasonable and practical, but the feeling would not go away.

She squared her shoulders and straightened her back, walking on further. She was confident that it was just a waste of time, but it wasn't as though she had any important appointments that she would be missing or anything of that nature. It was just some time that would be wasted and she had plenty of that. She scrutinized the area around her as she walked and, after about ten minutes, she saw something lying on the ground by some brush ahead of her. It looked like a person's legs. She cautiously crept up on the brush and slowly separated it, revealing a man lying underneath. Unable to tell if he was alive or dead, she kicked his foot with her boot. He moved like a rag doll, his limbs rolling loosely with the kick. His expression never changed as far as she could tell.

She pulled out her knife, leaned her rifle against a tree trunk and bent down a few feet back from him, to be as far out of reach as possible in case it was some kind of trick. She turned him over as much as she could and grimaced. The man was filthy. It looked like he had rolled around in the mud – he had leaves and debris stuck to his face and hair. She turned him a little more to get a good look at him and her heart almost jumped out of her chest in recognition. A breath caught in her throat, almost choking her. *Oh my, God, it's Junior*, she thought in total amazement.

She felt for a pulse and found it, weak but steady. She looked all around, trying to see if Clint was with him, but they were alone. She pulled the backpack off him and examined him closely. His shoulder had been bandaged and he also had a bandage on his back. He had obviously been shot.

There was nothing she could do without supplies, so she dragged him back into the brush and laid him down gently. Looking through his backpack, she found his poncho and covered him up. She quickly pulled off her coat and outer shirt, taking off the t-shirt she had on underneath. Quickly getting dressed again, she used her knife to cut her t-shirt into strips so she could mark the trail and be able to find him again quickly.

With a last glance at his unconscious form, she grabbed her rifle and took off running, stopping every few hundred yards and marking the trail back to him. She had to find someone to help her bring him home and she needed a few people to look for Clint. Hope and astonishment burned in her chest. Clint could be alive out here somewhere too.

Chapter 2

Clint and Junior

Katlin made it to the road and tied off her last piece of cloth, marking the spot to enter the woods. She raced for the cabin and burst through the door, her mind running faster than her mouth. She yelled out, "Quick, Junior needs help, medical surgery. Robbie and Gayle, get your stuff on." Both Robbie and Gayle had jumped to their feet and stood there looking at her.

Gayle asked, "What are you talking about? You found Junior and he's alive?"

Katlin didn't waste time explaining, "Robbie, go get help. We need men and a wagon. Junior is alive, but he's badly hurt. Gayle, don't just stand there! Let's go!"

Gayle replied, "Calm down. You have to tell Robbie where he's going and where to meet us." Then what Katlin had said hit her like a ton of bricks, the fact that Junior was alive. She became weak in the knees and her head started spinning.

"He's alive! My God, we have to go," she yelled, as she raced off to grab her coat.

She stopped and turned around, "Wait, what about Clint?"

Katlin shook her head no, unable to speak the words.

"Robbie, go tell them to meet us one mile down the road from here, and please hurry."

Robbie was off like a flash. Gayle and Katlin hurried down the road, talking a mile a minute. "How in the world did you find him?" Gayle asked, still trying to make sense of it.

"It was just luck." Katlin admitted. "I wandered the right way."

Even in the dark, they made it to the spot using their LED flashlight. They paced the road while waiting for the others. Gayle finally couldn't stand it anymore. "I am going to Junior; you wait for them here." She left, without waiting for a reply.

"Don't get lost." Katlin yelled as Gayle's light disappeared in the night.

"Come on guys, what is taking so damn long?" Katlin muttered to herself. *"Get here already. He needs medical attention now."* Finally she could hear voices and a wagon coming.

Gayle stumbled through the dark, finding the rag strips one at time, but it seemed to take forever. She wanted to run to him and was on the verge of losing it. "Junior where are you?" She screamed, her voice echoing off the trees. She paused to listen, holding her breath and straining her ears. Nothing. There was not a sound, other than a light breeze moving the tree branches.

She shone her light forward, walking slowly as she looked for each next strip of cloth. Once she spotted it, she would race to it, stop and scream out again, "Junior where are you?" She waited and listened, but there was still no reply.

Finally she came up to the last piece and saw a lump lying on the ground. It was Junior. She raced up to him and fell to her knees, reaching down to touch his face. It was cold. Looking closely, she could see his chest slowly rising and falling as he breathed. She cradled his head in her lap. "Hurry up Katlin! Tell me what to do!" She called back in the direction she'd come from, not knowing how far behind help was. "I should have taken a first aid course; I should know what to do." She cursed herself. "Where is everyone? Please hurry."

As soon as the men got out of the wagon, Katlin led them along the trail to Junior, carrying a stretcher between them. They asked if they should look for Clint. Katlin wanted them to so badly, but she was afraid they would trample any signs Junior left in the dark. "No." she said.

"Let's get everyone we can to track in the morning. Junior's trail should be easy to backtrack in the daylight."

They got Junior back to the cabin and laid him on the kitchen table. Katlin cleaned the wound with alcohol, carefully removing the pieces of clothing embedded in the wound. Luckily Junior was out cold, but he still moaned in pain when she hit a sensitive area.

He had lost a lot of blood. She remembered an emergency triage course she took back in college. The lecturer had told them a story of how, in a 3rd world country, an American doctor used a sugardine solution (sugar or honey and Betadine, or iodine solution, mixed into a paste) to prevent infection and promote healing for horse hoof wounds. That would be perfect for Junior's wound. They would still need to find antibiotics, but until then, the sugardine would have to do.

"Dean." Katlin said, "You know where the vet's house is. Can you go and get some Betadine?"

Dean nodded and said, "I'll go check."

"Thanks." Turning to Lenny, she asked, "Is there a pet store that sold fish and aquarium supplies anywhere near here? 'Cause if there is, I need antibiotics. They're the same antibiotics as those given to humans; they'd work for our purposes."

Lenny nodded, "Yeah, I know where one is, but its 35 miles away."

"Could you please go there and get some?"

"You bet. What are the names of the antibiotics I should be looking for?"

"Hang on and I'll write them down for you." She handed him a slip of paper with several brand names and added, "Please hurry."

"I'll be back as fast as humanly possible. I swear to God." And with that, he was gone.

"Now what?" Gayle asked.

"Now we wait and see what we can find to save his life."

Gayle said, "What, you don't know if you can save him or not?"

Katlin put her finger up to her lips and whispered, "Sshhh, follow me." Katlin began walking outside, with Gayle behind her. "Listen Gayle, I know you're upset, but Junior's subconscious mind can hear what we say. We don't want to say anything in his presence to make him think he's going to die, or he'll just give up. It looks like he is going to make it without a problem, BUT we need to pray that the antibiotic with the sugardine and fresh bandages will keep the wound clean and free of infection."

Gayle took a deep breath, "Okay, so he should make it but you're just not positive, right?"

"Yes, that's correct. We don't know how much blood he lost, or if infection has already set in. Other things can go wrong that could complicate his recovery. Right now I'm worried most about infection. The wound was a through and through, which is really good. I think he's going to be okay, but it may take a couple of months for him to get back to normal."

"A couple of months?"

"Yes, for him to be back to full strength again. That's a serious wound that must close up and heal."

As they hugged each other, Gayle said, "Thank you for being here and saving him. I would have been lost without you." She continued, "What about Clint? Do you think he's alive? Could he be hurt and Junior was trying to get here for us to go help him?"

"I don't know. Clint might be dead." Katlin said, as the tears began welling up in her eyes. She was trying to be strong for Gayle, but she couldn't think of Clint without crying; that was her weakness. It was easier thinking he was dead than to think he was lying somewhere suffering or slowly bleeding to death, with no one to help him. She said a silent prayer, *"Clint if you're alive, fight damn you! We are coming. I promise."* The tears were flooding now, like a faucet had opened. She shuddered and Gayle hugged her tight.

"Katlin, if he's alive, he's fighting. He's not the type of man to give up." Gayle reassured her. Katlin had said her prayer out loud, without even realizing it.

Dean returned with the Betadine and they set to work. There was no time to worry about Clint; it was all about saving Junior right now. That was the most important thing.

She mixed the sugar and Betadine together into a thick paste and applied it to Junior's wound, wrapping it with a sterile bandage.

Daylight finally came and the search party went out, trying to backtrack Junior's trail. By noon they had found Clint. He was still breathing and it took 4 men to carry him out and rush him to the Doc.

He had been hit in the chest, but the bullet had gone through the full magazine in his chest pouch, slowing it down. The AK-47's 7.62x39, full metal jacket bullet had still had enough power left to punch a hole and break a rib. The bullet was still in the wound, penetrating just enough to puncture the pleural space, between the ribs and lungs, causing a sucking wound, an open pneumothorax. Air was building in the pleural space so that every time Clint breathed, air got into his chest cavity and compressed the lung. It was like tightening a vise grip on the lungs, compromising his breathing. It was already slow enough to lower his respiration, but luckily not enough to kill him. It would have eventually, but they'd found him just in time.

Katlin removed the bullet first and then cleaned the wound with Betadine. Using plastic wrap to cover the wound, she taped three sides down so that when he inhaled, the wrap sucked onto the wound and no air got in. When he exhaled, the 4th side that wasn't taped down allowed any air in the chest to get out.

This relieved the pressure and allowed Clint to breath easier. He woke up, hours later, and looked around, straining his brain to figure out where he was. He remembered getting shot. Had he been captured? His eyes were having trouble focusing and it was dark in the room. He tried to sit up, but the pain in his chest was overwhelming. Who was helping him? Where was Junior? He puzzled over it until exhaustion overtook him and he drifted back off to sleep.

The next morning he woke again, finally recognizing the room. His throat was dry and he was only able to speak in a whisper, but when Katlin came in, he gave a crooked little smile and said, "Hey lady, need any work done around here?"

Katlin smiled at him, "You're awake. Thank God. How in the world did you get shot?"

"I forgot my Superman cape." He tried to laugh, but the pain in his chest reminded him that the situation was far from funny. He asked about Junior and she told him what had happened. He tried to sit up, but the pain stopped him.

"Now listen up Mister!" She scolded. "I have patched up your sucking chest wound and that means you have plastic wrap over your wound. When you breathe out, you have to let the air escape. Don't put your hands on the plastic wrap, okay?"

"Sure Doc, anything else? Was there only one bullet wound?"

Katlin looked worried. "I checked you all over and you only had the one bullet wound. Why, do you think you were hit somewhere else?"

"I don't know. I think it was just one. It felt like someone hit me in the chest with sledge hammer."

She nodded, relieved. "That's enough talking for now. You go back to sleep and get your rest and recover."

Chapter 3

Plans for an Army

Three months later Clint was almost back to full strength. He had thought it was over when he was hit. He was lucky they had found him in time. That was as close to a miracle as he ever wanted to get, but now there was a new problem. There was no rest for the weary. He needed to figure out how to get people to work together for the benefit of the community, for their mutual survival. It was a simple concept, until he tried to implement it.

Clint was never that good at dealing with petty issues. People complaining about things just grated on his nerves. 'Shut up and get to work' had always been his motto. There was always plenty of work to do, but the word was traveling and people were coming to find him and join the communities. Each had their own set of skills, but matching the talent and knowing how to apply it for the good of the community was the trick.

He had never wanted to be a leader, but he understood the need for them. Men needed a leader to follow, like in the military. In that chain of command, there was a job to do and one person to plan the mission, so everyone else could do their jobs, but civilians he never understood. Someone else needed to stand up and work the politics, so he could focus on the defense, but, before he could find someone for the job, news came in that the Rainbow Warriors were regrouping and trying to hook up with the Minnesota group.

Clint knew they needed to build an army to stop them this time. They needed men, supplies, food, cooks and medics, plus thousands of little things to fight them. In a way it was good, as it could really pull the small community together, but to be successful they needed more men. He talked it over with Junior and they made a plan.

"North of Duluth are some really good people that have been preppers for years." Junior said "Most of them have off-the-grid homes and supplies. If I could find my friends, we might be able to get two or three hundred men from that area to come over and help us. At worst we might only get ten, but if we can get the ten I am thinking of, they'll have lots of toys to bring to the party." He rubbed the stubble on his face as he was saying this.

"That would be great. What kind of toys we are talking about here?" Clint asked.

"The kind that the Rainbow Warriors are going to hate." Junior grinned. "One of the guys was working on a remote controlled gun mount, using a car battery and a solenoid from a starter. He had a tiny electric motor to swivel the gun to any position."

"That's great stuff, but do you think these toys survive the EMP?"

"I would say yes, because the guy working on it was prepared for an EMP. He thought 2012 was going to bring solar flares and cause a natural EMP, so he built a faraday cage for all his important electrical stuff."

Clint had a moment of thought and then said, "Good. Now who do you want to take with you, when can you leave and how long do you think it will take for you to get there and back?"

"I would pick Dean, unless you have someone else in mind?" Junior replied. "I'd guess two to three weeks, if everything goes perfectly."

Clint nodded his head and said, "I would prefer if it was you and me, but I have to start training the men we have. Dean is a good choice. Use the horses and travel at night, sleeping during the day. Avoid the big cities at all costs. There are just too many death traps you could walk right into."

Junior nodded in agreement. "Yes, of course. How do you think Gayle is going to take this?" He said with a pained look on his face.

Clint laughed long and hard and said, "The sooner you tell her, the better it would be, but I would explain to her we're not waiting for the Rainbow Warriors to come to us this time. We are taking the fight to them."

"Good point, but she's pregnant and not always easy to talk to."

Clint smiled. "Good luck my friend."

Junior playfully punched him in the shoulder and said, "Thanks. You're a lot of help."

"Okay, here's the plan. After dinner tonight I'll take Katlin and Robbie for a walk. We'll give you an hour, then come in, either to give support, or to bury you, whichever needs to be done." Clint laughed out loud.

Junior got a worried look on his face and said, "Do you really think she is going to be that mad?"

"I guess I won't know until I return from the walk," Clint said, still laughing.

"Knock it off. This isn't funny Clint."

As Clint wiped a tear from his eye, he said, "I know. Sorry, but it is funny as long as someone else has to do it."

That night after dinner, right on schedule, Robbie, Katlin and Clint left them alone in the cabin. He and Gayle were washing dishes and Junior was trying to work up his nerve to tell her.

Gayle stopped and looked him in the eye, "Are you going to tell me what is bugging so you so much tonight? You're acting weird."

Junior grimaced a little and said, "Uh, yes, there is something I need to talk to you about."

Gayle waited for him to talk, wondering what was wrong now. Junior looked at the floor, then the wall and then up to the ceiling. Gayle practically yelled at him, "Would you stop already and tell me. You're driving me insane."

He was so startled that he blurted out, "The Rainbow Warriors are regrouping. Clint wants to build an army to take the fight to them."

Gayle responded with, "That's a good idea. Why was that so hard to say?"

Junior took a deep breath, saying, "That was the easy part."

Gayle squinted her eyes and said, "Okay, okay, enough of the suspense. What is the hard part?"

Junior tightened up, like he was expecting to be punched, "I have to leave and go north of Duluth to help gather men."

Gayle had a look of fury on her face as she shouted, "Like hell you are! No way. It's not going to happen. I'm not going through almost losing you again. What the hell is the matter with you? You almost died last time and now you want to run off like some dumb fool on an impossible mission? Like those people over there would come all this way to help us."

As Gayle was catching her breath, Junior said, "It's not a fool's errand. I know some of the people over there and they will come and help. That's why I have to go. I have the contacts there and they know me."

With her face getting redder, she spat out, "I don't care. You are not going. Jesus, are you even at full strength yet? You're not totally healed and haven't regained all of your strength yet. No, no, no, you're not going. You have to start thinking like a man, Junior. I am your wife and you need to be here for the baby and me. What am I supposed to tell our baby if you die? That his father was a fool and got himself killed before he was even born?"

"Why the hell do you think I am doing this? It's for you and our baby. We must stop this threat once and for all, so we can live free."

Gayle was having none of it. "You think once this is over with that there isn't going to be some new threat, some other mad man taking charge that wants to play God? There will be threats for years to come."

Junior was determined to win this argument. "Good point, which is even more of a reason for me to go." He said, as his voice became more confident. "We need to form an army now, to handle this threat and any new threats. Building the army for mutual defense now just makes good sense."

With both hands balled into tight fists, she said, "Damn you. It doesn't matter what I want or think, because you've already made up your mind to leave me alone. This time you are going to die and I am going to be alone in this fucked up world. Left to raise our baby on my own. Thanks a lot, you selfish bastard."

Junior softened his tone and said in a quiet voice, "You don't believe in me enough. You think I am some rookie that I'm going to die. Thanks a lot. I'm doing this so we can have a family and live in a safe world."

She was crying now. "You don't care enough about me and the baby to stay here with us."

Junior shook his head. He wanted to scream that she and the baby were exactly why he was doing this, but she couldn't see that. Instead he took a deep breath. As he was trying to think of a new way to approach it, Gayle screamed, "You are not going and that is final!"

He tried to hold her, but she pushed him away, shouting. "Get away from me!"

She ran off to the bedroom, crying the whole way, and slammed the door behind her. Junior started to go to her, but changed his mind and walked outside for some fresh air instead. He look up into the night sky and said, "God, why is life so hard? Why is she being so stubborn about this?"

Just then, Clint, Katlin and Robbie walked towards him. Clint, half joking asked, "Did she throw you out?"

Katlin ask how badly Gayle had taken it and Junior said, "Not good. She's in the bedroom crying."

"Well I'll go talk to her. You guys had better stay out here." She walked inside, thinking that Clint should have let her talk to Gayle first. Stupid men.

Clint could see the pain on Junior's face and asked if he was still planning on going. Junior's expression changed to one of determination and he said, "Yes. I said I would and I'm the one with the contacts. No one else knows where to go, or how to find the place."

Clint put his hands up as a show of surrender and said, "Okay, I was just checking."

Robbie asked what was going on that had made Gayle so mad. Clint told him and then Robbie understood. "You should have told her mushy stuff first." He said, making both Clint and Junior laugh.

Junior said, "You're probably right; I should have tried that first."

Katlin came out and said, "Alright, go talk to her now. Be nice."

Junior walked into their bedroom and softly said, "I'm sorry, honey."

Gayle looked up at him with red eyes and said, "Just be quiet. I know you're going, but that doesn't mean I have to like to it. You had damn well better come back to me alive, or I'm never speaking to you again."

Junior smiled. "Well if I am dead it would be pretty hard for you to talk to me."

She threw a pillow at him and said, "You know what I mean. Just come back to me. Promise."

Junior ducked and said, "Yes, I promise I'll come back to you."

Meanwhile, outside, Katlin looked at Clint and asked, "How come you aren't going with him?"

Clint smiled and answered, "Because I was elected to run this rag tag Army and make them into a fighting force."

She gave a half hearted laugh and asked, "How are you going to do that?"

"Lots and lots of hard work." Clint shrugged. "We have to train and train and then train some more, until it all becomes instinct in their minds. We have tons of food to gather, as well as supplies. We are going to have a cavalry and an infantry. I have to find a leader to lead the cavalry. It has to be someone who knows how to inspire men and be a top horseman, someone who can shoot on the run." To illustrate his point, he quoted a General from the confederate army.

"[Stuart] is a rare man, wonderfully endowed by nature with the qualities necessary for an officer of light

cavalry. ... Calm, firm, acute, active, and enterprising, I know no one more competent than him to estimate the occurances before him at their true value. If you add to this army a real brigade of cavalry, you can find no better brigadier-General to command it."

General <u>Joseph E. Johnston</u>, letter to <u>Confederate President Jefferson Davis</u>, August 1861

"Tell me about him. Why would you respect a Rebel fighting against the North?"

"I respect the man for what he did. He fought for what he believed in. He could inspire men when they needed it most. We need a true leader like that, one that leads from the front. Men respect that and follow. Due to the thick cover in this area, our army can charge in on horseback, riding and firing pistols, coming in hard and fast. That's hard to defend against. It is also has its own kind of terror to the enemy."

"I don't understand." She frowned. "How can you use men like that? Wouldn't it be safer to have men behind barricades shooting rifles?"

"Their so called army is not trained as an army, in the sense that they are not accustomed to facing troops. They are used to fighting small, organized bands of people. We will train an army and cavalry so, once the battle starts, we can finish them off. We have to be offensive instead of defensive. If we stay in one position, hiding behind barricades, then we become defensive and loose the upper hand."

"What are you planning?"

"I'll let you know after I find out how many men we have. I am sure the word of mouth is traveling and anyone that survived them before will be coming to help us, but we still need more help."

"What else do you need?"

"A field doctor, front line medics, trained ammo guys and a tank. An attack helicopter would be nice too."

"Oh no problem. I can order all that tomorrow for you, off the internet." She smiled.

"Oh good. Order me two of everything while you're at it."

* * * * *

The next morning Junior was packing for his trip. Dean was coming at 8 am and they were leaving immediately. He grabbed what he thought he needed and was heading out the door when Katlin stop him.

"Wait. Here is your first aid kit, with battle bandages and more."

"Thanks. I almost forgot that. Now can I go load the horse?

Gayle said, "Okay and then come back and get your food. I have it all ready for you."

"Okay, be right back." He walked outside and Dean was waiting for him.

"You have enough stuff?"

"Not yet, the food is next." While he loaded what he had, Gayle brought the food out. He loaded it all on the packhorse and kissed Gayle goodbye. He shook Robbie's hand and gave Katlin a hug. "Tell Clint I'll be back in two or three weeks."

Katlin had tears in her eyes as she said, "Just come back in one piece. I don't think I can find you again, not where you are going."

He smiled at her and said, "Don't worry so much." With the confidence of youth, he jumped on the horse and said, "I'll be back before you know it." Then he rode off with Dean.

Dean said, "Damn. I thought I was going to be another hour waiting for you."

"Let's go. If we can cover enough ground, to the end of our territory, then we can sleep a few hours and we'll head off under the cover of dark."

"Giving orders already, are you?" Dean said with a smile.

"Nope. No orders. Just trying to keep you happy about hurrying up."

They rode for a few hours and stopped in with some friends to kill time as they waited for darkness. The last house was where they were staying. Jim Fleming was a bachelor, but he had his ear to the ground and always seemed to have the latest intel on what was going on.

"Hey Jim, what's the word?" Dean asked.

"Well Dean, it's funny you should ask. Word is you're never going to make it."

Junior had a quizzical look on his face and immediately asked, "Why? What's going on? Why would anyone say that?"

"Well, the rumors aren't good. You two are riding through hell. Well, maybe not hell, but you are going around the gates of hell for sure. They say the Rainbow Warriors already have control of Duluth. Before you even get there, you have to go through gangland and professionals that kill for a living to survive. Other than that, it should be an easy trip."

Dean had a stern look on his face and said, "Tell us everything you know."

Jim waved for them to come in and said, "Let me show you on the map where the danger zones are. Now don't take this as gospel, because you know things change daily, but this is the latest intel we have."

They walked into the house and in the living room was a coffee table with maps spread out on the surface.

"Okay, have a seat. Look at and study this map." He pointed one out. "The red circled areas are danger zones. I have mapped out all of the back ways to Superior, Wisconsin, so you can choose one after you gather the intel. You are going pass through there," He thumped his finger down, "and you are blind and totally on your own."

Junior studied the map a bit and said, "Yeah, we know that Jim."

Dean said, "Any groups we need to really worry about?"

Jim lit his pipe and a large cloud of smoke clouded his face, as he said, "Nothing big, just the normal 5-10 guys doing ambushes for supplies. You guys just follow the map I have for you and stay the hell off the main roads, you hear me?"

Junior waved some smoke away and said, "Yes, we understand. Why the paranoid talk all of sudden? Anything else you're not telling us?"

"With all of the death, disease and destruction, you two think you can sneak through all that and find your friends, then return with them to join us? Does sound little crazy if you ask me."

Junior laughed. "Okay, I understand, but we have to try. We need men to fight. Either we band together against a common enemy, or we get picked off one by one."

"Save your speech Junior. I understand why you are going; I'm just giving you my thoughts on the journey is all. Now you two get some sleep. I'll wake you for dinner and then off you go."

That night, August 20, they left at 8:10 pm. The weather was warm and the sky was clear, with a half moon overhead. Traveling on the pavement with horses seemed awfully loud in the still of the night, but it wasn't for long. In a couple of miles they would be on dirt roads and away from people. They planned on traveling the old logging roads as it was the safest way, but on the logging roads it was easier to ride into ambush areas, due to the roads being narrow with thick brush on either side.

Dean was leading the way and finally they turned off the on to the dirt road. Instantly the loud clop of the horseshoes on pavement was gone. Junior paused and looked back toward the security of his friends. Was Gayle right about this being a fool's errand? He shrugged his shoulders and rode off to catch up with Dean.

Chapter 4

Building an Army

Clint started the task of building an army and he soon found out that it was a nightmare in post Apocalyptic America. He not only had to find the men, but all of the food, supplies and gear, plus training and finding the leaders. His first task was sending the word out.

He was hoping for already trained vets to help train the others. Once the men came in, they would go through the quartermaster for their equipment and then be housed. He needed medics, scouts, riflemen, cooks, wagons and horses. The task seemed impossible and a weaker man would have given up in frustration, but Clint, being a natural leader, quickly found the right men.

He found the best horsemen he could, especially those that could ride and shoot, hitting a target at full gallop. The top man was put in charge of the cavalry division. The next man he wanted had to be a hustler, a guy who could come up with ice-cold beers and steaks in the middle of the desert. The type of guy that, no matter what, could find or make whatever was needed.

He found the man for the job in one Ron Mackey. He was a sawmill worker and knew all kinds of people in the area. If you needed something, Ron Mackey knew where to go or who to ask.

Clint told Ron, "I need you to save the day. Your first task is to get food, literally tons of it, as in enough to feed an army. I want you to pick three friends and get a wagon going. We need to start a supply line coming up with the food we need."

Ron absentmindedly scratched his head and asked, "What am I supposed to pay for it with?"

Clint looked up at him with a smile and said, "That's a good question. I guess you can just tell them that they don't have to help but, if they don't, they'll get no protection from us against the Rainbow Warriors. If they help us stop them by providing the necessary food, they'll have our support."

Ron looked at the floor and said, "Gee Clint, I think people are going to want something in trade."

"Well Ron, that's why I gave you this position. It's up to you to figure it out and food is just the beginning. After the food, we'll need weapons, ammo, horses, wagons and tons of other supplies. We're only going for the food first because an army moves on its stomach."

Ron stood up straight and said, "Okay captain, I'm your man."

Clint stood up. "Thanks Ron, we're counting on you. Please report to me at least once a week, or every time you return, so I have an idea what you are bringing in. Oh yeah, if you know any ladies that can knit, we are going to need socks. Plus, I need you to find me some guys that can repair boots."

They shook hands and Ron left. Clint turned to his desk and found the piece of paper he'd drafted with a list of names and reviewed them.

The next man he was looking for was a recruiter, someone with the gift of the gab that would be approachable and come across with friendly confidence. He found the man in Michael Newtown. Michael was 5'10" and about 200 pounds. He was a farmer with the gift of the gab and had that easy to approach personality. He always had a way to make people feel relaxed. His job was to literally go out and find men to join the army.

He was asked to report to Clint and, after learning of his mission, said, "Clint, that's a tall order. People are on edge and I have to cover many miles, plus there is no such thing as money now, so how do we get people to join?"

Clint used his persuasive smile and said, "We'll have to tell them that the supplies we capture from the Rainbow Warriors will be divided up and we need their help in stopping this threat so people can live in peace. Other than that, use your natural talent to say the right thing and convince them to join us."

Mike rubbed his rough callused hands on his chin, pausing in thought. "Captured supplies are all we can offer them?"

Clint leaned back in his chair and said, "Unless you have another idea."

It was obvious that Mike was thinking of solutions already. "I guess that is the best idea for now. Without money, payment of food and guns should sound good to them, I would think."

Clint sat up and said, "I want you to pick eight men and train them to ride with you. You must give the appearance of a clean, well-organized and trained group of men. People's first impression should be that you guys have it together."

Mike nodded and said, "Okay, do you have anyone in mind?"

Clint stood up and walked around his desk, letting Mike know the meeting was over. He said, "That's up to you. I trust you to pick the men and make them like our honor guard, the best of the best. I would pick men with military backgrounds that already have the training and know how to take orders and act like gentlemen."

Mike made a loose salute and said, "Yes sir, will do."

Clint saluted back and then shook his hand. "Thank you. I need you to report to me weekly, or every time you return to camp."

He answered, "Okay. By the way, what is the recruiting goal for the army?"

Clint had already returned to his chair and looked up saying, "I want three hundred cutthroat, murdering, hard asses," he laughed, "but six hundred men would be good goal for now."

After he left, Clint look at the piles of paper on his desk and mumbled under his breath, "Trying to get this all organized is a lot of work."

Katlin stopped in the command center, which was a farmhouse with tents set up for recruits, to see how things were going. She stepped into Clint's office and said, "Looks rather thin, with only about twenty men training. How is the recruitment going?"

Clint looked up and smiled at her, saying, "Oh just fine. I have twenty brand new recruits being trained by Sergeant Hannon and I have men scattered to the four winds, trying to find supplies. The funny part is that my biggest problem is coming up with a standard issue rifle."

Katlin scrunched up her nose and said, "Why is that important?"

Clint was pushing papers around on his desk as he answered her. "Because we have to teach all of our men field stripping, clearing jams and maintenance. If we have ten different types of rifles, it increases the training time, not to mention ammo problems. If we are all using the same weapons and ammo, it just makes life easier."

Clint found the papers he had been looking for and went on, "I need trained scouts the most. We need intelligence on the enemy, like where they are and what their plans are. A few good spies would really help. Once we win some battles against them, we can use their weapons and ammo, but until then, we only have the weapons and ammo we can scrounge."

Katlin put her hands on her hips and said, "You sure are confident that you are going to win this."

"Yes, Katlin, I am. Remember I saw them and their training up close. You have to remember that half of their troops are really not in the fight. The officers are fools and it will to be easy to take them out using snipers. We just need to get a functional army and pick the spot, and then we can take them out."

After glancing at yet another paper, he said, "Oh yeah, one thing came up. What are we going to do about money?"

Katlin was looking out the window at some men training. "I don't know, Clint. I suppose we could print some kind of paper dollars." Katlin shook her head and then went on. "But what would it be backed with? There isn't enough gold and silver around to even start an economy. Paper may be our only choice, but we should back it with something."

Clint thought for a moment and then said, "Maybe after we win and have the ammo, we could back it with that. Like tweenty rounds is equal to one dollar. We could adjust the value just like the government did, plus prices would be a supply and demand issue."

Rubbing her forehead, she said, "That might work, but right now I think we have bigger problems to solve."

*****

Mike started with two men and they rode from place to place, trying to convince men to join. Sometimes it was easy as they were eager to join and immediately headed off to camp for training, but other times people tossed them off their land. It was frustrating trying to make the people see that they would be under their protection and reap the benefit of an army when they continued to refuse to support it.

After leaving a house like that, Todd rode up beside Mike and said, "You'd think these people would be smart enough to join."

Mike replied, "Yes you would, but you have to remember that most of them have already survived almost a year with little to no help, so they figure they don't need us"

Todd nodded. "I understand that, but if they try to fight with just a family or small group, sooner or later they're going to lose and be taken out."

Mike looked back over his shoulder at the house they had just left and said, "Nothing we can do but keep looking for the right type of people to join."

Chapter 5

Finding More Men

Junior and Dean traveled the first night without any problems. This part of the isolated countryside seemed barren of life, or at least human life. There were no signs of people at all.

When they stopped for the morning, Dean said in a low voice, "Looks like we have clear sailing. This part shouldn't be a problem."

Junior replied, "Yes, so far so good. Tomorrow night we should be near Superior, Wisconsin and then we head south to avoid the city."

They removed their saddles and made sure the horses were fed and watered, taking turns standing watch. When daybreak came, they were quarter of a mile from the trail and well hidden in the thick brush.

That night, as they were heading out, they almost felt like early pioneers. They were in a stretch of land that might be considered "no man's land." They were traveling between two warring tribes. It was a buffer zone; neither tribe had the strength to control the land.

Just as morning was breaking it was difficult to see, but Junior spotted a man with his back to them. He appeared to be looking over the hill and then they noticed the light and smoke from a fire in the direction he was looking. In the distance they heard screams of someone in pain.

Dean, getting his AR-15 ready, and Junior with his rifle already up, approached the man. He turned and saw them coming, stepping immediately off into the shadows.

Dean called out, "Step out so we can see you."

The man stepped out from the shadows saying, "Good to meet you, gentlemen."

Junior took the man in at a glance. He noticed the man was carrying a Ruger 10-22 in stainless steel, the takedown survival model. It had the twenty five round extension magazine. It was hard to tell at a glance, but he thought it was genuine Ruger build, with steel lips to guarantee smooth, reliable actions for years. It looked like an Aim Point one thousand hour quick reflex sight was mounted on the rifle. The man wore the rifle with a quick attach sling, so the gun was carried at hip level and ready to go in an instant. The man also wore a medium size Alice pack, and was dressed in the newest high tech Real Tree 3D camo so that he blended in with the surrounding.

"Did you two want to stop here for the day?"

"Why is that?" Junior replied in a low tone.

The man was careful to keep his hands visible and was rubbing about three day's growth on his face when he motioned with his thumb towards the fire. "Trouble ahead that is best not to run into. It would be better for you to stay here for the day."

"Who are you and why are you so willing to help us?"

"Let's just say I had a run in with those guys last week. They're brutal and shoot first, asking questions later."

Dean asked, "Why are you only carrying a .22?"

The man glanced at his rifle and then said, "Simple really. You see, when the world came to end, this is what I had in my vehicle, along with six twenty five round magazines, a brick of .22 ammo and my survival gear. I can carry this light rifle with plenty of ammo and not be bogged down with extra weight. It has served me well. You see, I figured before I could get to my first cache, I would have to reload all my magazines twice."

Junior interrupted him and said, "Twice. How did you figure that?"

The man continued, "Simple really. I figured I would always be outnumbered and have to double tap everyone I shot, maybe even more. Most gangs are running with five to seven people in the group. I figured one hit for every three shots fired. I was wrong there; it turned out more like one person down per magazine. That's what happened when I ran into these clowns you were heading into." He pointed in the direction of the fire.

Junior relaxed just a little, as the guy didn't seem to be a threat to them. He asked, "So you got six of them?"

The man spit on the ground and nodded his head, "Yep, but the problem was that there were twelve of them. I was out of loaded magazines and had to beat feet to clear the area. After the first half mile or so, I lost them and took the time to quickly reload ten rounds in the magazine I had in the rifle. I then ran another half mile, before stopping again and reloading two magazines full. The only problem is that was my last fifty round box of ammo."

Dean and Junior pulled the horses off the trail and out of sight. It was quickly becoming daylight and time to stop anyway. The man led them off the trail and back into the woods about 100 yards, where no one could see their horses. They dismounted, removed the saddles and tied the horses to a tree.

The stranger had a fire going and was making coffee. They walked over and he handed them each a cup. "Names Stan. And you are...?"

Junior said, "My name is George Junior, but everybody calls me Junior. This here is Dean." Dean nodded to Stan and they stood by the fire to take off the morning chill. Junior said, "That coffee smells really good in the early cool morning."

They sat down on a fallen log and took a sip. "Real coffee?" Dean said, "How did you manage that after almost a year?"

Stan smiled as he wrapped both hands around his cup. "I am good at trading."

They finished their coffee and Junior stood up. Suddenly he felt wobbly and his head started spinning. "I don't feel so good," he said, "I'd better sit down." He half collapsed back onto the log. The world around him started spinning out of control and then he passed out.

Dean figured it out and tried to draw his pistol, but his hands felt like rubber and he slurred, "You ah . . . drugged us."

Stan smiled as he said, "That's right boys. Sorry about that, but I told you I am a good trader. Live healthy people with two horses are very valuable. Besides, I always wanted an AR-15," as he took it, "Thanks." That was last thing Dean heard before he passed out.

Four hours later, Junior woke up tied up on his horse like baggage. He was lying across the saddle on his stomach, with his hands tied together and the rope passing under the horse and tied to his feet. He was able to turn his head to see behind him and saw that Dean was tied the same way. Stan was walking ahead, leading both horses. It was full daylight, so he must not have been that worried about anyone attacking him.

Junior said, "Dean, you ok? What's going on?"

Stan called back, "You're going to be traded to the Rainbow Warriors. I figure you two will be worth about ten silver dollars each and your horses will be worth six months of food, easy."

Junior said, "What? Why are you doing this?"

Stan didn't even slow down or look towards Junior when he answered. "It's simple, I'm trader and this is survival -- nothing personal. Besides, it's really not that bad. You'll become infantrymen for the Rainbow Warriors. Just put up with their BS and you're going to survive this."

They rode like that for just over an hour, before arriving at Superior, Wisconsin. Walking up to the bridge that would take them to Duluth, Stan greeted the Rainbow Warrior that was standing guard.

The Lieutenant in charge came out to meet to Stan. "Stan, good to see you, my friend. You're back quickly this time. What did you find us?"

Stan motioned to the horses and said, "Two healthy men and two horses."

The lieutenant smiled and moved towards the prizes, "Let me see." He walked up and grabbed Junior by the hair, saying, "Open your mouth boy."

The Lieutenant didn't like what Junior said, so he grabbed his jaw and pulled his hair, forcing Junior to open up. The lieutenant moved closer and looked into his mouth, inspecting his teeth. He turned towards Stan and said, "Good teeth and he looks big and strong." Dropping Junior's head, he walked to Dean and did the same thing. He walked around the horses and looked them over, saying "Okay Stan. What do you want?"

Stan smiled and said, "You tell me what they are worth to you."

The man took off his hat and was quiet for a while and then said, "I can give two silver dollars for each man and a month's worth of food for each horse."

Stan laughed and said, "You're getting cheap in your old age. Try again. I am thinking more like fifteen silver dollars each and a year's worth of food for each horse."

"Stan, you know we can't go that high. Tell you what, I'll split the difference with you on the coins; fifteen dollars for both of them and six months worth of food."

Stan took off his hat and scratched his head. Looking up he said, "Toss in three pounds of coffee and you have deal."

They shook hands and two soldiers led Dean and Junior across the bridge. They were taken to a camp and tossed into a hole in the ground. Dean was dropped in the first hole, while Junior was put in the second one. The man in charge said, "Here are the rules, so listen up and make this easy on yourself. You will be in this hole until you give the right answers to our questions. The normal time is three days, but the stubborn ones take up to ten days. It's totally up to you to get yourself out with the correct answers. First rule is this - no questions. You will answer each question with 'yes sir'. You will be given food and water. Do you understand?"

Dean was in a hole with a steel top and it was slammed shut. The hole was ten foot deep and three feet wide. A small amount of light seeped through the edges of the steel top and, as his eyes adjusted, he looked around. His head was killing him from the drugs Stan had doped them with. The hole smelled of urine, sweat and defecation. He wished he could talk to Junior. The darkness was overwhelming. He found a spot to sit down, closed his eyes and thought, *find your center. Keep your mind. Get out of here quickly.* Escape crossed his mind and he stood up and felt the sidewalls to see if there were foot or handholds dug into the earth. Nothing. The walls were smooth and hard packed. He sat down again, feeling defeated. It felt like the walls were closing in around him.

In the next hole, Junior was thinking the same thing. This was some kind of twisted psychological break down of the human spirit. They had total control. A weaker man would break and go stark raving mad. Junior understood this was a game of control, a massive mind game. He just had to follow the rules, play the game and get out of the hole. If he could hook up with Dean, they could escape, but first they had to survive this hell.

At 6 am reverie was called, waking them up. They could hear men running around and felt the vibrations in the surrounding ground. Both looked at the steel lids of their prisons, wondering what was going on.

At 8 am, the hatch was opened and the bright sunshine blinded Dean. The fresh air swept in and Dean stood up, taking a deep breath and looking around for handholds. Nothing. He blinked the brightness away. A bottle of water and Tofu burger was tossed down. He reached to pick them up. A booming voice called down. "Stand up straight. You are not allowed to touch anything until you get permission. Do you understand?"

Dean didn't look up and just replied, "Yes."

The voice was deep and angry. "Yes what? What are the rules?"

Dean remembered, "Yes sir."

"That's better. That is your first mistake. Don't let happen again, or it's an automatic extra day added on. Do you understand?"

Dean wanted to climb up there and kick the shit out of the guy, but knew he needed to play the game in order to get out of the hole. "Yes sir."

"Much better. Now are you willing to volunteer and be a part of our Army?"

Dean had to fight back the feelings he was having and said, "Yes sir."

The man looming over the edge of the hole said, "The big question for today is, have you ever killed a Rainbow Warrior?"

Dean played dumb and said, "What is a Rainbow Warrior, sir?"

The figure said, "We are the Rainbow Warriors and worship the mother Gaia. Now answer my question."

Dean tried to make his answer sound honest and non-threatening. "No sir."

The man at the top yelled down in anger, "Liar. We know the truth and you had better have the correct answer tomorrow." Without another word, the hatch slammed shut.

Dean's mind was racing, *could they have Intel on us? Do they know who we are?* He had to really think about this and get the right answer. If he told the truth, would this become his grave? He sat down and mentally went over everything he had packed, trying to remember if there was anything that might give him away. Hopefully Junior was smart enough not to break.

The same process was done to Junior, with the same results. Now the fear Junior had was if Dean was smart enough to deny it, no matter how long they kept them locked up.

The next day the process was repeated. This time Junior was first. Dean could barely hear the man's deep voice asking questions, but he couldn't hear Junior's responses.

Junior stuck to his story, giving the same answer again. The man said, "Okay, say I believe you. You came from Wisconsin, so how did you survive the winter? Did you kill animals?"

Junior tried to be as subservient as possible and answered, "Yes sir."

"Good, a truthful answer from you. Do you regret killing the animals?"

Junior thought quickly, trying to remember everything about the beliefs of the Rainbow Warriors. "Yes. I have deep regrets, but it was survival, sir."

"You think you are more important than animals?" The man questioned.

Once again, keeping with what Junior knew, he answered, "I didn't say that sir."

"But that's what your actions said, loud and clear. How will you make it up to the animals?"

Junior was stunned by the question. What kind of fruitcake question was that? He said, "What do you feel I should do sir?"

"Wrong answer." And the lid was slammed shut.

Junior sat down and ran the question through his mind, trying to figure out what the hell the right answer was, or what he thought the man wanted to hear. He thought of Gayle and her warning for him not to go. He focused on thinking of her face and her laugh. He quietly voiced, *"I am coming back my love. No matter what, I am getting through this."*

The following morning Dean was first and the question was asked.

The voice called down, "How are you going to make it up to the animals you killed?"

Dean was quick with his answer. "In service to protect and defend them sir."

"Good answer. Here are two bottles of water for you today." And he dropped them down the hole.

Junior's answer was wrong again. He replied, "To do what I am ordered to do sir."

"Wrong answer." And the lid slammed shut.

Hold that anger but cover it up, he told himself. His day to take revenge would come, but right now he must think of an answer to the question. He had to guess what the correct answer would be for these people. What were they always talking about? Protect the animals...that had to be the answer.

The next morning was Dean's turn again.

The voice echoed down off the walls. "Have you ever killed a Rainbow Warrior?"

Without hesitation, Dean answered, "No sir."

"Are you sure? Because we know the truth. If you tell the truth, you will be released today. Have you ever killed a Rainbow Warrior?"

Again, without even thinking about it, he answered, "No sir."

A ladder was lowered into the hole. "Welcome to the Rainbow Warriors." He was hauled off to get a shower and then shaved bald.

Because Junior's answer was incorrect before, he had to spend an extra day in the hole. He was allowed out the next day and joined Dean, along with 20 others in training.

The brain washing technique was intense. The first step was to give a simple chant over and over again. After the end of every lecture, all solders had to chant three times, "Animals first, animals first, animal first." Each time louder than the last, with the third time the loudest.

All written material was based on a simple thought process and simple, bold headlines. 'Meat causes heart diseases, cancer, and diabetes.' 'Animals are sentient beings.' 'Animals have families.' 'Humans are cancer and inherently evil.'

It was obviously powerful brainwashing and meant to enter the subconscious and become part of the normal thought process. Soon they would start believing it. Repetitive constants were reinforced with fear and punishment, causing their minds to dismiss the truth. Their minds told them that they were smart, educated and caring people, so therefore they were correct. Their minds blocked all other information.

Group thinking was imperative as the whole group was graded as one. They all felt under the glare of peer pressure and shame if they weren't in step with the others. They didn't want the people they considered friends to be mad at them. Shame and ridicule are powerful tools.

The training was designed to make anyone want to be part of the group and not left out in the cold or, worse yet, tossed back in the hole for attitude adjustment.

Making it simple was key. Eating meat was bad and protecting animals was good. The choice was simply yes or no. Yes, they wanted to protect animals.

The Rainbow Warriors made them feel like they were now their family and that they stood together and protected each other. They were loved and cared for. They were Mother Earth Gaia's elite force of fighters, protecting the innocent. They were unique and a special band of brothers that must cleanse the earth of evil men.

The brainwashing was powerful and based upon a thousand years of brainwashing techniques, designed to induce people to kill those that didn't think as they did, or were a threat to their group. Tested and proven for generations, it could change the strongest man in a few months.

Only a select few that understood the process could protect their mind against it. They had to close their mind off to the propaganda and chant their own mantra silently in their head to protect themself.

Chapter 6

A Cavalry at Last

Clint kept himself separated from the troops at first. He focused on getting the food and necessary equipment for his men, rather than being a line commander. Each morning he would review the reports that came in. These included the number of recruits they had, amounts of food, supplies and weapons, plus housing for recruits and their families, if they had brought any along. He was now working on a plan for standard battle gear. Hunters had some great clothing, with better camo than the army, but they had no battle vests in which to carry needed supplies that they could grab quickly, like magazines, battle dressing, canteen, etc. He thought that they needed a ladies quilting bee group to sew some kind of standard battle vest.

He came up with a list of items that each soldier should have before going into battle. Of course they would need a battle rifle, preferably a military grade rifle, not counting the sniper teams. AR-15s would be great, but they were just a ragtag army right then, so he was sure they were going to have some SKSs, AK-47s and FALs, along with some AR-15s. Minimum ammo count should be 180 rounds per soldier, but they might have to compromise on that and say one hundred rounds each.

What about pistols too? He thought. *We should be able to come up with one hundred and eighty rounds for each person, for two weapons. One hundred and twenty rounds for the battle rifle and forty five rounds for a pistol, one hundred and sixty five rounds total, might work.*

Continuing with his list, he thought they could make canteens out of empty plastic bottles. They would have to be like a militia, with each man having to bring as much of their own gear as they could. The only problem with that was that the mismatched gear meant they wouldn't have any standards. He was once again feeling overwhelmed by the tasks at hand.

He was wearing his battle vest and was going to give it to the lady in charge of the sewing group, as a pattern. He walked out to grab a cup of coffee and the sergeant stood up and gave a crisp salute. "Good morning, sir."

He smiled and said, "Please stop calling me sir."

The sergeant responded, "Yes sir."

Clint laughed and asked him, "You're a former marine, right?"

"Yes sir."

"I guess I can't expect you to forget protocol. How's the coffee this morning?"

"Fresh as mud, sir."

"Fresh ground this morning?" he said, chuckling at his little joke. "Good" and he poured a cup. "Staff Sergeant., how is the salvage team getting on with hot water for our showers?"

"They are still working on it, sir."

"Okay, find the man in charge of it and have him come by my office at 10:00 please."

"Yes sir." He left to comply with the request.

Just as Clint had settled back in his chair, Mrs. Cathy McDonald walked in. "You wanted to see me this morning, Clint?" Cathy was sixty seven, straightforward and in good shape. At about 5'4", she looked to be close to one hundred and forty pounds. Her weathered face showed much wisdom from living on a farm her whole life.

"Yes ma'am." As he stood he said, "We need battle vests made for the front line troops." He pulled off his standard issue vest and offered it to her as a sample. "This is what the Army developed for our troops and it works very well." He opened the magazine pouch, showing her what it held, and went on. "It has a separate compartment for a first aid kit and compass. Can you sew something like this for our troops?"

Mrs. McDonald got a sour look on her face. "Of course I can sew it, young man. Don't insult me. The question is what are we supposed to use for material?"

Clint stammered a bit, apologized and then said, "You will need to figure that one out. Maybe the cloth can be salvaged from old clothes, or whatever you can find, but it has to be dark in color, or camo colors."

She was still inspecting the vest and said, "You don't want much, do you son?"

"Well ma'am, with all the talent you have, I'm sure you can figure it out."

She inspected the pockets and stitching, saying, "You have more faith in me than I deserve. How many do you need?"

"Well, five hundred would be great, but two hundred would be the minimum."

She looked him square in the eye and raised her eyebrows. "I suppose you want them by tomorrow? I hope you can find me fifty women to help. You know there are only six in our sewing group."

"Yes Ma'am, but please do the best you can."

"Okay young man, but you'd better get me some help."

Clint wrote a note and added it to the growing list of things he needed to do. "I'll see what I can do."

She stood up to leave and Clint stood up to walk her out. She turned before leaving and said, "Clint, I know you have a tremendous amount of work to do and you don't need my burdens, but please try to get us at least ten more women that can sew and we can do a great job for you. Maybe you could get that wily Mr. Mackey to come up with some sewing machines and some way to power them."

Clint nodded. "Yes Cathy, I'll do my best."

"Okay then. I'll get started on finding the material."

The SSgt returned and said, "Sir, Mr. Robert Wheeler will be here in a few minutes."

Clint nodded acknowledgement, saying, "Thank you, sergeant." He then added, "Make a note that we need to come up with ten more ladies that know how to sew. They need to join Mrs. McDonald to make us some vests."

"Yes sir, my wife can do that."

"That's good. Pass it on tonight."

"Yes sir."

Clint poured another cup of coffee. *God it's going to take a miracle to pull this off.* He was deep in thought when Robert walked in.

"Clint, what do you need? I'm busy."

Clint smiled and said, "Always straight to the point."

"Yes, and I don't appreciated being interrupted at work to come talk to you."

"I know, I know, but I need updates. You can't leave me in the dark."

Robert relaxed a little and said, "I'm sorry Clint, but I get busy and so involved in my work that I forget about acting like a military man, reporting to people all the time."

"Of course, but you have to change your mindset about it. Look at it as a refreshing walk. Get a cup of this delicious coffee, relax and brag about all of your great work."

Robert looked into Clint's face intently and said, "Clint, are you feeling all right? Do you have a fever or something?"

"No. I feel great. Why do you ask?"

"Because you're starting to sound like a mayor running for office."

Clint laughed. "Wow, now that's a scary thought. I didn't think of that. But come on, Robert. I do appreciate all the PFM you do and I'm grateful to have you help out."

Robert's face took on an almost pained look. "PFM? What the heck is that? Some military or scientific term I've never heard of?"

Clint laughed. "You've never heard of PFM? That's funny as heck. It means, *Pure Frigging Magic.*"

Robert busted out laughing. "I've got to remember that one."

"Okay, so what is the update on the hot water heaters?"

"Here's the straight talk; we're salvaging forty gallon hot water tanks and making solar hot water heaters out of some of them. We are also making some heat siphoning types, to store water heated up using copper coils in small wood stoves."

Clint tried to visualize what he was talking about. "Will you be able to get enough to handle five hundred men?"

Robert responded, "That's not a problem, as long as they use the navy shower method; you know, two minutes to wet down, turn the water off and soap up, and two minutes to rinse off."

Clint smiled. "Some of them will be grateful for that much hot water."

"Okay, anything else you want, Clint, or can I get back to work now?"

Clint stopped him from walking out and asked, "What else are you working on?"

Robert turned from the door and said, "I am trying to get a 1000-gallon plastic water tank to put up on the roof and work out a rain collection system to fill it."

"That would be amazing. I knew you were the right man for the job."

"Don't thank me yet, at least not until I get it rigged up."

"Okay my friend, keep up the great work. Please take the time to let me know what's going on a little more often."

"Sure Clint, but don't forget you can always drop by and see firsthand what we are up to. Think of it as getting some exercise and refreshing walk." And he gave a hearty laugh.

Clint walked him out, saying, "Okay, you got me there." He turned to the sergeant and asked, "Okay, whose next?"

The sergeant glanced at a pad on his desk, "Jeb Stuart just rode in and I expect he'll be coming to report to you shortly, sir."

"Don't call him that, sergeant. He is good guy."

"Yes sir, no disrespect intended. He is a great guy. I love the turkey feather in his hat and you have to admit he has certain flair."

"Yes he does, sergeant, and that's why we need him."

Clint looked around the office and it was anything but organized. Then again, did anyone expect overseeing all of this to be organized? He often felt like he was drowning in paperwork, and seeing all the different stacks told him why.

Mike walked in. "Reporting as ordered, sir."

Clint winced and said, "Mike, we're both officers in this ragtag army. Call me Clint."

"Okay Clint. Listen, I have some good news. I picked up another fifteen volunteers, but the good news is that five of them are expert horseman. What was your term? 'Get me cutthroats, murderers, rapist and hard asses'? Plus, they hate the Rainbow Warriors."

"Rapists?"

"It's just a term. These are the type of men that have seen the war up close and personal, with the scars to prove it."

"Good. Let's go meet them."

They walked out and headed toward the barn, where the men were still on their horses, looking at everything. They were trying to make up their mind if they were staying or leaving. Mike gave the order, "Attention." The horses swung around, with the five men lined up side by side. The men sat upright in the saddle. "Men, this is General Bolan."

They were ragtag group, but he could feel their energy and violence seething just under the surface. The leader was not the largest man, but his jet-black beard and cold uncaring eyes said a lot about him. He laughed out loud and his men joined him.

"General? Okay, whatever. You don't look that tough to me. Nor do I think your tiny little army is worth our time. We've been doing pretty well killing Rainbow Warriors without your help. You need us more than we need you."

Clint smiled and stared directly at the man. "And you are not the only men that have bled fighting this enemy."

"Yeah, we've heard of you. You're the miracle man. They say you turned back a huge army with only a handful of men. They say you were shot three times in the chest and then rose from the dead three days later, by the hand of Jesus himself."

Clint laughed out loud. He said. "We got lucky and I was only shot once in the chest. The doctor saved me from dying, so I was never dead, and Jesus didn't come see me. I am just a man like you."

The leader of the group continued. "So tell me why we should join up with you?"

Clint gave him a question back. "Why did you come here if you had already decided not to join us?"

"I wanted to hear what your plan is. Then I'll decide what we are going to do."

"Well, our plan is to take out the Rainbow Warriors, once and for all. I can promise you nothing but hardship, misery and possibly death. We will win and you will be rewarded with part of the captured supplies."

The man turned in his saddle to look at his men. "We're already doing that now."

Clint narrowed his eyes, not wanting to give away too much information, and said, "Yes, you take out a small patrol here and there and collect their food and weapons, but the odds are against you. Sooner or later you are going to be taken out." Clint took a wild guess and asked, "How many men did you start with?" He was hoping to put the horseman on the defensive.

The man said, "Okay, so we've lost a few men, but we still get what we want to keep us living well. Tell me what you want you from us. We're not playing military boys and marching; we fight on horseback."

Clint nodded. "And that's why I want you. I need you to train fifty men, or in this case forty five more men, to be the meanest, baddest cavalry in the world. You will fly a black flag and you will ride through the enemy and cast terror upon them. Your reputation will precede you and strike fear in the enemy."

The man looked at his men and got slight nods from them. He then said, "Sounds good, but I want the title of colonel."

Clint didn't completely trust the man and wasn't about to 'give' him anything until he proved himself, so he said, "No problem, colonel, as soon as I see you are worthy of the title. I want to see what the five of you can do." Clint barked out, "Sergeant."

"Yes sir?"

"I want you to set up three dummy targets at fifty yards in the back," he pointed in the direction he was talking about, "just at the edge of the woods." He then turned to Mike and asked him to get all the recruits, saying, "I want them to see this."

Turning back towards the horsemen he said, "Colonel, here is the scenario. If you five men can hit all three targets from your horses at a full run, without missing, you can have the job and the title."

The man exuded confidence, "When can we start shooting?" Clint smiled and said, "At whatever range you want. It's your battle plan, colonel, but at the end I want to see 15 bullet holes in those targets."

The man looked to his men and smiled. "No problem, General."

The course was set up with the dummies in place and the recruits lined up on the right, about fifty yards from the target, to watch the exhibit.

Clint was pointing at locations and said, "You come out of that ditch, like you are doing an ambush, colonel."

The men positioned themselves and he said, "Okay General, don't blink or you'll miss it."

The three man-sized targets were spread apart by about 10 feet each. The five men let out a rebel yell and charged. They split up, with the colonel in the middle and his other men split up on each side. They rode straight for the targets, yelling and charging, then at twenty five yards they opened up. Within seconds they had ridden past the targets, turned around and raced back, stopping in front of Clint.

Clint hollered out, "Sergeant, I want to see those targets."

The sergeant barked out orders to the recruits and the targets were quickly brought up to Clint.

"Sergeant, count out the bullet holes." He pointed to each of the holes and counted, "One, two, three . . ." all the way to 14.

Clint turned towards the mounted men and said, "You failed the test, Colonel. I think maybe Captain is a better title for you."

"Bull shit." The man jumped off his horse and walked over to the targets, saying, "Sergeant, do you need glasses?"

The sergeant looked at him and said, "No sir."

The man pointed at the target and said, "Look at this. There are four rounds in the center of this target, not three, don't you agree?"

The sergeant looked closely and said, "Yes sir."

Clint smiled and said, "Well, Colonel, looks like you have the job. You will have first pick of all the recruits, except for prior military scouts and snipers. I want you and your men to train away from here." He barked out, "Sergeant, show him the area we have picked for them."

"Yes sir."

Turning towards Sergeant Halloway, he said in a low voice, "I want a report on what the men thought of this exhibition in thirty minutes."

"Yes sir." Halloway returned to the troops.

Clint walked back to his office and started to rifle through some papers. He felt good now; having forty five men like that would make them dangerous and feared by the enemy.

Mike walked in and Clint told him what a great job he had done. He said, "Find us more men like that and we're going to win, hands down."

They shook hands and Mike said, "Okay, I'll see what I can do. See you next week."

Sergeant Halloway reported next. "Sir, reporting as ordered."

"At ease sergeant. Have a seat and tell me what you heard."

"The men were very impressed, sir."

"Did any of them want to join the cavalry?"

"Yes sir, several did."

Clint nodded. "I want you to test them on horseback first. Any that can ride like that can join, but no inexperienced men are to be sent unless the colonel wants them. Remember, the colonel has the final say."

"Yes sir."

He added, "Steer away any young naïve men. These are hardened men and they won't put up with it."

"Yes sir. Sir, may I speak freely?"

"Of course, go ahead."

The sergeant was uneasy and squirmed in his chair, saying, "Sir, these men are a bad idea. They are cutthroats and murderers, the lowest type of life. What would stop them from turning on us later, or killing you and trying to take over?"

"Yes, I had thought about that. I figure the Colonel and I might have a run in. We will just have to see, but for right now we need them. Look at how your men reacted to them. That's fighting spirit and the encouragement we need."

"Yes sir, but how can you trust them?"

"I don't think you understand men like them. They fight hard and fierce, but for different reasons than you and I. I would say they came together after the Rainbow Warriors wiped out their houses and killed their families. They have reasons for being as hard as they are."

"Yes sir, but are you sure?"

"Listen, let's do this. You pick someone to be your spy and get him into the group. Once he is accepted, get me weekly reports on them."

"Yes sir, good thinking."

"Okay sergeant, thank you for your honest report. Now back to work."

"Yes sir."

As Clint looked down at his desk, he felt good and believed the tide was turning. He could sense it.

With the day at an end, he walked back to the cabin. Weary from the long and busy day, he hoped for some down time. Robbie met him before he made it to the cabin. "Clint, Clint, what a great day. I caught four trout for dinner. It was so awesome. They fought like mad, twisting and turning and trying to get away, but I caught them."

He patted him on the back and said, "That's great Robbie. You are turning into quite the little woodsman. Great job."

Robbie then asked. "When do you think Junior is going to come back? He promised to show me his hidden fishing spots."

"Well, I'm hoping in a few weeks, but it may be longer."

They walked inside and Katlin was standing at the stove, cooking the fish. He walked up behind her and kissed her neck. "Smells great."

She smiled, thinking life was good. Gayle walked in and said, "Would you two stop that?"

Clint turned and smiled at her. "Sorry Gayle."

Gayle asked, "Have you had any word on Junior yet?"

"Nothing yet, but that's good news. I am sure everything is fine. He's smart and Dean is there to keep him from getting reckless."

She looked out the window and said. "I hope and pray you're right."

Chapter 7

Life at Rainbow Camp

The routine was intense: up at 6 a.m., on the field at 6:05 a.m., one hour of straight workouts - running, pushups, jumping jacks, pull-ups and other exercises. After that they marched back to the barracks, showered, cleaned up, and were out the door by 7:30 to eat, ready to march to classes by 8 a.m.

The classes were always based on the 'moral authority' of doing what was best to save Mother Gaia. The instructors were always upbeat, like they were letting you in on the hidden secrets of life. Their own beliefs were unshakeable, confident and positive, which naturally attracted others.

That old saying of 'take your time and think before you jump' was deliberately ignored in the training. They were never allowed time to think and sort things out in their own minds. They were fed constant propaganda over and over, reinforced with rewards or punishment. Lunch was for only thirty minutes and no talking was allowed. They got to eat and relax for a few precious minutes before being marched off to more classes.

At 5 p.m. they would have dinner. At 5:30 they would have to listen to one of the officer's praise them and reinforce all the brainwashing of the day. At 6:30 there was another work out time. At 7:30 they returned to the barracks for a shower. From 8:00 p.m. until 11:00 p.m., they were assigned some cleanup detail. That was normally the Officer's Quarters and they had to be perfect. If the inspecting officers found one speck of dust or one tiny thing wrong, they had to do it all over again. They all crawled gratefully into bed by 11:15. There was no time to think, no talking to others and no alone time.

After the second week, Dean and Junior had only spoken to each other a few brief times to confirm they were still a team and would stand firm, but they were never left alone or given any time to make escape plans.

As they were working out one evening, they heard a helicopter approaching. Everyone on the field stopped dead in their tracks. Junior gaped at the sky. Was the U.S. Government restored? Was this a rescue party?

The Officer in Charge said, "Spread out and cover the field. Whoever touches the briefcase will be highly honored and granted special privileges. Listen to me, you are only allowed to grab it after it hits the ground, do you understand?"

"Yes sir." Echoed across the field as the twenty men spread out across the area, about fifty feet apart.

At first glance, Junior thought it was an American Blackhawk, but something was different, not quite the way he remembered it. As it came closer, he could see the missiles on the side and the cannon on the front. They all reminded him of the Blackhawk, but the shape was different. He would later learn it was a Chinese WZ-10 armed helicopter. It was a medium range anti-tank attack helicopter, with helmet mounted targeting and night vision for the pilot. It was formidable weapon.

The helicopter flew overhead and hovered, dropping an aluminum briefcase. Junior raced for it and so did another man that was close. It was between the two of them and the race was on to see who would be honored. Junior was slightly closer and the finish was going to be tight. Once he was within a few yards, Junior dove for the briefcase. He grabbed it in a roll and came up straight in front of the other man, who angrily smashed his fist into Junior's face, trying to steal the brief case. The officer arrived and grabbed the man, pulling him off Junior by his shirt. The man was enraged and not thinking clearly and he swung at the officer, hitting him square in the face. The officer reeled back from the blow and yelled, "Attention!"

The officer, a young lieutenant, yelled attention again and Junior stood up and snapped to attention. The other man was still fuming with anger, but turned toward the officer and stood at attention.

The lieutenant looked around and, spotting a sergeant, called him over. "Have this man arrested for assaulting an officer. He'll be brought up before the General for court martial tomorrow. For tonight, throw him in the hole."

The sergeant was still holding a salute and said, "Yes Sir." He hauled the man away.

The officer turned to Junior and asked, "What's your name?"

Junior was still at attention and said, "Junior, sir."

"Junior, you are now going directly to the General's office. You do not let go of that briefcase until you hand it to the General. Do you understand me?"

Junior had been clutching the briefcase against his chest. Releasing just his right hand, he snapped a salute, saying, "Yes sir."

The Lieutenant was rubbing the now red welt on his face as he turned and barked an order. "The rest of you form up and march back to the barracks.'

Junior followed the man, wondering if this was a good thing or not. The helicopter had flown off and headed southeast as soon as the drop was made. He thought it must be low on fuel.

After the lieutenant knocked on the open door, they entered the General's office. Junior took the room in a sweeping glance, trying to memorize as many details as he could. The General was sitting behind a highly polished mahogany desk, in a leather executive chair. Everything was in perfect order.

The lieutenant spoke, "General, this man has been the only man to touch and hold the briefcase."

The General interrupted him when he noticed the bruise on Junior's face. "How did you get that bruise, son? Did one of my officers hit you?"

Junior stood at attention, "No sir. Another man tried to steal the briefcase from me."

The General smiled and said. "So you wouldn't allow that to happen. That says a lot of good things about you."

He directed his attention to the officer and asked, "Lieutenant, what happened to this other man?" As an afterthought, he told them both to stand at ease. Junior remained at attention to play to the General's ego of authority.

The lieutenant began, "General, when I arrived the two were fighting over the briefcase and I grabbed the other man to pull him off. He turned and slugged me in the face. I had Sergeant Henderson arrest him and put him in the hole for you to decide what should become of him."

The General looked over his reading glasses and addressed the lieutenant. "He struck an officer, but we can talk about that later lieutenant. Right now is a moment to praise this young man. Hand me the briefcase, son." Junior took two steps forward and presented it to the General. "You may sit down, both of you." They sat down in plush leather chairs, facing the General's desk.

"Now," the General looked at Junior, "tell me, what do you think is in here that is so important?"

Junior was sitting at attention and said, "Sir, I have no idea. It's not my job to question, but to do as I am told, sir."

"You have demonstrated that you are a superior young man. For this, I will tell you what is inside." The General worked the combination lock on the aluminum briefcase and opened it up. A huge smile crossed his face. "This is excellent news, my friends. We are going to be reinforced and resupplied in the spring. Because we have secured the northern part of Interstate-35, we are going to be rewarded with a tank and some machine guns."

Junior's mind was racing and he tried not to let his expression give him away. A tank? What in the heck was going on? Who was supplying them? He dared not ask any questions, so he only smiled.

The General had a large map of the US on the wall behind him and he noticed Junior looking at it. "You seem confused. Let me tell you what is going on. First, this is top secret information. If I ever hear of you breathing one word to anyone about this, I will have you executed on the spot. Do you understand me?"

Junior sat up straighter and answered, "Yes sir."

The General went on, "The U.S. Government owed China over a trillion dollars. They want to collect. They are here for our resources, to collect on a legal debt. Our job is to clean out any resistance force. Then they are going to allow us to retire in any part of the country we choose to live a peaceful life. You see," he turned toward the map, pointing, "I-35 is straight up from Texas. The Chinese want our wheat fields and soybeans to feed their people. They also want the iron ore from the North Country. They are taking control of the west coast and the fertile land of the Sacramento valley in California. They will help to restore power and pay people to work for them, under their rules and laws."

Junior nodded his head, indicating he understood what the General was saying.

The General went on. "The Rainbow Warriors will be allowed to live anywhere we want, in tribes that live in harmony with the land, in perfect coexistence, where no animals will be hurt. We are almost done with our job and, by next fall, this will be our land and we'll walk away. I am thinking of Florida. Living on the beach would be a good place. Where would you want to live?"

Junior was unsure what to say, but thought fast and said, "Florida on the beach sounds great to me, especially after last winter."

The General continued. "China has helped us all along and that's how we were able to strike so fast."

Before Junior could stop himself, he blurted out, "China, sir?"

The General smiled and leaned back in his chair. "Yes, China has supplied us. We had to prove ourselves with victories. It would take too long to explain it all right now. For your reward, I am promoting you to corporal in charge of your unit. That will be all for now." With that remark, the General began shuffling papers and they were obviously dismissed.

As they got up to leave, he said, "Lieutenant, come back we need to talk."

The lieutenant made an abrupt stop and turned around, "Yes General."

The lieutenant told Junior to wait outside as he shut the door and spoke with the General.

Junior spent the time well, memorizing the layout of the building and where the windows and exits were. After about 5 minutes, the LT came out and said with a big smile,

"Wow, you did really great. Keep doing well and you will move up fast." He patted Junior's shoulder.

Junior had to bite his tongue to keep from laughing and said, "Yes sir. Thank you, sir."

As they walked down the hall, the LT said, "You and one friend are granted a free night, with no duties. You can go to a private room, where you'll be given two beers each and you can relax and listen to music. Who do you pick?"

Junior had to make it seem like a hard choice, pretending not to be too eager, so after a pause, he said, "Dean, sir."

"Isn't that the man you were brought here with?"

Dean nodded and said, "Yes, sir. He's the only one I really know."

The Lieutenant was happy too and said "Of course." They walked back to the barracks and called out Dean, who answered, "Yes, sir?" The Lieutenant motioned for Dean to come to him and then led them to a private room, allowing Junior to tell him of the free night. He gave them each two Budweiser beers. Pointing to the shelf, he said, "Here's the radio. Just crank the handle and you can listen to music from the CD collection."

Junior couldn't have wished for a better opportunity. Once they had some music playing, they made their plan to escape the next night. Dean said they would go at midnight, during the guard change. They drank their beer and sat down to listen to some music until it was time for them to return to their barracks.

Chapter 8

Training with the Men

Clint had given a lot of thought to his new and growing army and how he could weed out the troublemakers and untrustworthy men. The following week he put his plan into action. He called all the officers and sergeants together. "Here's my plan. I am going to go undercover as a recruit for a week. I want you to treat me like any other recruit. I'll eat the same, work out the same and march with them."

Sergeant Halloway had a puzzled look as he asked. "What's the purpose of this plan?"

Clint responded, "Simple. I want to get a feel for the men and weed out the troublemakers. I also feel that it would help earn the respect of the men. It's very important that you treat me just like everyone else, and don't worry, nothing will be held against you." He paused and then added, "But don't go overboard either. Do you understand?"

Sergeant Halloway nodded and said, "Yes sir, I get it."

Clint added, "And you have to drop the 'sir' when addressing me for this to work."

The following day Clint was inserted into the ranks of the soldiers. He would get up every morning and work out with the men, not saying much, but observing and listening. He was watching them and evaluating each man's strength and weakness, making mental notes. He firmly believed that every man had a special gift, something they were great at. To learn each man's gift is the skill of a good leader.

They did their morning workout on the obstacle course, running, crawling over barricades and crossing the creek on a tight rope. Once they were back at the beginning, they started pull-ups, push-ups and sit-ups.

With calisthenics over, they were off to breakfast. Clint watched the men carefully, noting which ones grouped with others. Within the group of men, there were small groups, or 'cliques' forming. Men that had things in common would form a friendship, which was good, but he wanted a full team and not individual groups. He needed all of the men to work as one. In the course of observation, one troublemaker stood out. He was a former truck driver and a know it all. There was always one loud mouth who knew it all. His name was Jim Blinder and he would brag about being able to shoot freehanded and hit a target at one thousand yards, using his AR-15. He made it known that he was part of a militia and didn't have to follow orders and they could walk off the battlefield if they didn't like the plan.

Clint had worked out a signal that he could give to Sergeant Halloway, to indicate a problem like this. He gave the signal and the sergeant called Clint over and started chewing his ass and then told him to go outside and give him fifty pushups. The sergeant walked outside with him and then Clint did the pushups. When he finished, he stood and the Sergeant, in a loud voice, told him to straighten up or he was out of here.

Under his breath, Clint said, "We need to put Blinder in his place. You must have heard him bragging already. After chow, get my AR-15 and say we are going to see a demonstration of someone shooting a target at one thousands yards. Get a sixteen-inch steel plate set up. If he can hit it from one thousand yards, we are going to put him in charge of teaching marksmanship. If not, hopefully it will embarrass him enough to shut him up".

Clint returned to his breakfast, acting contrite, and finished eating. The other men noticed him, but didn't say anything to him.

When they had finished breakfast, they had a tent inspection and then formed up. The sergeant said, "We have a man that claims he can shoot a target at thousands yards out, using an AR -15, free hand. We are going see if this is true. Would the man making this claim step forward now?"

Blinder didn't move and people started looking at him. Sergeant Halloway walked over to him. "Looks like you're the one making this claim." Pointing down range, he said, "If you can hit that sixteen inch steel plate at one thousand yards, with this AR-15, you will be put in charge of marksmanship training."

Stunned and putting forth his best bravado, Blinder said, "Okay, I'll be glad to show you how to shoot."

The sergeant tried to hand him Clint's rifle, but he held out his hand in a stopping motion to refuse it, saying, "No, I want my rifle."

The sergeant said, "Okay, that's fair, go get your rifle."

He turned to other men and said, "The rest of you form up on the road. The course has already been set up. There will be absolute silence so you can hear the ding of a hit."

Blinder returned with his rifle and Sergeant Halloway said, "Do you want to be in the prone position, or do you really think you can do this free handed?"

Blinder said, "I can do this. Just watch me."

He stood up on the front line and, after about a minute of preparation, he fired his first shot. The bullet hit three feet short and about five feet to the right of the target. The dust it produced was clear to see.

His next shot was ten feet past the target and eight feet to the right.

The sergeant said, "Last chance, so make it count."

This shot fell about twelve feet short and three feet to the right.

The sergeant called, "Put your rifle on the bench and turn and face the others."

He did as ordered and then the sergeant said, "You have to give us twenty five push up for each shot missed." He then turned and directed his next comment to the rest of the men. "Let this be a lesson to everyone. I don't want to hear any more bragging or lies. Ammo is way too precious right now to put up with people bragging about themselves. If you say you can do something, you damn well better be able to do it."

He turned back to Blinder. "Well, what are you waiting for? I want to see those pushups now, so get going."

Everyone could see the anger building in Blinder's face and finally he said, "I am not doing them. I quit. Who's going to join me? These clowns have no idea how to command an army. Follow me out of here and we can do this ourselves, without their help."

The men moved uncomfortably and a few made comments under their breath. That was when Sergeant Halloway started laughing, long and hard. He turned to the troops and said, "Anyone that wants to follow this braggart is more than welcome to leave." He then slowly turned back to Blinder and said, "You have ten minutes to gather your things and leave."

Blinder was beside himself and yelled at the sergeant, "I want to see the General. You're just a piss-ant sergeant and you have no authority to order me out."

The sergeant smiled and said, "The General is gone right now and he left me in full authority." Glancing at his watch, he said, "You now have nine minutes." He turned and pointed to two men and gave an order. "You two escort Mr. Blinder back to his tent; make sure he gathers his gear and is off this property in nine minutes. Anyone that wants to join him is free to go. As for the rest of you, we have foxhole training in the woods. Now move it."

As the troops walked past Blinder, several were laughing at him and making comments like, "Mr. thousand yards, yeah right. More like Mr. thousand inches." And then everyone broke out laughing.

The two men escorted Blinder back to his tent and watched while he packed his gear. He was grumbling the whole time, trying to talk the men into leaving with him. They ignored him and, when he was packed, they walked him off the property. He was still grumbling and yelling as he walked off.

The first man looked at the other, saying, "I have never met such a loud mouth, arrogant, blowhard in my entire life. Who would follow an idiot like that?"

The other man laughed and said, "Come on, let's get back to the others." As they walked, he added, "I'm sure glad he's gone. He's the type that gets men killed. Too arrogant to admit he's ever wrong, and that is very dangerous on the battlefield."

They worked on building foxholes with top covers, for protection against the 105 mm cannon the enemy had. It was hard work and the day flew by.

That night Clint listened to the troops. He wanted to hear what they thought about getting rid of the man. Most of the men were laughing at the fool he proved himself to be. Two men tried to stick up for him, saying; "He said he had all kinds of gear back at his house, like .50 caliber sniper rifles, reloading equipment, medical supplies and food."

One of the other men said, "That's all good, but my God, what a relief not to hear his mouth anymore. The look on his face was priceless." They all laughed. "I kept waiting to hear all his excuses. It was the wind, the ammo was bad, the gun's sight was knocked off, or the sun was in my eyes." They laughed again.

Throughout the week, Clint kept a mental record of all the men. Who were the natural leaders? Who were the hunters, the target shooters that were the best? What talent did each man have? He listened hard and seldom talked, except to answer the sergeant or just polite small talk.

Chapter 9

On the Lam

The next night, at lights out, they waited for the guard change and easily snuck away from the camp. Within an hour they were traveling hard and fast, covering as much ground as they could under the cover of darkness.

Somewhat winded, Dean asked, "Where are we heading?"

Junior said, "To my friend's place. We have to head up to Two Harbors and turn north there."

"How far is Two Harbors from here?"

After a short pause to think about it, Junior said, "About twenty eight miles. If we travel at a trot, we should be able to make five mph. It will take us just under 5 and a half to six hours. It would be good to get there before daylight."

Around 3 a.m. they stopped for a break. "I am thinking we need to get back to Clint and tell him what you have learned," Dean said.

"But what about our mission, getting more people to help us?"

"Don't you understand? If Clint is building an army, he needs to know this information now. If we die before next spring, they are going to be cut to ribbons by that tank and the machine guns. I hate to say it, but we would be the cause of hundreds, if not thousands, of people being killed."

Junior thought about that for moment. "How are we going to get home unarmed? We're the wrong side of Duluth and heading in the wrong direction."

Dean was stumped by that and said, "I guess we should have talked about that before we ran off in this direction."

"I say we head to Two Harbors and salvage what we can from houses. We can get some sleep and decide what to do later."

Dean gave it some thought and then said, "Sounds like a plan."

In the still of the night, they heard the clop of horse hooves on pavement. They quickly ducked out of sight, hiding off the road. If they were coming from the east and not coming from behind them, it would be good news. It meant the Rainbow Warriors weren't looking for them.

The sound of the horses coming closer seemed to go on forever, but they never arrived. The night was clear and the starlight allowed for only dimmed vision in the shadows. They strained their eyes, trying to see. Their minds played tricks on them, turning shadows into Special Forces tracking them.

Where were they? Why weren't they there yet? The suspense of listening to the hoof beats allowed doubts to creep in. Should they have run off into the woods and never looked back? Had someone spotted them? Did they have night vision? Doubt, darkness and the power of the mind could drive even the most hardened person to scream.

Clop, clop, clop, it came closer. The shadows danced across the road. A feeling of dread crept into Junior's mind. The General had said he would have him executed on the spot, so there was no surviving if they were captured. This was it, the end of the line. They had nothing to fight with, but sticks and rocks. He clutched a rock the size of a baseball as he lay next to the road.

Dark shapes of gloomy figures materialized out of the darkness. There were at least fifteen men on horseback. Were they Rainbow Warriors on patrol, or a resistance force? Friend or foe? There was no way to tell in the darkness. As they rode past, Junior breathed a sigh of relief.

Dean whispered, "Let's cover some ground."

Off they trotted into the night. Just before dawn, they cut off the main road and found an abandoned house. It had already been ransacked, but the beds and blankets were still there, so they crawled in slept.

Dean woke up around noon and checked the area. There were no signs of a patrol. He looked for food and water, something they needed right away. In the basement he checked the hot water heater, drained it until it ran clear and then filled up a couple of one gallon jugs.

Having water covered, he found a cupboard in the basement with some over looked food. It was just a couple of cans of tuna and some dried Ramen noodles. Dean, thought it should cover the day, but he wasn't sure how he was going to get the cans open. He walked up the stairs and set the two jugs of water and food on the kitchen table. He searched and searched for a can opener, but there was nothing, not even a sharp knife.

As he was still searching, Junior walked out. "What do we have to eat?"

Without looking up, Dean answered, "Some tuna, but no can opener."

Junior smiled and said, "Let me show you how to open a can without one." Dean followed Junior out into the attached garage, where he placed a can on the concrete floor. Dean had a puzzled look on his face as Junior began rubbing the top of the can back and forth on the concrete. A short while later, he turned the can right side up and slowly squeezed its edges, all around, until the lid popped off.

Dean smiled, "Cool trick. Where did you learn that one?"

"On a YouTube zombie survival video."

Dean said, "Well, no zombies, but it is the end of the world. Good trick."

As they were eating, Dean said, "No patrols coming this way, so do you think we are in the clear?"

Junior licked some of the tuna from his fingers and said, "Yes, for a few days probably. I'm betting they look hard on the way to Wisconsin, thinking we would head home. What's the plan now?"

"I am thinking we need to get some more food and water and then gear up with what we can find. A couple of rifles and some ammo would be nice, but food and water is what we need first." Dean added, "How far is your friend from here?"

Junior looked into space and then said, "About sixty miles, if we can go straight north, maybe a bit more."

"I vote we gear up and head back. We have to get the plans to Clint, no matter what."

"Okay, let me get this straight. You want to go back through the hornets' nest, around the city, cross the Mississippi and back to our homes, unarmed and on foot, with no food?"

Dean shook his head and said, "Don't be such a buzz kill. You make it sound impossible. I am thinking a sailboat. If we sail straight across, it's only thirty miles. With a good wind and a sail boat, we would be there in about three or four hours."

Junior finished chewing and looked at Dean. "I hate to be a buzz kill, but all the working sailboats are pulled out of the water and we would need a lift to launch one. I don't see any working lifts with a sign saying 'free sailboats'. Not to mention, any left in the water were crushed and sunk from the ice last winter."

"You are a buzz kill." Dean chuckled, "Okay, tomorrow we'll find some gear and get some food put up, because, no matter what, we need to eat."

That night they took turns sleeping and standing watch. The night was quiet and nothing passed through the area they were in.

The next morning they started searching houses. First they wanted packs, like daypacks or something to carry everything in, so they could haul their water bottles, flint and steel, food and clothes. They were working in one garage when Dean found a 10' x 10' Military Camo Mesh Netting. It was in woodland camo pattern. Dean had a big smile on his face. "Look what I found."

Junior looked at it and said, "Great, we can camo the sailboat when we get it. I am sure no one could see a camo sailboat sailing away on the water." He had a noticeable sneer on his face.

"There you go being a smart ass again. You don't know how this is made, do you?"

Junior looked at the netting and said, "No clue. Why? How is that going to help us now?"

Dean held up a portion and said, "It's made out of netting, with the material tied on it. All you have to do is leave the top one foot of material, strip the rest of it off and you have an instant gill net for fishing."

Junior's eyes lit up and a big grin appeared. "Dean, you are a genius. We can put it out on the river and fill it with fish by morning."

"I don't know about filling it, but we should be able to put some food up, that's for sure. We need to find some window screens so we can dry the fish, along with some salt and pepper for seasoning."

Junior looked at the netting again and said, "Why leave the top foot of the material on? Wouldn't we catch more fish if we stripped it all down?"

"Maybe, but we need a natural looking debris pile, like the fish would normally see in the river. It should look like leaves and we can tie sticks on top to keep it floating. Anyone looking at would just think it was debris floating in the river, which is something you see all the time. We can tie rocks to the bottom to keep it more or less in one place, and we are all set. Plus the leaves give fish cover and they would swim in to get shade from the sun and get caught."

Junior slapped him on the back and said, "Dean, I am so glad I chose you to come with me. I would have never thought of that."

At the end of the day they had come across enough useful items, finding that indeed one man's junk is another man's treasure. They found two small daypacks, along with a flint and steel on a magnesium bar, a couple of camo rain ponchos, light jackets, socks and spare clothes. They didn't fit perfectly, but at least they could wash the clothes they were wearing and have some clean clothes to put on. They had walked out of town, heading east along Main Street, until they came across the Stewart River.

Just before dark they put the gill net out on the river, in a slow spot where the current was practically still.

"We'll find out in the morning if this works." Dean said.

"I sure hope so, 'cause all we found for tonight's dinner was rice."

"Well, that's better than nothing. Hopefully tomorrow it will be fish and rice for breakfast." While at the riverbank, they washed out their clothes, beating them clean on the rocks.

"We can hang these up in the house and let them dry overnight. Thank God for those clean socks. They feel wonderful." Junior added.

Dean nodded in agreement and said, "In the morning we can pull this net in and hopefully be eating some fresh walleye."

They stayed in a house near the river and got inside just as it started raining. Dean was worried that if it rained really hard, the net could be flooded out or smashed by floating logs coming down the river. They would just have to wait and see in the morning.

It was a light mist of rain all-night and just before daybreak they were back at the river. As they approached the net in the pre-dawn light, Junior thought he saw the far float being moved around. He wondered if his eyes were playing tricks on him. Dean pulled on the paracord they had tied the net off with. He had to pull hard and said, "Hey man, we have something. I can feel it fighting the net."

Junior raced over to help him and together they hauled the net in. There were two steelheads, with one being about six pounds and the other around eight pounds. Once out of the water, the fish fought wildly to free themselves. Junior used the jackknife he had found to kill the fish immediately.

They quickly filleted both and had about eight pounds of fish. Junior smiled. "We will eat like kings this morning. I wonder why the steelhead were in the river this time of year?"

Dean said, "I think some of them stay in the river, or near the mouth, all year round. The rain must have caused them to swim in, looking for easy food." Together they reset the net and secured it. The plan was to check it again just before dark and then again in the morning.

They kept looking for supplies throughout the day, going from building to building. At noon they saw two men on horses, traveling by on the road. They were both armed, but didn't look like Rainbow Warriors. Junior and Dean were both inside a house as the men went by and Dean whispered, "How come the Rainbow Warriors are not coming this far?"

Junior shrugged and said, "Not sure. They must not control this area, or they have no reason to come this way. Their job is to control Duluth."

After the men were long gone, they kept looking for supplies, finding a few more items. Dean began making a sun dehydrator out of window screens and they cut the large fillets into thin, long strips. They sandwiched the strips on to the screen and heavily salted and peppered each piece. The salt would help cure them and the pepper was for added flavor. In the hot August weather, the fillets would make good fish jerky. Dean said, "If we can do this for a few days, we should be able to put up enough food that we'll be ready to travel."

They spent any spare time they had continuing to search houses, until they finally found a gun. It was an AR-7 model, which was a .22 semi auto rifle that broke down so the barrel fitted into its own stock and was capable of floating. It had three rounds in the magazine. Junior said, "With only three rounds, it's almost useless."

Dean shook his head and said, "Not at all. Do you know the story of the Jewish uprising in World War II? They started with one pistol and three rounds. That was all they had."

Junior shook his head. He had really never heard this story before. He asked, "What happened?"

Dean continued, "Well, you see the Nazis were rounding up the Jews and hauling them off to the death camps. When you know you're going to die and have nothing left to lose, you have an edge on the enemy. You are going to die either way, so you might as well go down fighting. One man took the pistol and shot a lone German soldier. He returned with a rifle and a new pistol. They took those three guns and took on three more Nazis, returning with nine new guns. It all started from one man, who had enough and said that it's better to stand as a man, fighting to the death, instead of being helpless sheep led off to be slaughtered."

Junior looked at Dean and said, "So they were able to drive the Nazis out and won their freedom?"

Dean was looking down at the magazine and three shells. "No, unfortunately the majority of the resistance force was wiped out, but the important thing to understand is that the uprising itself started with one gun with three bullets, and it changed history. The Germans were beaten back and had to send in a Panzer division. They used poison gas in the storm drains where the resistance fighters were hiding." Dean continued, "The fighting was intense. Young people in their early twenties, men and women of the Jewish resistance, were fighting against a superior firepower. They stood up to the Germans and fought against tanks and machine guns for eleven days."

"When you no longer have anything to fear and swear to fight to the death, you become a fighting force feared by all armies of the world. The number of people in the fighting force varies depending who is telling the story, but some say it was just fifty fighters, while others say it was between two and three hundred."

Junior said, "That was an amazing story and to think it all started with one pistol and only three bullets."

"Yes it was amazing, so don't knock having only three bullets. We are armed now and, if the Rainbow Warriors come this way, we shall fight to the death."

"I swear I'll fight to my death if they come this way, but I would prefer to escape and get back to our place. What is your idea on that?"

"Well, I figure we will be ready to travel in about two days. I would like to get at least three days' worth of food and then hit the road."

Junior asked, "What do you think about us still going to look for my friend?"

"I say we skip it and get back to Clint. In fact, I would say it's the most important mission of our lives. He has got to have our information, and the sooner the better."

They caught more fish and found more cans of food and by the third day they had a week's worth of food.

As they were collecting the canned goods and dried fish, Junior said, "I think we should head out tonight and sneak around Duluth, heading back that way."

The plans changed at once, as that afternoon a patrol of twenty Rainbow Warriors entered the town and began searching every house and building. As the patrol worked its way through the town, they were heading straight for Junior and Dean. They heard them coming and, peeking out to look down the road, they saw the patrol.

Their daypacks were already packed as bug-out bags and, as they were making ready, Junior asked, "Dean, should we grab the last fish in the dehydrator?"

Dean said, "Yes. We'll grab it as we run out back and then head for the woods. They can't help but notice that someone has been staying here. The search is going to be intense in this area."

They ran for their lives and cleared the woods, just as the patrol hit the house they had been staying in.

They headed back along the river and didn't stop, running like a band of demons were chasing them. After an hour, they stopped to drink some water and catch their breath.

"Do you think we lost them?" Dean asked.

"I have no clue if they were even chasing us. I just wanted to put as much ground between them and us as we could."

"We covered a lot a ground. What about the gill net?"

"I say we go back after dark and retrieve it. It's way too valuable as a food-gathering tool to lose it. Plus we can do a night recon of the area and see if they left."

Just before dark they slowly worked their way back to the road. They listened, watched and waited, but nothing was in sight.

"I guess we were lucky to have the time we had." Dean whispered.

"Yes, we got lucky and we have a chance now."

"The big question is where did they go? Are they still here, moving back, or did they keep going east?"

"That's all we have, questions. Let's just get the net and then get out of here."

They snuck over to the riverbank and quietly retrieved the net. It had two small brook trout in it and, after killing them, they ate them raw. They took a chance that the patrol wasn't in the area and stretched the net between some trees to let it dry for a while. Being wet made it too heavy to carry, so they finished eating before packing up and heading out.

They snuck back into town and looked for horses or any sign of the patrol in the moonlight. They couldn't find anything. At daybreak, they stayed in a cabin near the river, packing the net and being ready to run at a moment's notice, taking turns at watch.

Junior was on watch and wondering how they were going to get back. It would take them weeks on foot. They had already been gone almost three weeks and Gayle would be freaking out. He wished he had listened to her and stayed home.

That afternoon, when Dean was on watch, he walked out and looked at Lake Superior and the thirty miles straight across the water. If they could get a sailboat, they could be back home in three days. The lake was calm and they could even row across. He'd have to talk to Junior about it.

Their brief relaxation was over all too soon and it was time to move on.

Chapter 10

Who is this Guy?

On the last day of his undercover work, they had bayonet training. He volunteered to be the test dummy. They used sticks with rags tied on the end, in lieu of the real thing. Any blow to the chest or head was considered a lethal strike.

A ring was drawn on the ground and the men stood in a circle about twenty feet apart. Clint stood in the middle, calm and relaxed but at the ready. When the sergeant gave the word, a man yelled and charged at him. Clint deflected his blow and it bounced off. He used his 'bayonet' to stick the man straight into the heart. The stunned look on the man's face was priceless.

Another man charged and Clint did it again. The sergeant said, "It seems we have a man that has been trained already. Let's see how good you really are." Pointing to two men, he said, "You two men, take him out."

Clint was light on his feet and dodged the first man, making him miss. He popped him in the head and then slammed the other man in the chest. It happened so fast it was hard to see what happened, but both men were down on the ground.

The sergeant said, "Just who the hell are you soldier?"

Clint smiled and said, "My real name is Clint Bolan, or General Bolan to you, sergeant."

There were audible gasps from the group and the sergeant snapped a salute and said, "Yes sir, General Bolan," and he yelled, "Attention!"

The troops stood at attention in amazement. This was *the* General? The man they had worked side by side with for a week?

Clint gave the order, "Sergeant, form these men up."

"Yes sir General." He gave the order and they gathered in formation, leaving little doubt that this was indeed the General.

"At ease men. Listen up. I pulled this little charade because I wanted to see what kind of men you truly are. I can proudly say that I now trust all of you with my life. You should be proud of the progress you have made in becoming a top fighting force. I am not any better than any other man here. We all eat the same food and we all train the same way. I will lead you from the front lines. If we want a fighting force that causes the enemy to shake in their boots, then you are the men to do it."

The men let out a loud cheer, showing their approval.

"The sergeant and I are going to decide which of you are going to be our corporals. Please, no worries about any comment you made about the General being too good to be seen with his troops."

That caused the men to laugh.

"We have procured some cattle and, believe it or not, a few cases of beer. Every man is going to eat steaks tonight and have a beer. Dismissed."

The sergeant called them to attention and then dismissed them.

There were more cheers and then the men wandered off.

Clint turned to the sergeant and asked, "Was this successful?"

The sergeant smiled and answered, "Yes sir, I believe so, General."

"Good. Now tomorrow, give everyone two days off so they can go home to see their families and relax. Tell them to report back Sunday night, no later than midnight."

"Sir, do you think all of them will return?"

"We'll find out Monday morning. If my plan works right, they will be bringing friends and family members back to join or help us."

Snapping a salute, the sergeant said, "Sir, may I say that I am proud to be part of this army?"

Clint returned the salute and said, "Thank you sergeant. I'll talk to you tomorrow."

"Yes sir."

After a week as one of the soldiers, Clint walked back to his cabin thinking of everything he had learned. The pressure was easing and things were coming together. He was thinking that they just needed a couple of breaks. He hoped Junior was back soon; it had been two weeks. He reached the cabin after dark and the door was locked. He knocked on the door and Katlin let him in. She gave him a kiss and a big hug. "Good to see you survived boot camp."

"Yeah, it was well worth the time. Did you save me something to eat?"

She turned to lead him into the kitchen. "Yes I did. Come in and have a seat while I warm it up for you."

Hearing Clint's voice, Robbie came running into the kitchen. "Clint, Clint, you missed an exciting week! I was fishing back on the beaver pond and guess what I saw? Come on, guess. You will never in a million years guess it. Go on, guess what I saw."

Clint smiled at the boy's enthusiasm and said. "A beaver?"

"That's not it, but I did see some beavers. Come on, come on, and guess again."

"Okay, a deer?"

Katlin was stifling a laugh, trying to give Clint a hint with pantomime.

"No, no, not that, but I did see a deer. Okay, ready? I am just going to tell you. Ready?"

Without giving him time to answer, he blurted out, "A bear. A great big bear. He had to be 8 feet tall and 900 pounds. A monster! I thought he was going to eat me."

Clint looked over at Katlin, not knowing if he was supposed to believe it or not. She was no help as she was doubled over laughing.

Clint played along. "What happened? Did he eat you?"

"No, silly, I ran all the way home. I forgot my fish and then the next day when I went back, the bear had stolen and eaten all my fish."

"You went back all by yourself?"

"No, mom came with me. She is so worried about me. You know how moms are."

Clint laughed out loud at the face he made.

Katlin served him dinner and said, "Yes, we moms want to protect our cubs too. You are not a man yet and you had better remember that."

"Yeah, but I'm okay. Nothing happened. You worry too much."

Clint swallowed a bite and said, "Robbie, that's her job to worry about you."

Robbie made another face and said, "I know Clint, but I can take care of myself."

A very pregnant Gayle walked into the kitchen and said, "Junior is still not back and it's been two weeks. Something is terribly wrong, I can feel it."

"You really didn't think he could travel all of that way, gather men and come back in two weeks did you? If he does it in three weeks it would be a miracle." Clint said.

"Clint you don't understand. My gut tells me they're in serious trouble. You have to send a patrol to go rescue them, please."

"I am sorry Gayle, I really am, but we don't have the men to spare to go on a rescue mission. We don't know the facts and wouldn't know where to go and look. Where are they supposed to go? We don't even know if there is anything wrong."

Her hormonal imbalance wasn't helping and she started crying. In between sobs she said, "I am telling you something is very wrong; he is in great danger and you're doing nothing to help him."

Clint looked up at Katlin with the *help me talk to her* look.

Katlin said, "Calm down, Gayle. This stress isn't good for the baby. It's going to work out and they'll be back soon, so relax. Junior and Dean are smart and you're not giving them enough credit."

Gayle was near hysteria and said, "He's going to die and I am going to be alone, raising a baby by myself. It's not fair, Clint. You should have never let him go. This all your fault." She stormed out of the room.

That night, lying in bed, he thought of Junior and all the millions of things that could have gone wrong. He hoped it wasn't the worst mistake he'd ever made, sending Junior on that mission. He prayed that Junior would pull it together and get back to them. He had too many other things to do to send men looking for his young ass.

He had so many other things to worry about. They had some beef, so they needed to make jerky and parch corn. He remembered reading about the Rebel army surviving on two tablespoons of corn meal, a quart of water and a few pieces of beef jerky to keep going.

Ammo and weapons were a top priority. The way it was shaping up, they might just have enough for one fight. One fight...talk about pressure, live or die. It would have to be a victory that would go into the history books, or this ragtag, half-starved militia army was going to be a faded memory.

What would Alexander the Great do? He thought of THE BATTLE OF GAUGAMELA, which took place in 331 BC between Alexander the Great and Darius III of Persia. Alexander was only twenty years old, with an army of 47,000 men, yet he was facing the mighty Persian Army, and whose numbers were over 250,000 men. Alexander's army was outnumbered five to one.

Alexander's troops were well trained and he understood the enemy battle tactics very well. They would deploy the two hundred-scythed war-chariots, which had sharpened swords coming out the center of the each wheel. These were designed to cut through enemy troops, but they were horse powered and horses don't like charging into a group of men holding spears. Alexander had his troops in battle formation, sixteen across and sixteen deep for a total of two hundred and fifty six men. When the chariots arrived, they spilt up, making a "U" shape, and the horses gladly ran into the opening. The soldiers in the rear ranks had the job to spear and kill the horses. The job of the men on the sides was to kill the drivers and their archer. The plan worked so well that The Persian chariot crews were quickly slaughtered.

At the same time, Alexander took his cavalry parallel to the front lines, working his way across so he could flank the enemy from behind. He had men that were called peltasts running beside his cavalry but out of sight of the enemy. They had shields and their weapons were slings, javelins and short bows.

Darius fell for the trap and sent his cavalry to block Alexander from flanking him. Once the distance was great enough, and a gap was open behind the cavalry and the foot soldiers, Alexander timed his turn and charged for the opening. His peltasts opened fire on the Persian cavalry, pelting them with rocks, javelins and arrows, keeping them busy long enough for Alexander to gain the opening. He headed straight for Darius, planning to kill him and end the battle. Darius fled the battlefield, running for his life. Before Alexander could reach him, word was sent that his left flank was failing. He had two choices: to go and save his men, or to go after and kill Darius. Alexander made the right decision and turned back to save his men.

What could Clint learn from this? First, well-trained men could take out fearful weapons, even when outnumbered. Second, his cavalry was well trained and changed the course of the battle. He also couldn't ever forget the most important third lesson - always take care of your men.

He knew the enemy had the 105 mm cannon and they needed to take them out, or steal them. He was forming his cavalry to be well trained and fierce. Most importantly, he would take care of his men and not needlessly waste their lives.

As he drifted off to sleep, he thought they needed trained scouts and sniper teams. Intel was the most important thing right then and to gather it, he needed scouts.

Chapter 11

A Sailing We Shall Go

When Junior woke up, they talked about Dean's crazy idea of making a sailboat out of a canoe.

"Of course we can do it. Countless voyagers and natives paddled these waters in craft a lot more rickety than that aluminum tub." Dean said as he and Junior gazed southward from the Minnesota shore, where they stood on what was left of Two Harbors Lakeview Park. They were eyeing an old aluminum canoe on the backside of an abandoned garage.

Junior responded, "Yeah, by staying along the shoreline and only crossing small bays. What you are suggesting is a thirty mile paddle across the Wolf's Nose to the wilds of Wisconsin."

"That is one long paddle, no pulling up on a beach to rest. Once started, no stopping. If we can make a good five miles an hour, that is around six to eight hours of paddle pulling, probably closer to eight. We would also need a day with no head wind out of the south, but I guess that doesn't really matter and canoes don't leave tracks. We are really between the Devil and the Deep Blue Sea and those devils are coming this way. We are outnumbered, not to mention outgunned. That limits our choices - we have to do it. And that, my friend brings us to this old black and white photo, from some long gone magazine, that the owner had stapled to his garage wall," Dean said as he slapped down a photo of a couple in a standard aluminum canoe with a sail mounted. "Look at what they used for a keel - a spare pair of paddles, somehow held upright on both sides at the center. I can't quite see how they are rigged, but we sure could come up with something like that, including the sail. With a northwest breeze, that would at least help move us along, or maybe even move us without having to paddle very much. Whoever left this canoe beside his garage probably won't be back to use it ever again."

"Okay, assuming we can make a rig, we would need to go on a calm night. That's going to be a hope and prayer, because it's not like we can check the weather forecast before we go. We need perfect weather with a slight breeze, but not really enough to bring on heavy waves. We'll also need at least a gallon of drinking water where we can both reach it."

"We'll be riding over the largest body of fresh water in the world. We won't be far from a drink," Dean replied.

"Non-salty maybe, but hardly fresh. That stuff has runoff from a thousand sewers and fuel drips from a thousand engines. We'll fill something from that rain barrel."

"It would be nice if we could just rush out and buy a canoe sail, all made up and ready, but we'll have to make up our own rig, thank you very much. The fact that there's no stores left standing helps make that decision easier."

Behind the abandoned garage on the eastern section of Two Harbors, they propped their newly acquired aluminum canoe upside down on a pair of sawhorses and examined the bottom as though they had never seen one before, although they had slept under similar ones many times. "This center joint is almost a bit of a keel as it is. It's more than an inch deep. It's passable for a lake canoe, but if we hoist up a sail I think we would want more of a bite on the water. We don't want to heel over so far that we are dumping the gunnel into Lake Superior," Dean said.

Without a word, Junior rummaged in the stockpile of garage stuff, too good to be thrown out by the previous owner. He came up with a stiff quarter inch thick piece of white plastic. They cut it to a suitable size and shape and then, using an old hand powered Yankee drill, which was hanging on the neat tool rack, they drilled three holes through the canoe keel and bolted it to the bottom at the center. Righting the craft, they turned their attention to the mast and rigging.

The mast was quickly crafted from a hollow aluminum tube, like the one from the old photo they were using as their guide. It had a previous existence as a TV roof antenna. Next, they found a piece of capped iron water pipe that the mast would fit over. They mounted it towards the bow by drilling through the front bench seat, which they had strengthened with a U-bolt clamp and all of the scrounged epoxy glue they could find.

The sail was next on their list and the top of a quickly condemned old nylon tent was cut to into a triangle shape. Using a pipe clamp, they bolted the spar to the mast. Heating a Phillips head screwdriver over a candle, Dean melted several perfectly round holes through the doubled over edge of the sail. He then snapped metal shower curtain loops, which they found in a box of useless old plumbing parts, in each one of the holes. They slid nicely over the mast, allowing the sail to be raised and lowered as needed. Scooping a bit of the hardening epoxy, Junior wiped some on each shower curtain loop to prevent them from opening under a strain.

They used the paracord they had to rig the necessary halyard and lines for the sail. Dean had Junior lightly melt the ends so it wouldn't fray.

"We are sailing men," Dean announced, "or soon will be."

Junior responded, "We are not about to set off without a bit of a plan. Time for a map study, gathering our gear and any useful stuff we can round up in here. We'll take that Yankee drill for sure. If we pump it up and down with a dry twig in it, that will make just about the best fire starting bow we could ever imagine."

Laying out their tattered forestry map, they decided if they left the shore of the park and sailed straight south at 180°, they would miss the peninsula and be out on the open lake, or, worse yet, end up on one of the many islands in the Apostle Islands National Lakeshore. It was decided that, to be sure of making land, they would sail at least at 190° bearing and choose a suitable landing site somewhere along the Wisconsin shore.

"There's been no sign of the patrol closing in on us here, so I suggest we stuff ourselves with whatever food this family left behind and get some shut-eye until dark. I don't think we want to start out at this time of day, if we can help it." Dean suggested.

"Sounds about right to me. We'd better get everything ready for a quick launch, just in case those Rainbow Warriors do move up during the day. Let's grub up on whatever we can find and then each take two hour watches. We will want to be at least a mile out before anyone sees us. Remember they have some .50 caliber stuff that can reach a long way. Not only possibly hitting us, but one bullet hole in the canoe could be a death sentence in that cold water"

Dean said, "That reminds me, let's make sure we have a bucket or can to bail water and some type of material to patch holes in both the sail and the canoe. Maybe a plastic shower curtain would work for both. We could sew it to the sail or wrap it under the canoe to cover a leak."

They had lucked out finding the home of a previous owner that had enjoyed the outdoors for some time. They discovered fishing rods, four life jackets and a very old Coleman stove, which they scrounged and lashed into the canoe with fishing line. Finding an old four-gallon boat motor gas tank caused them to scour every inch of the property, seeking a motor, but none was found. "That would have been nice, but we can make it with what we've found," Dean said, while mouthing down the Rice-A-Roni.

They fitfully tossed and turned with shallow sleep in the small garden tool shed beside the garage. They wanted to stay as close as possible to the canoe in case they had to make a fast departure. Being trapped in a house would definitely be bad for them. They were thankful the August night was warm, as they were escaping their pursuers with little more than the clothes on their back. They were also happy to have found the AR-7 rifle that was capable of floating.

With darkness over the lake, they heard what sounded like several horses somewhere off to the west. "I would say we don't bother to stay around to greet whoever is coming. It would probably turn into a fast goodbye," Dean said.

They struggled with the partially loaded canoe to the water's edge and discovered launching it with a keel was a problem. "We don't have time for niceties like a dry feet put-in. Just carry it out to two feet of water and let's get to where we ain't," Junior said. "We'll dry off soon enough in this weather."

The pair slid the canoe out to where the new keel cleared the bottom, then Junior slid expertly over the bow and Dean pulled himself into the stern and said, "We are at the most vulnerable point right now. No cover and easily within range of shots from shore. Let's leave fiddling with the sail until we put some distance behind our backs."

Junior turned his head and spoke over his shoulder. "Yeah." From experience, he knew the stern paddler would not hear the bow paddler if he spoke straight ahead. "Let's dig deep and stroke fast and quietly until the shoreline begins to blur a bit."

With the muscles in their arms and backs straining to pull, they threw all their effort into steaming straight ahead. As an experienced canoe paddler, Dean matched the timing of his strokes to the bow paddler. Sweat from the constant effort beaded on their foreheads for nearly an hour, until Dean said, "Okay, let's stop and evaluate our position." He eased the canoe into a slight turn and looked back. "Plenty far enough. One enemy beaten and only the endless expanse of water to conquer now." Junior pulled the sail up using the halyard they had knotted to the top of the sail and passed down through the mast. He secured it on the thwart behind him. The sail immediately swung with the slight breeze and stopped on his shoulder. Dean pulled it around to near ninety degrees and snugged it in front of him. The result was an immediate but sluggish forward thrust. Dean looked at the small bow wave and announced. "It's working, we're sailing the Crazy Cheese Head."

Dean popped the lid cover on his lensatic compass and watched the card settle down. "One-ninety degrees we had decided," He set the rotating arrow on the top glass at that. "We are already a lot less than that. Time for a course correction." A stronger puff of wind heeled the canoe slightly to the starboard. Dean thrust his paddle into the water and braced it against the side. Turning the blade slightly outward righted the canoe. "Looks like I'm going to need to hold this hard and use it as a steering tiller. Gets me out of paddling, but it will take constant effort. If we get any strong gusts and this thing starts to heel over, unhook the halyard immediately to drop the sail. Cut it if it's going to take too long to untie it. We can't afford to capsize out here."

"Well I may as well paddle, because we are not here for a pleasure cruise. The faster we cross, the better. We had estimated about six hours, but I think it will be at least twice that. We would probably move faster with pure paddling rather than sailing, but it's a good assist," Junior said.

"You do that, but switch paddle sides about every twenty strokes or so, or we will be constantly pulled off course." Dean managed to tie the thumb ring of the compass to the center of the rear thwart in front of him, where he could monitor it at a glance, and they settled back to a fairly straight and uneventful few hours, sliding almost straight ahead. Both gobbled snacks during the calm and straightened their cramped legs whenever they could. The wind dropped to totally calm, around 2 a.m. Dean left the sail up, but resumed paddling. "I don't like the look of the dark sky coming up behind us. A dead wind spot could be the not so proverbially calm before the storm."

"Yeah. Maybe we should be somewhere else when that storm hits." Junior said. "What do you figure, four hours we have been on the water...at five miles an hour we should be about twenty miles across, don't you think?"

"I think we should take advantage of the calm to take a piss over the side, drink, eat and rest for a few minutes."

They rested in the still darkness. It was an eerie feeling to hear nothing around. There was no sound and no wind, just the water and darkness. The clouds were coming in behind them and blocking out the stars. The first gust arrived with an unannounced blast that snapped the sail taut and heeled them over, almost dipping the starboard gunnel under the water. The blast of wind signaling the weather front immediately slacked and the canoe righted. Dean clutched the paddle as a tiller and stopped the sideways scudding and heeling over. "There's going to be more of that pretty soon." Dean yelled.

"Let's hope we can beat the storm to shore, because that's about the only choice we have."

"The choice is straight ahead and try to stay upright. Keep ready to drop that sail. It damn near spilled us over on that leading gust." Dean was soon glad of the fluorescent numbers glowing on the compass face. They were being pushed toward one ninety degrees and he strained the paddle until the magnetic north needle was again under his preset course arrow. For an hour they cruised at a good speed, with Junior paddling hard. The winds steadily increased from their right rear and the thin aluminum mast leaned almost at the bending point. Two of the shower curtain rings stretched out flat and then finally ripped through the thin fabric. A sudden gust grabbed the frail craft, pushing the stern sideways. They both heard the snap from below as the keel ripped loose and the craft rolled to the port side.

Junior had prepared for the event by tying his army surplus jackknife to the thwart behind him. A quick twist of his wrist sent the razor edge through the halyard, dropping the sail into a flopping mass of rayon and tubing. The canoe righted itself and rode the swells evenly.

It was near total darkness around them and the rollers were up to a couple of feet in height. The white wave tops snarled at them as they both paddled on the left to keep from being pushed out into the unseen bay ahead. Like a cold, uncaring devil, the waves laughed at them, like a patient predator waiting for that one mistake that would claim their lives. They stroked forward with lagging muscles, but never stopping. Dean kept staring at the compass and trying to constantly return to their chosen heading. Time was measured only by distance into the blackness and snapping waves.

Exhaustion slowly slipped up on them, until only their doggedness kept them slowly pulling forward, but always in time together. In the pitch blackness the compass fluorescence had faded to dimness so only the two main arrows remained visible. A sharp increase in both wind and sound brought their tired heads up as one, peering into what appeared to be a line of solid whitecaps stretching across their front as far as they could see in the inkiness.

Dean could hear the breakers smashing on the shore. He yelled above the storm. "Listen to me good, Junior. We only have one chance at this. The waves are going to start breaking about two hundred yards from shore. Whatever happens, we don't want a wave to break behind us and flood the canoe. When I say stop paddling, stop immediately, and when I say paddle for your life, that's what I mean."

Junior turned around and yelled, "Got it." Just then the wind had kicked up and rain poured down in fast, hard-hitting waves. In the pre-dawn light, he prayed this was a beach and not some rocky area they were going to be smashed to bits on.

They could see the white caps in front of them. *Gray-black waves, the sign of death*, Junior thought. Dean was trying to time the waves and yelled, "Paddle." They both dug their paddles in deep, just in time as a wave crashed behind them and the surge lifted the canoe up. "Stop." Dean yelled. "Wait for it, wait for it, paddle." Again they beat the wave and were lifted up and surged forward.

Dean yelled, "Can you see the shore line?"

"Not yet. I feel like we are in the Edmond Fitzgerald. 'Where does the time go when the waves turn the minutes into hours?'"

Dean yelled. "No time for that, paddle."

They were a little late getting their paddles in and the last part of the wave broke over the stern of the canoe,

134

soaking Dean's back, but not swamping them. "Paddle hard." Dean yelled.

He was thinking that they had to be close, because the waves were breaking faster. No sooner had that thought crossed his mind than he had a chill down his back. What if this was not land, but a small island? Without nautical maps, there was no way they knew for sure that this was the mainland.

There was no time for thinking, he reminded himself. "Paddle." He yelled. They barely beat the wave and Dean was treated to another soaking on his back.

Junior turned around and yelled, "I can see shore about fifty yards ahead at the most." Then he yelled, "Oh My God." In the pre-dawn light he saw a rogue wave coming at them. It had to be six feet tall, looking all black and menacing. He snapped his head back and paddled for all he was worth.

Dean had turned and seen it coming also and with pure adrenaline they pumped forward as fast as possible. The wave broke over them, pushing them toward the bottom. The predator snapped its icy jaws around them. The pressure let up from the wave and they were washed out of the canoe. Luckily they were wearing their life jackets and they popped up and took a deep breath, but as soon as they did, another wave crashed over them and sent them back under water. They hit bottom quickly and popped back up. Junior yelled, "Swim for shore"

They swam for all they were worth, but the cold fifty-degree water was cramping their muscles. Junior thought, *No, I am too close. I am making it to see Gayle, no matter what.* He swam forward and felt his feet kick the bottom, just as the next wave washed him up on shore. He crawled up until he was completely out of the water. Dean washed up right after him. Their strength gone, they were completely exhausted. They heard the canoe bang on the shore in the waves.

Dean yelled, "Come on Junior, help me drag it on shore and see what we can save out of it." He was exhausted, but forced himself to get up and they both walked stiff-legged over to the canoe. The wind was pounding the rain in their faces and they shivered against it. They pulled the canoe up about half way out of the water, but the back half was filled with water, making it too heavy to move any further.

Junior looked around and saw a piece of driftwood. "Dean, let's roll that over here and tie the bowline to it. We have to get out of this storm."

Dean nodded. "Sounds good, but let's hurry. My fingers are going numb."

They quickly rolled the log over. It was a heavy piece of timber, about eight inches at the base. They tied off the

136

line and looked in the canoe. "I don't see anything we need right now." Dean said

"Junior, grab my daypack, it has the flint and steel we need to get a fire going." As hard as Junior tried, the strap just didn't want to come off, so he unzipped the pack and fished around until he found the flint and steel. Pulling them out, he said, "Let's go."

They walked inland about three hundred yards into thick cover. Dean started collecting birch bark and Junior collected small dead sticks from standing pine trees that were dry, as the top of the tree protected them. They got a fire going and the warm orange glow brought a happy smile across their tired faces.

"We made it, Junior. We beat Lake Gitche Gumee. Remember that Gordon Lightfoot song?"

Junior shivered. "Yeah, we got lucky and I never want to try that again. Next time you have a brilliant idea about sailing the Great Lakes, make sure I am not around."

Chapter 12

Putting the Plan Together

Monday morning rolled in and Clint smiled at the sight. Not only did all the men return from their two-day pass, but they brought forty three more men with them. Clint turned to the sergeant and said, "Get these men in tents and let's start their training. I want Tim McBride promoted to corporal and put in charge of the new troops. I want the new recruits to run through the boot camp this week to catch up to the rest of the men. You take the rest of the troops on a ten-mile hike, set up camp and assign watches for defense around the camp."

The sergeant saluted and said, "Yes sir. Right away, sir."

As Sergeant Halloway was about to leave, Clint added, "I want you to come back tomorrow and give me a full report on how the men are doing."

"Yes sir." He turned and walked away.

Clint walked over to the barn, saddled a horse and rode off to check on the cavalry, or cutthroats as some were calling them. As he rode up they were doing horse drills, racing at a full gallop using just their knees to guide the horse. It took hours and hours of practice to do well, the rider becoming one with the horse.

He saw the Colonel over by some drying racks and rode over to him, saying, "Morning Colonel. How are the men working out?"

The Colonel looked up and said, "The General arrives to check up on us lowlifes? We're doing well, General. Come on over to my tent and have a cup of coffee." He dismounted and walked over with him. In front of the tent was a fire, with a coffee pot off to the side. Clint tied his horse off and walked over. The Colonel motioned towards one of the tree stumps around the fire and said, "Pull up a stump, General, and talk to me."

After Clint sat down, the Colonel handed him a cup of coffee. Clint took a sip, made a face and then said, "I need a report of your strength and when you think they will be ready for battle."

"Straight to the point. I like that. We are thirty eight strong right now and I would say we would be ready in two weeks."

That was music to Clint's ears. "Good. Anything you need?"

The Colonel set his cup down and looked Clint in the eyes. "Yes. Ammo. We need about twenty five hundred rounds for practice. It would also be nice to have some better grub, more men and a couple of strippers."

Clint laughed. "Right now ammo and strippers are worth their weight in gold. We'll be doing good just to have enough ammo for one major battle. My procurement officer did come up with some paint ball guns to practice with."

The colonel smiled, saying, "That's great. By the way, I heard about the stunt you pulled last week, acting like a recruit and being put in with the men. Smart move."

"It wasn't a stunt. I am no better than any man here; I just have skills in this area. Besides, it worked as we now have forty three new men that came back with them." Clint stood up, throwing the remainder of the coffee on the ground. "Ride with me back to camp and you'll get your pick of the ones you want to test."

The Colonel stood and threw his remaining coffee on the fire, following the General back towards his horse. He had one of his men ready a mount for him and then the two of them headed out.

They walked the horses so they could talk along the way. The Colonel asked, "General, what do you think our chances really are? If we try to go head-to-head with them, they can use those cannons and take us out."

Clint looked straight ahead, saying, "We are going to make sure that they can't set up those cannons. We set a deadly trap for them. "

"Trap? How do you plan on doing that?"

"With good Intel, that's how. We will find the perfect spot and get set up before they arrive. Your men are going to ram fear down the throats of the enemy. After we launch the attack, I want you to smash through their lines and finish them off. By the way, call me Clint. What is your first name?"

The Colonel reached over to shake his hand and said, "Albert is the name, Clint, but my friends call me Bert because my grandfather was Al."

They finished shaking and Clint said, "Okay Bert, now here's a question for you. If you had to send five men on a search and rescue mission, who would you send?"

Bert rubbed his beard. "I'd have to think about that. Where and what is the mission?"

"It may be nothing, but I want you to pick five good men that are willing to go and send only one of your own men to go with them."

"Sure. No problem, Clint. I will let you know the names later."

Arriving back at camp, Clint said, "Now pick out the troops you want and get your numbers up to fifty. I have to leave you now to take care of a lot of other things."

Bert gave him a relaxed salute and said, "Clint, thanks for allowing me to lead these men."

Clint stopped and turned his horse to face him. Looking him straight in the eye, he said. "I want to you understand that your job is to train men. You are going to lose some good men and you'll blame yourself for not training them better. You are going to worry about a thousand things. In the end, your one chance to change the battle has to be decided quickly and followed through on firmly. Men hate wishy-washy leaders."

The Colonel nodded. "I understand, Clint. I've already lost some good men."

"I am sure you have, Colonel. I have to leave you now, but I feel better about putting you in charge of this."

"Same here, Clint."

Clint rode off to the barn and then walked back to his office. He was thinking about being just an enlisted guy, with no responsibility, just doing what he was told to. That was the simple life. It easy to talk about being a leader, but not so easy to be one. A leader must have ESPRIT DE CORPS, pride and loyalty to the army they are building, to the unit they are in and the men around them.

******

Thinking back, Clint was glad he had gotten rid of Blinder. Obedience to orders means that when an order was given, it was obeyed without question. He couldn't have a man that said he didn't like the plan and walked off the battlefield. In order for the military to work, men had to follow orders without question.

Those who appreciated true valor, courage and leadership were the men you wanted beside you. Thousands of years ago, Sun Tzu said the battle would be won by the General with the best-disciplined troops. Discipline is more than treating men harshly. If you whip men, you just create animals. Discipline must be fair and just. Discipline needs to go hand in hand with respect. Having soldiers that fear you isn't creating respect or loyalty. Encouraging individual contributions to the greater whole is important – one may provide what others have missed - but once the battle plan is in motion, it must be carried through without question.

Clint had read the research showing that the largest groups that could effectively function as "teams" were composed of no more than eight-twelve people. For the next step of training, Clint wanted all of the men to be broken down into ten man units, with a corporal in charge of each unit and a replacement right beside him. These corporals would be required to attend leadership training after their normal duty hours.

The dignity of labor and an acceptance of hardship was one thing all men had to understand when they joined. Since money had no value at that time, the only incentive was reward with booty they captured, but only from the enemy and never from innocent civilians.

All this was running through Clint's mind. He needed scouts out in the field, like yesterday. He placed a high premium on unconventional warfare and unconventional warriors, like sniper scouts and recon teams.

"Sergeant." He called out, as he walked toward his office.

"Yes, sir?"

"Grab a cup of coffee and join me in my office."

Upon entering, Clint said, "Sergeant, sit down and listen. I have a new assignment for you. I want you to give leadership training to our newly promoted corporals. The first thing I want you to teach them is discipline. It is too often focused on insanely stupid and irrelevant stuff. I want fighting men, not pretty peacocks. The focus from here on out must be on unit effectiveness."

"Good idea, sir."

"Sergeant, don't kiss my ass. I want this written out and on my desk by tomorrow at noon. I want you to show me what you plan to teach them. Each corporal is going to have ten men assigned to them and I want it set up so that if he dies, his right hand man can immediately take over. I want it set up all the way to the last man."

"Yes sir." Clint could see the slight confusion on the sergeant's face.

"Let me ask you this, sergeant. Do you know why the Germans hated to fight us?"

"Because we are a feared fighting force?"

"That's only one reason. What the European military hated was our command structures. They trained their snipers to take out the officer first, thinking it would break up the command. They were amazed at how well our troops would adapt and keep on fighting, even after the officer and senior NCO were killed."

"I see where you going with this, sir."

"Good. Now using that as your basic plan, put it together."

"Yes sir."

Shifting gears, Clint asked, "Now what else is going on?"

"Jeb Stuart-... I'm sorry sir, Mike, came back while you were gone and reported a fighting team is coming to talk to you. Also, your 'Catch 22' trader is as crazy as ever, wheeling and dealing like mad. He has found some reloading folks with single stage reloaders and they are making common ammo like .223 and 9 mm." The sergeant continued. "They brought in the cattle and tons of parched corn, oats, rice and beans, but you really are going to have to talk to him about payments, because he has made some crazy deals that is for sure."

Clint had been organizing some papers on his desk and he stopped, looking up. "Crazy deals? What do you mean?"

"Sir, I don't want to screw it up trying to explain it you, but the way I understand it, he traded with one guy to get the gun powder, to trade to another guy to reload, who needed chickens from another guy, who he traded rice and beans to get it all together. I was lost the first time he tried to explain it to me."

Clint smiled. "Good. We picked the right man for the job."

"There's more sir, like we are going to owe some captured AK-47s and ammo for the cattle."

"Okay, we can work that all out. I hope to God he is writing this all down."

"Sir, we also have something you need to hear about. Supposedly a former lieutenant from the Rainbow Warriors wants to talk to you."

Clint dropped the papers in his hands and listened to the sergeant. "Mike the engineer is talking to him right now."

"Go get them both and ask them to come over here."

The sergeant hurried off and soon they all arrived back in Clint's office. The lieutenant gave a report that the Wisconsin Rainbow Warriors were trying to establish a clear route across Highway 8 to Interstate 35. This would enable them to transfer food and receive reinforcements from the Minnesota Rainbow Warriors. After some questions and answers, Clint dismissed them.

Later that afternoon, Scott and Fred came in to talk to Clint. They wanted to volunteer their help.

Clint welcomed them and said, "Okay gentleman, what we have heard is that the main battle force from Green Bay is traveling across Highway 8. First we need scouts and recon snipers to take them out. Find a bridge and blow it up to stop them from easy access across the state. We need sniper teams to harass them all the way back to Green Bay and I want reports on positions every other day."

Fred had some questions and, once they were clarified, Clint went on. "You need to scout and find us a perfect ambush spot, so we can set up before they arrive. Let them walk into the trap and we'll take them out, but your sniper teams are to harass and slow them down as much as possible."

Both Scott and Fred acknowledged his orders and then Fred asked, "Anything else you need from us?"

"Yes. As many men and as much food, ammo, medicine, wagons, horses and anything else you can spare."

"Sure Clint. We'll send what we can to help out."

"Thank you. I really appreciate any help you can give us."

As they left, Clint had a glimmer of hope. Things were coming together.

Within days he had to have 500 men and whip them into fighting force. No problem...yeah right. He finished up some notes and paperwork and then headed for home. It was late when he got to the cabin.

Gayle was still bugging him to send out a search party to look for Junior.

"Gayle, I promise if he's not back by the end of the third week, I will send out a five man search party. I'm sorry, but that's all we can spare." Clint could see the relief in her face.

She said, "Good. I feel better." She was waddling around and her stomach was the first thing he saw when she came into the room.

Clint gave her a gentle hug and said, "You need to relax and stay calm, for the baby's sake."

She responded, "I am. I feel better now. Thank you."

Robbie came running in to report. "Clint, guess what, guess what?"

Clint ruffled his hair and said, "Robbie, I am really tired right now. Please just tell me."

"Okay Clint. Remember I told you about the bear?"

"Yes Robbie, I remember."

"Well now I found a great big buck deer. I've been watching it all week."

"Good deal Robbie. Maybe later this fall you and I can go hunt him."

"Okay Clint, you've got a deal. I'll be your guide."

Clint smiled and said, "Okay Mr. Guide, but there are two of us hunting, so you had better find a buck deer for me to hunt too."

Robbie's face changed to a frown and he said, "Oh, you're right." You could see his mind racing and his face brightened up to a smile and he said, "You got it, Clint. I can find another buck, one for you to hunt."

Later that night, Clint and Katlin were talking in bed and she asked, "What do you think our wounded rate is going to be and how much surgical and medical supplies do I need?"

Clint propped himself up on one elbow and said, "I have no idea, but I would say at a minimum we should plan for at least ten percent dead and twenty percent wounded. About one hundred wounded men would be my guess."

"One hundred men?" she almost shouted in his face. "That's way too many! We would be doing well to take care of twenty men. What do you think I am Wonder Woman that I could handle one hundred wounded men in one day? Jesus?"

Clint sighed, "The sign of good leader is delegating to others. You have to get the nurses and field medics ready to handle that many. Don't take on this task by yourself; let your staff take on some of the responsibilities."

"Jesus Clint, that's one hell of a tall order."

"You can do it. You're my miracle worker. You saved me and I have faith in you."

"Faith is one thing, believing I am ready to handle that many people is a totally different story."

"You have the people around you, so trust them. Train them properly and it will all work out."

She let out a loud sigh and said, "Okay Clint." They drifted off to sleep.

Chapter 13

Lucky Landfall and Gunpowder

Once Junior and Dean had warmed up, after the sun came out, they checked the canoe. The rain had stopped and now the wind was blowing, causing the waves to smash against the canoe. It was making a heck of racket. Dean said, "Let's grab our stuff and get it all up to the camp area where we can sort and dry things out." Junior started pulling things from the canoe. His pack was soaked and heavy now. After looking over the items, he asked Dean, "Do you see the gun?"

It wasn't in the canoe, but they needed to haul the gear to the camp area before they could take the time to look around. When they finished, Dean said, "Now let's get that canoe bailed out and hauled out of sight. It's a big beacon saying we're here."

"Why, do you think the Rainbow Warriors are sailing after us?"

"No, but I don't like advertising that we are here. We need to haul the canoe off the beach and stash it in the woods. We'll take today to dry out our gear and get a plan together. We'd better get that fish jerky out and drying in the sun again. I'd hate to lose the food we already have put up."

Junior said, "Yes, in this wind it shouldn't take long, that's for sure."

Once the canoe was off the beach and out of sight, they split up. Junior went to look for the gun and Dean tended to drying the fish.

They had a couple cans of beans that were okay to eat, but the rice was soaked. Dean wondered if he could somehow dry it out, but thought the birds and mice would make quick work of it.

Junior was smiling as he came back with the rifle, saying, "It was about one hundred yards down from where we landed. That water proof floating stock saved the day, but I am pretty sure the ammo is useless."

Dean looked up. "Maybe it will still fire. We'll just have to hope for the best."

Junior asked, "How we doing on food?"

Dean was still spreading the fish jerky out on the sail. "The fish are drying, but we lost the rice and other dry goods. The canned food is still good, but we only have two cans of beans."

Junior put the rifle down and picked up a can. "The labels got washed off, so how do you know they're beans?"

"Because that's all we had in cans, remember?" He answered in an irritated voice.

Junior thought for a minute and nodded. "How long do you think we have?"

"Depends. About three days at best, unless we ration it."

"Well we still have the gill net, so we can get more fish or set it up in the forest and try to catch birds with it."

Dean smiled. "Good idea. Why didn't I think of that?"

"What are you talking about?"

"Well, your idea just gave us the solution to our wet rice. We can use it as bait, suspend the net above it and, when we have enough birds feeding on the rice, we can drop the net on them."

Junior agreed that sounded like a good idea and set about rigging up the net. They used sticks and the paracord, suspending it about three feet off the ground, and then they put four trails of wet rice leading to large pile in the center.

When they finished, they stood back to admire their work and Dean said, "Simple enough set up. Cut the cord and the net drops on them. We can use a club and bash them in the head."

Junior smiled. "This net sure is one of the best things we have found. I am sure glad we didn't lose it in the lake."

When they finished, Dean said, "Okay, it's sleep time. You take the first watch and get us some meat to eat."

Junior sat down behind a large log, where he could still watch the net area and not scare the birds off. After a while the forest calmed down and the wind subsided as the day was warming up. A grey squirrel found the trail of rice and was working the main pile. Just as Junior was about to cut the cord, he spotted another squirrel coming out of the corner of his eye. He was eating the rice on the trail and taking his sweet time. *Wait for it,* Junior thought, *come on, hurry up.* Two squirrels were better than one. The first squirrel spotted the second one and took off at a dead run. They raced off into a nearby tree, chattering back and forth at each other. The first squirrel had claimed all the food for himself and was not about to share any of it.

They leapt from tree to tree and were soon out of sight. Junior cursed under his breath, "One in your hand is better than two in the bush. Don't get greedy." He scolded himself.

He couldn't hear the squirrels anymore and thought he'd blown their chance at having fresh meat. Time ticked by and Junior was still mad at himself. It wasn't like they had plenty of bait to play games with. The more he thought about what had happened, the madder he got.

Finally the largest squirrel returned, but this time he was stopping and eating all the rice on the trail as Junior watched. The squirrel came within three feet from the net. *Come on already get back under the net.* Junior got ready to move. Now the squirrel was two feet away. *Oh come on already.* Impatiently Junior noticed that the second squirrel

154

had appeared in a tree above them. It was just watching and waiting. *Don't get this chase going again,* Junior thought. The big one was less than a foot from the net and the second squirrel was slowly creeping down the tree.

When the second squirrel hit the ground, he took off at a dead run for the pile in the middle. He raced past the first squirrel, which was sitting up eating his rice. Then the race to the center was on again. As soon as both of them were under the net, Junior cut the cord and dropped the net on them both. The squirrels start chattering and making a racket, fighting to get out of the net. Junior ran up and clubbed one and looked for where the net was bouncing up and down for the other. He spotted it and ran over to bash the club down on the second squirrel, but he missed and the squirrel started chattering and yelling at him. The second blow connected.

With a big smile on his face, he thought they would eat well for lunch. He quickly got the squirrels skinned and cleaned and then put them on a stick to roast over the fire. He woke Dean up by saying, "Come on lazy bones. Cook your lunch."

Dean sat up; wiping his eyes and said, "Lunch? You caught some birds?"

Junior was still smiling and said, "Nope, something better - two gray squirrels."

Dean rubbed his hands together. "Good for you. I can't wait to eat. I'm starved."

As they were eating, a voice called out from the forest. "You two need any help?" Junior had the AR-7 up in a flash.

"Who are you and what do you want?"

The stranger said, "Calm down there, son. I'm friendly."

Dean said, "Come out where we can see you."

The man said, "Okay, but you point that gun somewhere else first."

Junior kept the gun up, but pointed it to the right of where the voice was. The man walked in to view. He was a stocky older man, around 5' 8", with a gray-black beard. He walked towards them, carrying an old Iver Johnson pump 12 gauge shotgun. He stood off about 10 feet from them with the shotgun cradled in his arms. "You two need some help?"

Junior laughed and said, "No thanks. The last time a friendly person helped us, we ended up as prisoners."

The man shook his head and said, "Oh that must have been bad. How'd you end up on my property?"

Dean had a surprised look on his face, "Sorry, we didn't know. It's a long story and we're not too trusting right now. As soon as our stuff is dry, we'll be moving off your land, if that is okay?"

The man rubbed his beard and said, "There's no hurry. Tell me what happened."

Junior explained that a nice guy had invited them to have a cup of coffee, but it was laced with some kind of drugs. He told him about waking up tied to their horses, and how the man traded them to the Rainbow Warriors in Duluth, where they'd tried to re-educate them for two weeks. Dean finished the story by telling him how they escaped and made it to Two Harbors, made a sail boat canoe and sailed here.

The man looked astonished and relaxed his posture. "You crossed Lake Superior in a canoe? You two are as crazy as a loon, or lucky as heck."

"Well, we had to swim the last thirty yards." Junior said.

The stranger was shaking his head and then said, "Name's Jim."

Junior and Dean both introduced themselves and then Jim asked, "You guys heard the news?"

Almost in unison, they both said, "No. What news?"

"The Rainbow Warriors in Wisconsin are hooking up with the Minnesota Army. They plan on controlling this whole Northern route by winter. You guys need my help."

Junior said, "Why is that?"

"Because I know how to make gun powder out of chicken shit."

Dean and Junior both burst out laughing. Dean said, "Are you crazy?"

The man shook his head no. "I know it sounds funny, but it's based on reality. I have fifty chickens and have been making my own gun powder for almost a year now."

Junior said, "Okay, you have our attention, so show us this chicken shit gun powder."

He said, "Well all right then, come with me."

They followed Jim through the woods to a beautiful log cabin made from solid twelve-inch thick logs, with a green metal roof.

He turned to both of them and said, "Stay here for a minute" as he walked inside. Dean leaned over to Junior and said, "I think he is as crazy as a loon. We should just pack up and leave."

Junior said, "Hold on. I am not sure if he is telling the truth or not, but if he is, we could sure use this powder in our fight."

Jim reappeared at the door and walked outside. He had a little tuna can in his hand and he said, "Look at this." They both leaned in to peer into the can. Inside was a gray looking powder. He set the can on the ground and said, "Watch this." He lit a match and tossed it into the can. The powder immediately flared up and burned, just like gunpowder.

"Wow that is amazing. How do you make it?" Dean asked.

Jim pulled an old folded up magazine from his back pocket and pointed to the open page.

Junior took the magazine from him and began reading it aloud.

* * * * *

Recipe published in the Backwoodsman, May of 2013. Reprinted with permission.

BLACK POWDER FROM CHICKEN MANURE

Ever since mankind noticed the grass grew greener where the chickens left some fertilizer, they knew there was power in manure. There is. It's nitrogen. Where birds have gathered for thousands of years, such as the coast of Peru, their droppings are mined for nitrate fertilizer. French revolutionists in the 1700s were ordered to collect bird droppings to produce potassium nitrate, also known as saltpeter, for black powder production used by their busy revolutionary army. And to think most of us usually don't even collect it and keep a pail full around the house!

The following is a list format of materials, production steps and formulas to make your own black powder – from the VERY start.

I PRECAUTIONS: DON'T DO THIS IN THE HOUSE IF YOU ARE MARRIED!

1. WARNING: Production of explosive materials may be restricted in your area. Consult local and federal authorities.

2. This process provides the potassium nitrate for use in explosives, principally black powder. Other chemicals (below) are required for the black powder.

II MATERIALS

1) 5 gal. (20 L.) pail

2) 2 gal. (8 L.) <u>wide</u> container

3) 2 pieces fine weave cloth the diameter of the 5 gal. pail

4) 1 gal. (4 L.) rubbing alcohol

5) paper towel

6) 2 cups wood ashes

7) 5 gal. chicken manure

III PRODUCTION STEPS

1. Punch tiny holes over entire bottom of 5 gal. pail.

2. Cover inside of pail with one layer fine cloth.

3. Spread two cups **wood ashes** evenly over cloth.

4. Cover ashes with second cloth layer.

5. Fill pail with chicken manure, softer is better.

6. Place pail over equally wide two gal. catch container.

7. Slowly pour two gal, (9 L.) <u>very hot</u> water over manure. Stop frequently.

8. Allow liquid to settle in lower pan for two hours.

9. Drain liquid, discard settled sludge in it.

10. Boil two hours or until common salt grains begin to appear floating *in solution.*

11. Scoop these out with screen scoop and discard them.

12. Evaporate liquid volume to about one gal. (4L). Cool 30 minutes.

13.Add equal volume about 4 qts. (4 L.) rubbing alcohol(methanol).   Stir

14. Pour the liquid through porous paper. Collect the white crystals that form on top.

15. Further purification is possible by redissolving the crystals and evaporating to dryness.

16. Dry the **Potassium Nitrate** crystals. They are ready for use or may be ground finer.

IV BLACK GUNPOWDER FORMULAS

1. Potassium Nitrate *75%* weight

2. Potassium Nitrate *70%* Sulfur *10%* Sulfur *20%* charcoal *15%* Sodium Sulfate *10%*

Charcoal may be obtained by scraping it off any partially burned log. Choose any one of above formulas, grind each powder fine separately. Mix thoroughly. No. 1 is best for firearms. All will ignite **easily** by spark / flame / fuse. Many other recipes are available over the internet. This is finer grained than even FFFg.

Further improvement can be done by wetting the gunpowder, drying it into a cake (Photo) then making it into granules of whatever size preferred.

* * * * *

Junior read this and was amazed at how simple it seemed. He asked the man, "Can we have this magazine?"

The old man shook his head. "No, son, but you are welcome to write out a copy to take with you. But the real reason I approached you two was I wanted to do some horse trading."

Dean laughed and said, "Well, our horses were stolen."

The old man laughed. "Okay, canoe trading then. Are you planning on taking the canoe when you leave?"

Junior looked at Dean and he said, "We're not sure; that kind of depends on where we are."

"You're about two miles from Highway 2 and about thirty miles from Bayfield."

"What are you willing to trade for the canoe?"

"How about ten pounds of gun powder?"

Dean came back with, "How about ten pounds of powder, some food and a one hundred rounds of .22 ammo?"

The man looked at Junior's rifle and said, "That takes long rifle, right?"

"Yes."

"Okay, tell you what, how about fifty rounds of .22, ten pounds of powder and three days' worth of food."

Dean smiled. "You have a deal mister, and we can copy the recipe too, right?"

"Of course." The old man answered.

"We want canned or sealed food. No offense, we are just a little gun shy right now."

"I understand. No problem."

Junior sat down on the porch and wrote out the recipe while Dean took care of the trade.

"One last things, boys, I need you to haul the canoe over to the beaver pond for me."

"Sure, no problem."

They hauled the canoe to the beaver pond. Walking back, they saw a minivan and Junior wandered over and looked inside. The seats and all the carpeting had been stripped out, with racks installed instead, going to the ceiling.

They stopped in to say goodbye to the old man and Junior just had to ask. "What's with the minivan and all the racks?"

"Oh, that old thing. It's my dehydrator. You two ever see that commercial about not leaving your dogs in a car in hot weather? It said that in ninety minutes, when it's ninety degree outside, the car can hit one hundred and thirty eight degrees on the inside. I decided to convert that van to see if it would work for drying food and it does."

"That is good thinking."

"Yep, and I sealed it up so the bugs can't get in, or the mice and birds either."

Dean smiled, "Thanks for the idea."

They both shook the man's hand and he said, "You two travel safe and thanks for the trade."

Chapter 14

Getting Ready for War

Things were happening fast now. He was given the reports on where the Rainbow Warriors were and he was mapping out their route. He needed recon scouts to pick his battlefield.

Mr. Wheeler showed up with some awesome news. He had found two machine guns. One was a .30 caliber WW II machine gun and the other a Gatling gun.

The Model 1881 Gatling gun was designed to use the 'Bruce'-style feed system, accepting two rows of gravity fed .45-70 cartridges. While one row was being fed into the gun, the other could be reloaded, thus allowing sustained fire. The gun required four operators to maneuver and fire. By 1876, the gun had a theoretical rate of fire of twelve hundred rounds per minute, although four hundred rounds per minute was more likely in combat. As the barrels rotated, it allowed them to cool and the idea of allowing the barrels to cool in between shots persisted to modern day in mini gun designs. The main drawback of the weapon was that it was heavy and had to be wheeled like a cannon, using a two wheel cart.

The round used, .45-70, was based on the old military way of explaining what you had. It was a 45-70-405, but was also referred to as the '.45 Government' cartridge in commercial catalogs. The nomenclature of the time was based on several properties of the cartridge: .45 was the nominal bullet diameter, in decimal inches i.e. 0.458 inches; 70 was the mass of black powder in grains and 405 was the weight of the lead bullet in grains, i.e. 405 grains. It was considered a slow moving bullet at 1,394 feet per second.

While Clint was happy to have it, it used a center fire rifle bullet and the man that owned the gun only had three hundred rounds for it, but could reload another three hundred if he had primers.

Clint said, "That's great news, but how do we find primers for it?"

Wheeler smiled and said, "You're going to love this one. I ran into a guy who had stored up fifty thousand rounds of .22 ammo and he gave me a recipe for taking them apart to get the primer material out, allowing us to remake the discharged primers."

Clint screwed up his face and said, "What? How in the world do you do that?"

Wheeler retrieved and unfolded a piece of paper from his pocket, showing Clint the written instructions.

Clint carefully studied the directions, reading each line a couple of times so he completely understood it.

* * * * *

Pull the bullets out of the case - it doesn't matter what brand ammo. Holding the case, bend the projectile over with pliers and they'll come out of the case.

Save the powder and lead for homemade hand grenades or reloads.

Put about 50 empty shell cases in a Mason jar and fill with enough distilled water to cover the brass. You can use filtered water or rubbing alcohol, but it does not dissolve the primer mix as fast as distilled water.

Shake the jar a couple of times a day and you'll notice the water turning green as the primer mix begins to dissolve.

After 3 or 4 days you'll have enough solution to make several large rifle primers. It will take about a month to dissolve all of the primer mix that is in the rim fired .22 cases.

Pour the now green water onto a cookie sheet and let it dry - you could expedite drying time in an oven at about 120 degrees.

Now remove the used primer from the spent shell with a punch or other small tool and remove the anvil. Keep your parts secured so they don't become lost. A used

167

egg carton works well. Using another appropriately sized tool, flatten the dimple in the primer cup, left by the firing pin.

Next, as the mixture begins to dry, it will become "pasty" and this is the time you should put it into the primer cups, filling them to the top.

Using tweezers or some other tools, place the anvil back in the cup.

The mixture becomes volatile and sensitive after it's completely dry. Now dry the primers in the sun or an oven - this may take 10 to 24 hours.

Once the paste is completely dry, it is pressure sensitive, so handle with care.

Reload your spent casings using the new primer and you are good to go.

Remember to be careful, as this is an explosive - wear protective equipment such as glasses or goggles. If you light a small piece on an ashtray it burns so fast it pops.

The green primer mix has mercury compounds in it and is corrosive - so keep it off your hands, or it could cause serious medical problems. You should also clean the bore frequently to prevent rust.

* * * * *

Clint called for one of his men that knew explosives and had reloaded for years. He had the man read the

168

directions and asked if this was a possible way to make new primers.

The man carefully read the information and then handed it back to Clint, saying, "Yes. That would work. The only difference between primer material and gun powder is that the primer material is pressure sensitive and has to ignite easily and burn fast to set off the gun powder."

Clint asked the man if black powder could be used to make a primer and the man said no. He went on to explain that gun powder burned too slowly to be used. If gun powder burned as fast as primer material, it wouldn't allow the bullet to move down the barrel in front of the explosion and would just blow the barrel up. The material for primers needed to be a pressure sensitive, fast burning material. Match heads or caps could be used, if enough were available.

Clint thanked the man and dismissed him, saying he may need his services to fulfil this task. He turned to Wheeler and said, "Please tell me you are writing down all these trades."

"Of course, Clint. All the unfinished trades are written down and I've given people vouchers for things I've received. Relax."

"Thank you. You are doing amazing work."

* * * * *

Katlin brought Clint lunch so she could talk with him. She started talking about how they could build a successful nation again. She had been reading the historian Niall Ferguson's book *Civilization: The West and the Rest*. It was about the six steps, or "apps" as he called them, that made America a successful nation and she told Clint the steps.

1. Competition

2. The scientific revolution

3. Property rights- the rule of law based on property rights

4. Modern Medicine

5. The consumer society

6. The work ethic

She added on #7. Laws and rules invented for a good reason.

She was passionate about this and Clint allowed her to expound on her thoughts. She went on to tell him about the seven easy steps to destroy a successful nation.

1. Pass laws to destroy competition. As an example she pointed to raw milk. It was illegal to sell or buy it. The government controlled it and only pasteurized milk could be bought. That was just the tip of iceberg on laws passed to destroy competition.

2. Discourage science by dumbing down students. She quoted a good book to read on that; "The Dumbing down of America"

3. Destroy property rights. That was an ongoing assault, and was happening each day prior to the EMP. She quoted the endangered species act. Wolves could destroy your livelihood, but they were still protected in a couple of places in the United States, New Mexico being one. Nothing can be done to the wolves because they were considered an endangered species. She went on to mention the Gibson Guitar raid in 2012 by SWAT teams with assault rifles, all over some fake endangered tree. Building steam, she told him about the farmers in California being denied irrigation water over an endangered delta smelt, which was nothing more than a minnow. Property rights were being destroyed.

4. Health Care – it was made free and Americans were taxed to death to pay for it. The "Affordable Care Act" caused large employers to reduce work hours from 40-28 hour work weeks, making workers part-time, all due to the high cost of mandates to cover full time workers with so called free health care.

5. Destroy the consumer buying power. As an example, she asked him to guess how much money, in the days before the EMP, would be the equivalent of $100 from 1980, using the CPI Inflation calculator. Clint guessed $150

and was wrong. He was surprised when she told him he would have needed $282.20. Inflation was killing the consumer.

6. Destroying work ethic was another way. There was growing unrest before the EMP about the 20-something kids and their work ethic. They came in late, left early and missed days, barely working 5 out of the 8-hour day. Of course there were still good workers out there, but this was just an example.

7. Corruption in politics - the difference between any 1st world nation and a corrupt banana republic is that laws are to be applied to each man or woman equally. No one should ever be above the law. There was scandal after scandal and no one was being held accountable. An easy example was the Fast and Furious fiasco, with Americans being killed as part of a failed ATF plan to demonize guns in America.

Hitler said it best; "The best way to take control over a people and control them utterly, is to take a little of their freedom at a time, to erode rights by a thousand tiny and almost imperceptible reductions. In this way the people will not see those rights and freedoms being removed until past the point at which these changes cannot be reversed."

Clint listened to her thoughtfully and then said, "That's all well and good, but don't you think we should win this battle first? We know the problems of the past, but we have the immediate future to take care of."

Katlin made a face and said, "You are such a kill joy. Your thinking is too short term. Of course you're going to win. Start thinking long term."

Clint didn't want to go into it with her and said, "Okay, as soon as this battle is over we can talk long term."

She left and Clint went back to work studying the map. His mind was racing, trying to remember how smaller forces won major battles. The unknown factor in battle was the desire of the men to fight to the death. How much heart did his men really have? Was the loyalty to their friends beside them enough to drive them to the end? Fighting was always about so much more than just shooting.

He was dwelling on the fact that they only had enough ammo and spirit for one major fight. The pressure was mounting on him again. They had to have one solid victory, or it was over. He had to instill in his men that running was the worst thing they could do. Throughout history any army that broke and ran was slaughtered. It gave the other side a superior feeling; they loved the chase and finishing off the other side.

In WW I, the U.S. 77th Division, called the Lost Battalion, was testimony to the fighting spirit of Americans. In October 1918, they had advanced far into enemy lines in the Argonne Forest of France. Those five hundred and fifty four Americans were isolated by the German forces and fought a battle that was studied extensively for many decades afterwards. After some of the most intense battles of the war, the Americans had one hundred and ninety seven dead, one hundred and fifty missing or captured and one hundred and ninety four men that were finally rescued. For six days they fought on, with no resupplies and no communications. They were following their orders to the bitter end.

Most of the men were from New York City and the German Officers could not believe how long they fought on. One called them American Gangsters. The American side was led by a major, whose orders read:

"It is again impressed upon every officer and man of this command that ground, once captured, must, under no circumstances, be given up in the absence of direct, positive and formal orders to do so, emanating from these headquarters. Troops occupying ground must be supported against counterattack and all gains held. It is a favorite trick of the Boche to spread confusion...by calling out "retire" or "fall back." If, in action, any such command is heard, officers and men may be sure that it is given by the enemy. Whoever gives such a command is a traitor and it is the duty of any officer or man who is loyal to his country and who hears such an order given to shoot the

offender upon the spot. WE ARE NOT GOING BACK, BUT FORWARD!" –General Alexander.

After battles they would strip the dead Germans of their food and water. For six days they had no way of knowing what was going on. They were sending carrier pigeons with messages to communicate when they came under friendly fire. Their own artillery was bombing them and the only reliable way to communicate that was by carrier pigeons. One was sent out with this message.

WE ARE ALONG THE ROAD PARALELL 276.4. OUR ARTILLERY IS DROPPING A BARRAGE DIRECTLY ON US. FOR HEAVENS SAKE STOP IT.

They lost over half of their men in the intense six day battle. They dug in and held the ground they had captured, just as ordered. It was why Americans were a feared fighting force.

Clint thought about what they knew about the enemy. They were not committed to this fight as much as his troops were and their officers were arrogant. They thought that, because they had the largest fighting force, they were unstoppable. They had never had to face anything but small bands of poorly armed men.

The scout snipers would be his weapon to use that thinking against them. They had to harass them and let the enemy think they had the superior forces, until they were in the trap strike zone. He remembered a story about the battle of El Bruc, where a small band of local militia stopped the undefeated army of Napoleon.

Napoleon's army was three thousand eight hundred men strong and the Spaniards only had two thousand men. How they stopped them was the story. They used the terrain to their advantage. The French losses were insane, with three hundred and sixty dead, eight hundred wounded and sixty captured. That was a total of one thousands two hundred and eighty men, almost a third of their fighting force. The Spaniards had twenty dead, eighty wounded and one hundred men captured. Clint studied everything he could on their strategy. How did they stop the undefeated army?

The legend was that a young drummer boy saw the French coming and played his drum so loudly that it echoed off the valley walls, sounding like the drums of thousands coming to slaughter the French. A statue had been erected in honor of the brave drummer boy.

The real story was that the men used the terrain to ambush the French and held the high ground on the mountain pass. Clint realized that was what he needed to do, find a place where they could have men on both sides of the road and they could be shooting down into the enemy. They needed to find this perfect spot and get set up so they could have the victory they desperately needed. That would boost the men's morale, not to mention the weapons, ammo and equipment they would get.

Chapter 15

The Assassin

Clint came home on Friday night and it had been a long week. He felt like the walking dead. Robbie of course was waiting for him before he even reached the door. With the exuberance only a young boy could have, he said, "Clint, I did it. I found you a buck to hunt."

Clint tousled his hair and said, "Good job, Robbie. Is he as big as your buck?"

Robbie looked at the floor and said, "Ahhh, well, you see, uhm, well not as big, but he is a really fat four pointer."

Clint laughed at that. "And how big is your buck?"

Robbie shuffled his feet and answered, "Ahhh, he's a skinny 8 pointer."

Clint laughed again and raised his voice in mock surprise. "A skinny eight pointer? Are you sure?"

He looked up at Clint. "Okay, he's not too skinny, but Clint, I found them both so I should get the chance to hunt the biggest buck."

Clint smiled and said, "That's okay with me, Robbie. Thank you for finding a buck for me to hunt."

They walked into the cabin and Gayle was sitting on the couch, looking uncomfortable as her belly stuck out a mile. She smiled at Clint and, looking at her stomach, she said, "I bet it's going to be a boy."

Clint raised an eyebrow and said, "Why is that?"

She laughed and said, "Because he is kicking and moving around like a mad man. I can't wait to let him out."

"I bet so. When do you think that will be?"

"I don't know, but I hope it's soon because my back is killing me."

Clint walked into the kitchen and asked, "What's for dinner?"

Katlin was at the stove and said, "Your favorite, rice and beans."

Clint rubbed his stomach and licked his lips and sarcastically said, "Oh yes, my very favorite."

She threw a hand towel at him and said, "I have homemade bread to go with it, so stop complaining or you won't get any."

"Hey, I'm not complaining at all. I'm thankful for food and safe place to live."

She turned towards him with a surprised face and said, "Safe? Really? You've already won the war?"

"Honey, please don't give me a hard time. It's been a long week." He leaned over and whispered in her ear, "Still nothing on Junior."

Katlin frowned and whispered, "That's not good. What are you going to do?"

He had an almost pained look on his face and said, "Give me until Monday and then I'll send out a search party. What should I tell Gayle?"

She looked at him. "Not one word. Okay? Now have a seat and relax, dinner will be served in a minute." Just then Robbie came bounding in.

"So ahhh, you know, I was wondering, how did the baby end up in Gayle's belly?"

Clint looked over at Katlin, who turned around without a second's delay and said, "It's not polite to ask questions like that. When you get older we can talk about it."

Robbie frowned and kicked at some invisible thing on the floor, saying, "It's always 'wait until I get older'."

Clint jumped in. "So Robbie, tell me again about this fat four pointer you found for me to hunt."

That instantly switched the conversation and Katlin smiled at Clint. "Well I was off in the woods and I was looking for a buck for you, and I was hiding under this cedar tree, quiet as mouse. I saw some squirrels and chipmunks and birds, you know, the little stuff. All of a sudden this doe walked out into the clearing. I was real quiet and watching. She looked around and smelled the air, making sure the coast was clear, and then she started feeding and wagged her tail. I think that was a signal for the buck to come out."

Clint's eyes got real big and he asked, "Really? Are you sure she wasn't just wagging her tail to get the bugs off?"

Robbie had a very serious look on his face and said, "No. Listen, I am serious. A few minutes later this little – ahhh -- I mean this fat four pointer walked out into the clearing."

Clint laughed and said, "Wait a minute, did you said little? I thought you said this was big fat four pointer?"

Robbie looked embarrassed and looked down at the table. They could see the wheels turning in his head and then he perked up. "Clint I ahhh, I, okay he is a little buck compared to my 8 pointer, but Clint, I want that 8 pointer."

Clint smiled. "Robbie it's fine. I'm just teasing you."

Robbie breathed a sigh of relief. "So I can still hunt the great big buck?"

"Yes, of course you can."

Gayle waddled into the kitchen and sat down. Looking at Clint she said, "I have to ask. Is there any word on Junior?"

Clint looked at Katlin and then to Gayle. "We have nothing yet, but I am sure he will be back soon. You just worry about the baby."

Still looking at Clint, she asked, "What are you going to do?"

Clint wished he could avoid this conversation, but she needed to know. "If he's not back by Monday, I have put together a special team of five men and I will send them out looking for him."

That brightened her spirits up and, with a smile, she said, "Thank you Clint."

While lying in bed later that night, Katlin rolled over and said, "Now Clint, seriously tell me what you are really thinking about Junior."

He adjusted his pillow and said, "Well, I think they may have run into some trouble. What kind, who knows? He might come back, or not. The worst part is we may never know what happened to him. Remember that line in the movie Dance with Wolves? When they found the skeleton. "I'll bet someone back east is going, "Now why don't he write?"

"You don't sound too hopeful? You think he is already dead and a skeleton is what you're really saying?"

"Honey, I'm just telling the truth."

"What?" Her voice went up an octave. "If you knew he didn't stand a chance then why in God's name did you allow him to go?"

Clint just wanted to roll over and go to sleep, but he could see she was troubled by this situation. "I didn't say that. In case you haven't noticed, we are living in a very dangerous time frame of history, if you will, a new modern dark age. People die, people disappear."

"So you think he's dead, is that what you are really saying here?"

"Stop drawing conclusions about what I say. Look, I have no idea. For all we know he is fine and, knowing Junior, he might stay longer to try to gather more men. Or they might be trying to sneak around Duluth with two hundred men and they have to take an extra wide and longer route. I don't know. What I am saying is that if he doesn't come back, we might never find out what happen to him."

"Jesus, Gayle will be crushed if he doesn't come back. She is going to feel abandoned, hopeless and lost. She'll hate you."

"I think hate is a pretty strong word. I am sure she's going to blame me in the end, but let's stop buying trouble. We don't know and I want to give him another week before I will really be worried."

They left it there and drifted off to sleep.

*****

With the flood of new recruits coming in, there was a hidden assassin among them, a specially trained killer from the Rainbow Warriors, whose soul goal in life was to kill Clint and break the spirit of this ragtag militia once and for all. In the fighting last year, his brother had been hit and killed by one of the homemade cannon. He was burning up with rage. His single focus in life was to kill Clint, the man behind the homemade cannon.

He had trained in hand-to-hand combat, using knives, and his personal goal beyond any other, was the desire to kill Clint. For months his mind and body were one, becoming stronger, faster and deadlier.

If he had only joined this army earlier, he could have met Clint and knew what he looked like. He'd heard the rumors of a man that was unstoppable, having been shot in the heart and still lived. They said he'd been shot three times and lived, as the legend went. The story was growing by word of mouth, getting exaggerated and making him into a super hero, but he was just a man that bled like everyone else.

But the people believed in him. He inspired his troops and they would follow him, fighting to their death to be part of this army. He had to be stopped before he became too strong.

The assassin was patient, waiting, watching and listening. What did Clint look like? He still didn't know, but he knew one thing for sure - he would have to catch him alone and kill him with a knife if he was to survive and escape this assignment. Not that he feared death. After his brother's death, he was the last surviving member of his family and he no longer cared if he lived or died. He just wanted the world to know that he was the man that killed Clint Bolan.

The problem was that, while he knew where Clint's Office was, the man was always on the move and never kept to any set schedule. He would have to catch him at night, but where? No one knew where the man slept. He was committed now and his only choice was to play the game and wait for an opportunity to kill the legend.

*****

Clint had a Lieutenant come by to talk him on Saturday and, as they walked outside, he asked Clint point blank. "What do we do with the men that won't kill, but want to help?"

"The natural instinct of most humans is not to kill their own kind, so it's unnatural to want to kill your own species. Surprisingly, reading military history you will hear about some of the bravest men on the battle field that risk all to save their fallen comrades in arms. But never fired a shot at the enemy."

Clint stopped and looked at the lieutenant. "You have these people help in other ways. We need messengers, medics, cooks, and people to haul supplies and take care of animals. You never turn a man down that is willing to help, but doesn't want to fight."

The Lieutenant said, "I never thought of that. Thank you, sir."

Clint asked, "Did you ever read Lt. Col. Dave Grossman's book, *On Killing: The Psychological Cost of Learning to Kill in War and Society?*"

"No, sir. I've never heard of it."

Clint began walking again and the lieutenant followed. "Too bad. He talks about how in war even soldiers did not want to kill their fellow humans being. In WW II, I'm not sure on exact numbers, but I recall that only twenty percent were actively trying to kill the enemy, while eighty percent of the men did not shoot, or shot over the enemy's heads. Later they learned it was because they were taught to shoot only at paper targets, just round circles. Before Vietnam, they switched to shooting at paper targets that looked like humans."

With a puzzled look, he asked, "Okay, so what I am missing here?"

"In Vietnam, ninety percent of the soldiers were doing their very best to kill the enemy."

"Wow, what a radical change from something so simple."

Clint went on. "The author also wrote an article called *On Sheep, Wolves, and Sheepdogs*. In that article he really did a great job explaining the three types of people in the world. The vast majority are sheep, not in a negative sense, but they choose to live life in a kind, gentle, productive way and never intentionally hurt anyone else. Physically hurt them I mean, with violence."

Continuing, he said, "Then we have wolves. These are evil men that want to do great harm to the sheep. In our case it would be the Rainbow Warriors. They want to inflict great harm to others and use force to control people."

Pausing to let this information sink in, he then went on. "Last we have the sheepdogs. The sheepdog's job is to protect the flock and confront the wolf. He has the moral superiority and he is itching for a fight. He's not fighting for the sake of the fight, but more because he knows there is evil that must be confronted and he is the only one to do the job."

As they were approaching the office, he finished by saying, "The major problem with sheep is that they live life in denial. I called it the *utopian dreamland*. These are the people who believe that if all guns were banned, life would be perfect. The problem with these types of dreamers is that when the wolf comes knocking at the door they react with fear, helplessness and horror. They live their lives based on hopes and dreams. Nothing wrong with hopes and dreams but it is denial of the real world. Our job is to turn our fighting men into sheepdogs, rugged, hard and ready to fight to defend those sheep. We are the warrior class and we must act like warriors. Our time has come and the wolf is at the door. It's our job to stop him."

"Good point. Okay, so how many men are truly going to fight?"

"You tell me Lieutenant."

He was stumped for an answer, but managed to say, "From what I have seen, we're in about the seventy-eighty percent range right now."

Clint nodded. "Things are coming together for us. We just need the time to train. We have the sniper scouts out to buy us the time we need. But, and this is a big but, we are going to have to pull this all together quickly and be ready to move. I want to hit the Rainbow Warriors when they are on the road and they are most vulnerable."

"Thanks for the talk, Clint, it gives me something to think about. Have a good night."

"You too, Lieutenant."

Clint wondered how this had all happened. He was in charge of hundreds of lives in a country that was a wasteland, fighting an enemy that was well supplied. This was his worst nightmare. The pressure was continuing to build on him. A victory had to be assured.

Before he could get back inside, two more horses rode into the yard. It was Mike and he said, "There is man here that wants to talk to you."

Clint said, "Who is that?"

Before Mike could respond, "Retired Major Charles Windham the third," was called out.

The two men climbed off their horses and walked over.

Clint offered his hand and said, "Welcome, Major."

Without any niceties, the man said, "Clint, I am taking over this army and you are going to follow my orders."

Clint burst out laughing and said, "In case you haven't noticed, Major, America is in shambles and you have no authority to take over anything."

"I beg to differ, sir. You can't appoint yourself General in charge of militia because you have no experience."

Clint didn't know whether to laugh or get mad. "Major, you are not going to waltz in and take over. Men don't follow fools. Especially my men."

In a huffy voice, the Major said, "I have the authority and, unless America has surrendered, you have to respect military rank and order."

Clint laughed long and hard, saying. "Listen, Major, I would love to have you work with us, but unless you have tanks, attack helicopters and military support, you have nothing. Tell me what you are bringing to the fight?"

"I have ten men under my command. No tanks or attack helicopters."

Clint couldn't help but smirk. "Are your ten men equipped for battle?"

The major, still posing as a statue said, "Yes and they are ready to fight and follow my orders."

Clint continued to stare into the face of this pompous man. "Great, are you going to join and be part of the team?"

In a huff, he responded, "No. I am taking over the whole army."

Clint said, "I would love for you to take command, Major, I truly would, but we have come too far to lose it all now. We have enough men and equipment to do one major battle, but if we don't win, then this ragtag army is going to split apart."

"That is exactly why I have to be in charge."

Clint was losing his patience with this infuriating man, but was trying to show decorum. "Major, I am not going to play this game of who is in charge. You have two choices; you can either join up and come under my command, or leave." Raising his voice to a command level, he added. "Do you understand?"

The Major was taken back and said, "I am not sure about this. I will give you my answer in the morning."

They left and Clint was thinking, *God it would good to be able to turn command over to him, but the people we have now are following me and, like it or not, I have no choice but to lead them into battle.*

Chapter 16

Home Again

At dusk the next evening Dean and Junior headed out. They whispered back and forth. "What do you think? We have what, fifty miles to go and we should be able to maintain three mph and walk for eight hours a night, so we should be back in our area in two days."

Junior smiled, "Sure, as long as we don't run into any problems. No patrols, no ambushes, no friendly traders with laced coffee, no dog packs, no . . ."

Dean cut him off. "Okay, I get the picture. Do you always have to look at the bright side?"

Junior laughed and said, "Just telling the truth. I'm a realist, not a pessimist."

"Okay mister realist, you take point, and watch out for dogs." He ended that statement in a snicker.

They traveled on the pavement to make better time, but without road crews working, the pot holes and upheavals from the winter were a new problem, especially at night. They walked and more often stumbled along.

The night was clear but cool, making good traveling weather. They traveled until about midnight and then stopped for some food. They didn't want a fire for this short stop and just chewed on some fish jerky, drinking plenty of water to wash it down.

Whispering, Junior said, "How long have we been gone?

Dean sighed, "If you start that 'are we there yet' crap, I'll find out if those wet .22s will work. We've been gone three weeks. Don't worry. Gayle is fine; I am sure she is being well taken care of."

Junior almost whined, "But I promised her I would make it back, no matter what."

"And you will. We are doing pretty well so far. We travel on, that's what we do. No matter what demons and hell we have to face, we are too close not to make it now."

"I know, it's just hard, that's all." Junior handed the little rifle to Dean. "It's your turn for point."

Just before day break a shot rang out and Dean was violently tossed on his back. Other shots rang out and Junior heard the bullets' angry ricochets off the pavement.

He ran up to Dean and kneeled down beside him. "Where are you hit?" He was met with silence. Dean's eyes were wide open and staring at the sky. He was dead. The bullets continued ricocheting around him, bringing him out of the shock. The AR-7 lay about twenty feet off to the right. It was too far and in the open, so he ran straight for the cover of the woods. He saw the dirt kick up on his side as the shooting increased and he raced for safety. He heard the footsteps of men chasing after him, but he never turned to look. He increased his speed into the woods, running for his life.

The thieves stripped Dean of his pack and grabbed the AR-7. The leader called out to the rest of his men, telling them to leave him. "He's not worth the energy to chase in these thick woods at night." Not that Junior heard any of that, as he ran for over a mile before stopping to catch his breath.

Tears welled up in his eyes. "Why? Why let us come so far to be cut down less than a day from the safety of home?" He sat down on a fallen log and listened. No one seemed to be in pursuit. He kept waiting for Dean to say, "We lost them. That was easy." But Dean was no longer with him; he was alone.

He closed his eyes and sat for a long time, then thought, "What is taking Dean so long to catch up?" He opened his eyes, half-way expecting to see Dean, but shook his head, trying to clear his thoughts. *No, Dean is dead. But he can't be dead, this must be a dream, this isn't real.* He denied the reality of the situation. He was in shock.

He mumbled to himself, "So close. Only one day away. This can't be happening." He began to wander in shock, feeling like the world had cheated him. It was shortly before noon when he realized he was lost in the woods. He had headed east towards the morning sun. By noon he had no clue which way was east. Dean had the compass. Dean had the rifle. He was still in a stage of shock where he felt like he was in a dream state. He kept thinking he would wake up soon, or Dean would find him. His face was scratched and bleeding from blindly running through the forest, but he didn't care. The pain took away his dark thoughts.

As the sun set and the last light of the day faded, he stopped and curled up under a pine tree. Uncaring about anything, he slept through the night. His dreams were bad. Dean came to him in his dream, waking him up. Dean was in ghostly white form, with a large bullet hole in his chest, but no blood.

Dean said, "You're going the wrong way. You're heading south instead of east. When you wake up, you have to head northeast. You are about five miles from the road."

Junior answered in his sleep, "Dean, are you alive? Do you have the compass?"

But the ghostly vision only said, "No, you are on your own now. But you must remember this in the morning; head north east. Keep the sun on your right shoulder. You must get back to Gayle. You have to tell Clint what is going on. You are their only hope. You must survive."

Junior turned and looked in the direction Dean was pointing, into the darkness. "Dean, you'll show me the way in the morning, right?" When he looked back, Dean was gone. The realism of the dream startled him awake and he looked around, but saw nothing but the blackness of the night. "It was a dream." He said out loud.

As the first morning light filtered through the forest, he awoke and his first thought was to tell Dean about the dream. He looked around and was disappointed to see he was still alone. The dream had been so vivid, so clear.

As he began hiking northeast that morning, he kept the sun on his right shoulder. He understood that Dean was dead and it was just a dream. Anger welled up inside him. Whoever had shot Dean was going to pay. He would avenge his friend, no matter what. He thought, *Dean this is your fault. You left me alone and made too much noise in the lead. That's why you got shot. This is all your fault.*

He was walking in a semi-trance when a branch smacked him in the face. With his built up anger, he attacked the branch, tearing it off and pounding it into the ground. He vented his pain and anger by yelling and screaming at it. After several minutes, he caught his breath and said to himself, "You are acting insane. Get ahold of yourself."

He remembered that he had not eaten, so he sat on a log to rest and chew on some fish jerky. It was tasteless to him. He ate it like a robot, more mechanical than human. He washed down the last bite with a large gulp of water. He said, "Dean told me to keep the sun on my right shoulder, but why would I believe him, it was just a stupid dream. Not even real." He thought that he should head east and into the sun instead. But northeast would cause him to hit the road if he had wandered the wrong way.

Confused and feeling guilty for not being on point last night, he stumbled on. If he had been on point, he would have seen the ambush and Dean would still be alive. It was Dean's fault for being so careless. He was mad and hurting all over again.

He stumbled forward, no longer caring if he headed into the sun or not. The forest never seemed to end and, just before dark, he sat down to rest. He ate some more tasteless jerky and was still feeling the stages of grief. He began having evil dark thoughts of what he wanted to do to the person that killed Dean.

Looking up at the sky he prayed aloud. "God, give us a 'do over'. Take us back in time to the night before Dean was killed. Let me be point man and take us off the road earlier so Dean can live." There was no answer. The clouds rolled in and darkness fell upon him.

That night, as he slept fitfully, his dad came to him in a dream. He told Junior, "You have to stop acting like a baby. Dean is dead and you have a wife with a baby coming, so man up and get your head on straight."

"But dad, you're dead. You can't be here talking to me."

Dreams having no common sense, his dad said, "Listen to me, son, you have to pull it together. A lot of people are depending on you to make it back alive." In his dream, his dad was wearing his bow hunting camo. He kept waiting for him to say it was time to go hunting, or it was daylight in the swamps so get moving, but he didn't. He said, "Head east in the morning; you're almost there. Hit the road and head east. It's clear all the way through."

Junior, tossing and turning in his sleep, said, "How do you know it's clear?"

"Listen to me, son, I don't have much time. Man up now and remember Gayle and your soon to be born child. You are so close to safety. Head east in the morning. Don't forget, head east." And then his father's image dissolved into the night. Was he awake or asleep? He no longer knew whether to believe what was happening or not. His mind was playing tricks on him.

At first light, he woke up and understood that he was truly alone. Depression clouded his mind and he felt overwhelmed. He walked east, straight towards the sun, more like he was on autopilot than remembering the dream. His darkness and misery were searing his soul. *Why does the world have to be so evil?* He thought. *Why so much killing? Will this ever end?*

Around noon, he walked out of the forest and onto the road. He was thinking that it was a strange dream, but it was right. Junior wondered if it was clear to walk on the road in the daylight? In his depression, he no longer cared, so he walked right down the middle of the road in broad daylight. Just before dark he came to realize the reality of his situation and accepted that Dean was dead. He was on his own and, once he came to that conclusion, calm overcame him.

He saw Jim's house just before dark. He had made it, but under the circumstances he was not excited and almost didn't care. He walked up on the porch and knocked on the door.

A voice behind the door said, "I have a double barrel shotgun pointing right at you. Don't move."

Junior said, "Jim, you don't own a double barrel shotgun."

In a surprised voice, Jim said, "Junior is that you? Is Dean with you? I had given up on you two. I figured you were dead for sure." He opened the door and Junior walked in on numb legs, feeling exhausted.

He practically fell into the chair at the table and said, "Dean is dead. He died two days ago, after all we had been through together. He was shot down for no reason by some stinking thieves."

Jim took the seat across from him and said, "I am so sorry, Junior."

Exhaustion overtook him and he let his head fall into his hands, saying, "It's my fault. I should have never asked him to go with me."

Jim didn't know exactly what to say, but tried to comfort him, saying, "Come on now, you know he wouldn't have gone with you if he hadn't wanted to. He knew what he was getting into."

Junior was quietly crying, keeping his head buried in shame. His filthy face was all scratched up and caked with dried blood running down in crazy patterns. He looked like the walking dead.

Jim reached across and put his hand on Junior's shoulder, trying to comfort him. "Relax now; you are safe. We have to get you cleaned up. You don't want Gayle to see you this way, do you?"

Junior used his shirt to wipe his tears away and said, "Gayle was right, it was a fool's errand and I should have never gone."

"Now, now, I don't want to hear it. You come with me right now. You need to take a bath and get cleaned up. I was just heating some water on the stove. I'll bring it to you, so go get out of those filthy rags and get cleaned up. I think I have some clothes that might fit you and then I'll fix you something to eat."

Junior slowly got up and shuffled into the bathroom, with his head hanging down. Jim took him the bucket of hot water.

He looked in the mirror and saw the hollow eyes and dried blood on his face. He felt empty inside. He stripped off his clothes and suddenly realized just how badly he stank. He stepped in the bath tub and poured half the water over his head, soaping up. By the time he had finished scrubbing himself clean, he began to feel human again. He rinsed and then dried off and put on the fresh clothes that Jim had given him.

He did feel a little better, but that empty feeling was still there. He walked out and sat down at the kitchen table. Jim looked him over and said, "Good timing. Here's some venison steak and potatoes. Eat up and relax." Jim walked over the cupboard and pulled down a bottle. "Here, take a shot of whiskey and relax. You are safe now." After dinner Junior asked for another shot, or the whole bottle, to numb the pain.

Jim poured him a small portion, saying, "No, you have to keep your wits about you. I am going to send word to let Gayle and Clint know you are back. Here is one more shot, but you promise me you will drink no more when I leave."

Junior picked up the glass and said, "Sure Jim, thanks for your help."

As soon as Jim left, he slammed the shot down and walked over to the cupboard and grabbed the bottle of Johnny Walker. He poured himself a double shot and drank it down. He felt that one cruising down his throat, burning and warming his insides. He went to the couch and let himself drop on to it. As he sat down, he was feeling numb and closed his eyes. Dean was dead. Now he must pull it together for Gayle, but he didn't care. She would have to help him.

Within an hour Clint was there. Jim had reported that Junior looked half dead and he seemed empty inside, blaming himself for Dean's death.

Clint wondered what the hell they had been through. It had to have been a nightmare. He walked inside and found Junior asleep on the couch. He gave him a slight shake and said, "Junior, I'm so damn glad to see you, son. So glad you made it." He made sure not to refer to Dean in any way.

Junior rubbed his face and looked up with empty eyes. "Yeah, I made it, but Dean is dead."

Clint put his hand on Junior's shoulder and quietly said, "I know. I heard and I'm truly sorry. Dean was a good man."

Junior became a little defensive and said, "You have no idea what a great man he was. He saved me and he came up with the plan to build a sail boat canoe to cross Lake

Superior. He showed me how to catch fish. He made the trade for the chicken shit gun powder. He kept me strong through the Rainbow Warriors' brainwashing. But then he was careless two days ago while walking point and was killed. I should have never asked him to come with me. It's my fault he is dead."

Clint's mind was racing. They were captured and somehow they escaped and crossed Lake Superior in canoe? They were tortured? He shook his head, trying to focus. Junior was in shock and suffering from survivor's guilt. He was letting it consume his soul. Clint firmly gripped him by both shoulders and said, "Listen Junior, you need to sleep here tonight. Rest and pull yourself together before you see Gayle."

"Gayle?" He said absent mindedly. "Did she have the baby yet?"

"Not yet. She's not due for a couple of days. You'll be there to see your baby born. How does that sound?"

"I need to see her right now. I need to hold her. Let me go see her." He tried to get up and was going to head out the door, but Clint stopped him.

"Not tonight, son. You've been through one hell of an ordeal and you need to get your head together."

Junior had a need to spill all of his information out at once and said, "Clint, I have to tell you the worst news. The Rainbow Warriors are being supplied by the Chinese and they're going to be reinforced this spring with a tank and machine guns." Before Clint could even absorb the information, Junior went on. "Dean's ghost told me I had to tell you this." He looked up at the ceiling and said, "Dean, you can rest in peace. I finished the mission." Tears were running down his face, but he didn't care.

"Junior, relax. You are rambling. Tell me what's going on. What Chinese are you talking about?"

Junior kept rambling on, telling Clint about the helicopter, grabbing the briefcase, earning the right to take it to the General. Clint grabbed Junior and sat him at the table. "The Chinese helicopter dropped it off? Did you see it?"

Junior continued. "They're getting resupplied this spring, with food, a tank and machine guns. We don't stand a chance once they get the tank. We have to move, leave this part of the country. We need to stay away from Interstate 35. They are going to control the country from Texas to Canada."

"The Chinese? That must be who set off the EMP." Clint said, thinking out loud. "Now they are going for our bread basket to feed their own people. Of course...the iron ore from the north too. I should have figured it out sooner."

Clint was pacing the kitchen and said, "Junior, listen to me, calm down and tell me what you know. This is vital information that I must understand."

Junior's eyes flared with anger as he yelled at Clint. "What you need to understand is a great man is dead because of me. Damn you Clint for letting me go on this fool's mission. I should have listened to Gayle and stayed put. Dean would still be alive. This is my fault."

Clint wanted to slap some sense into Junior, but he knew he was suffering from the events he had been through. He understood that Junior's young mind was trying to deal with the tragic event of Dean dying.

Clint lowered his voice to calm Junior down and said, "You need to get some sleep and clear your head. We'll talk in the morning."

Junior's expression went blank and he stood up. "I'm going to bed." He stumbled off towards the spare bedroom.

Clint and Jim watched him walk down the hall. When he was gone, Jim said, "Wow, they have been to hell and back. What should I do?"

Clint was feeling a little guilty that he had sent them off on a fool's errand, but this Intel was worth it. How many lives would be saved because they knew what was coming? He said, "Let him sleep. I'll be here in the afternoon. Whatever you do, promise me on your life that you will never say one word about what you just heard to anyone."

Jim nodded. "Ah yeah, sure, but why?"

Clint's mind was going a mile a second. "Several reasons, with the main one being we don't want the

Rainbow Warriors to hear what we know. Chances are they think Junior and Dean are dead. The other reason is that we don't want our troops to get scared out of their minds and scatter into the wind. We can take whatever they are going to throw at us, but only after we are a fighting army. Don't you dare tell a soul, not one single person."

Jim held his hands up. "Okay Clint. I understand."

"I don't mean to be a hard ass, but if a word of this is leaked to anyone, I will kill you myself."

Jim was stunned. "Hey, I can keep my mouth shut. That's pretty harsh Clint." As he stepped back from the demon that Clint had become.

Clint looked him square in the eye. "Better to be harsh than having no fighting force to stop this threat. I am sorry Jim. If I'd had any idea that what he was going to say was this important, I would have ask you to stay outside, but I can't undo what has already been done."

"I understand Clint, but calm down a bit. I won't say a word, I promise."

"Okay Jim. I'll see you in the afternoon. Fed him in the morning and make sure he has his head on straight" Jim nodded as Clint let himself out the front door.

Junior had fallen into a deep sleep. He was exhausted and the whisky just added to it. Around 4 a.m. Dean woke him up in a dream. "You did good, Junior. I am proud of you. I am in a better place now. You have to go to Gayle right now. She is going to have the baby soon."

Junior opened his eyes and Dean's ghostly form was standing beside the bed. He still had the large hole in his chest. It hadn't healed yet. "Dean, I am so sorry. We shouldn't have ever left here. It's my fault you are dead."

"No Junior, I volunteered to go. It's not your fault. Go to Gayle now, time is short."

Junior asked, "What are you talking about 'time is short'? How is Gayle doing? Is she is having the baby?"

The apparition only said, "Go now." and then faded away. Junior woke up with a start. He looked around the room, but there was no Dean. It had just been a DREAM. *Go back to sleep*, he told himself, but the nagging feeling would not leave him. Dean had been right the other times, so why not believe him now?

Junior quickly got out of bed and got dressed. He walked right out of the house without waking Jim up, and headed for Gayle.

Chapter 17

Little Dean

Junior walked all night and it was close to high noon when he was in sight of the cabin. He stopped and thought about what Dean had said in the dream, about the baby coming, so he managed the strength to run the last fifty yards and burst through the door.

The noise startled Robbie, who was in the kitchen boiling water, and he grabbed for his rifle, but then noticed it was Junior. He let the rifle go and ran to him, grabbing him in a death-like hug.

Junior finally peeled him off and asked, "Where is Gayle?"

Robbie said, "She's in the bedroom with Mom. She's having the baby."

Junior ran to the bedroom and stopped abruptly, seeing Gayle being cared for by Katlin and another woman. Gayle was screaming as the women were trying to help her push through the contractions. He could only stand there and watch. He was petrified by the scene and couldn't move.

Soon, he heard the women say, "It's a boy!" and then a baby cried.

Junior gasped and fell to his knees and that was when Katlin first noticed him. Katlin rushed to him and her moving aside allowed Gayle to see him. She screamed and cried for joy, saying, "Junior. Oh my God, you made it. Come meet your new son."

Katlin helped Junior to the bed and he sat at the edge, admiring his new son and kissing Gayle gently on the face. He was beside himself with joy and felt lucky that he had made it home in time to see his son born.

Everyone had a thousand questions for Junior, but he could only think about being home and his new son. He said, "What shall we name him?"

The room fell silent and everyone looked to Gayle. She said, "I don't suppose you'd care for the name 'Wild Man', would you?

Junior looked at her with a frown and said, "Wild Man? What kind of a name is that?"

Gayle explained how the baby had kicked and turned during the last part of the pregnancy and she began calling him The Wild Man. Junior laughed and then got a serious look on his face. He looked at the baby and said, "We shall name him for the greatest man I know. Dean."

Gayle asked, "Where is Dean?" Junior shook his head and tears began rolling down his cheeks. Gayle understood and wiped them away, saying, "It's alright. You're home safe now and we have a son."

Junior smiled weakly and said, "I know, I just wish he could be here to see his namesake."

Katlin and the other lady left them to be alone and Junior laid down next to Gayle, with the baby on her stomach nursing, and they all fell asleep.

* * * * *

Clint needed to talk to Junior again. He was hoping the new baby would cheer him up and help snap him out of the tragic events he had gone through. He also prayed that he hadn't told anyone about the information he had shared before. Having heard that Junior was at the cabin, he rode out to talk with him. "Are you feeling better today?"

"Yes. Sorry about yesterday Clint, I was just over tired and hurting deep inside."

"It's okay Junior. Let's take a walk" They went outside and headed towards the pond. "Now tell me what is going on with the Chinese."

Junior took a deep breath and said, "Okay, from what I could piece together, the Rainbow Warriors knew the EMP attack was coming and had already been supplied with weapons, food, medicine, etc. That is how they rose to power so fast. The Chinese want to control the middle of the country and get the fields producing food again for their people. They also want the iron ore for steel. They are coming up through the Great Lakes and their next resupply is scheduled for this coming spring. The Rainbow Warriors' job was to clear the way and wipe out resistance forces to make it easier for the Chinese."

Clint had a sneer on his face. "Those damn fools. What did the Chinese promise them?"

"The Chinese promised to give them land anywhere in the U.S. that they could use for 'their tribes' and they would leave them alone so they can co-exist with the animals."

Clint was pacing back and forth now, filled with rage. "Those fools. The Chinese hate traitors. They will use these people up and then slaughter them. The Chinese way of thinking is that if you're a traitor to your own country, sooner or later you are going to turn on them. They must have heard of the Green Bay Army having trouble with us and want to end it quickly, by giving them a tank and machine guns. You did well getting this information back to me and you must not mention any of this to anyone. The Rainbow Warriors or the Chinese cannot know what we know and I want you to stay out of this fight. You have done your job and we are grateful, but you have new son and wife that need you now. So you are staying here."

Junior stood up. "Wait Clint, what? No way am I staying. I am going to fight with you, just like last time."

Clint put his hand on Junior's shoulder and looked him in the eye. "This is not like last time. We have an army of five hundred men. This is totally different. Plus I promised myself that if you made it back, I was not going to put you in danger again. You have a wife and son now and you have already been through hell. Besides, I want you to teach Robbie how to live off the land."

Junior looked dejected. "You mean baby sit."

Clint tried to soften it. "No, that's not what I mean. You have a special set of skills. Not many people know how to trap and snare. You need to teach this to Robbie. What if you died? Your knowledge would die with you. We need you to teach Robbie how to find food and be self-reliant."

Junior thought about it for a minute and then said, "You're right. I should teach him about trapping snapper turtles, bullfrogs and crayfish to eat in the summer."

Clint was nodding his head to reinforce Junior's comments. "See, that's what I told you. You have special skills and Robbie needs you to teach him. So will you do it?"

While Junior wasn't wearing a happy face, he said, "Of course I will."

"Good. Now let me worry about the fighting. Please stay close to Gayle for a couple of days before you take off again. I have got tons of stuff to do."

"Clint, when am I going to get over Dean's death?"

"You'll never get over it fully, but you must learn to accept it. You don't know; he could have died here falling off a horse. When your time is up, that's it. You can only accept it and move on. Remember the good times you had and that it wasn't your fault. He was a great man, so remember him for that."

"That's a lot easier said than done."

Clint rubbed his shoulder and said, "It takes time, my friend."

* * * * *

While Clint was riding to the army, he was thinking that with so many new men they had to find a way to get the best ones up front quickly. How to do it? Then he remembered something an old drill sergeant had told him.

Throughout history, as far back as three thousand years ago, armor weighed in at about seventy pounds. Even modern equipment for the military was seventy pounds. Clint thought that to speed up the process of who would be on the front line, they would have a test. In order to pass this test, the men had to carry a seventy-pound pack for five miles. Those that passed would be considered fit enough to be on the front line. There was no time to get people in shape.

The Major rode up to him before he reached camp. "Sir, I and my men have decided we would like to join up and offer our help in this campaign."

Clint smiled, knowing it took a lot for this man to say that. "Good. And Major, please relax and call me Clint." The Major's posture never changed, but he did seem to relax. Clint went on, "Please tell me you have at least one drill sergeant in your ranks."

"Yes, I believe we do, Clint."

"Good Charles, so grab your men and have them report to the head drill instructor and help wherever they can. If you'd like to come up to my office, we'll come up with a plan to win this battle."

The Major agreed and rode off to get his men. Clint was reading the scouts' report when Charles returned. Clint told him to grab a cup of coffee before they started, but the Major passed, saying, "That stuff makes me shaky." He then asked, "What exactly are we facing?"

Clint said, "First, I'd like your resume of experience so I can put you to good use. What did you do in the army?"

The Major stood up straight, almost at attention and said, "I was liaison officer for General Mark Hughes at the Pentagon. Gen. Hughes was responsible for military and civilian departments' procurement. I liaised between him and other departments, including FEMA, on securing supplies."

Clint nodded and then asked, "And the men you have with you, where did they come from and what did they do?"

Again the major responded. "Most of them are from the reserve unit that I joined after retirement. Two were friends of mine that lived in my area. All are trained military fighters."

Again Clint nodded his understanding. "Thank you for that information, Major. Aside from the drill sergeant, do you have any armory guys?"

The major nodded and said, "Yes. Sergeant Aims is a master armorer."

"Good, good." Clint said. "I know we can definitely use his services."

After the Q and A session, Clint moved on. Pulling out a map, he pointed to an area, saying "The main force from Green Bay is traveling across Highway 8 to set up a supply and reinforcement route, allowing both armies to aid each other." He pointed to a specific area on the map and said, "We have scouts and sniper teams harassing them. On their return trip I want to hit them hard and take them out. Then we'll go to Green Bay and finish this once and for all." Clint had respect for the Major and his years of service, so asked, "Any thoughts on the plan?"

The Major hesitated and then said, "But they travel with artillery. How do you plan on avoiding that?"

Clint smiled and said, "We steal it from them, or set up an ambush that is so deadly they will never have time use it."

"Okay, so what do you have in mind?

Clint said, "A morning assault with the sun in their eyes. A scout of mine gave me a recipe for making gunpowder. We can make up enough gunpowder to make bombs. We have two machine gun nests and, in case you haven't heard, we have fifty mounted cavalry that are fearsome in their own right."

Charles smiled. "I see what you are saying."

Clint continued. "We catch them going up a hill, one that has high banks on each side, so we can catch them in the cross fire. The cavalry stays out of sight, just over the hill. We drop bombs on them and have the machine guns and everyone else open up. Once we have enough of them down, the cavalry comes in for mop up."

The Major was silent for a moment, thinking, and then said, "Clint, I see nothing wrong with your plan, except what measures do you have to stop them from retreating?"

Clint said, "I thought about that. The largest majority of them are on foot, so they can't out run a horse, plus retreating would mean leaving everything behind. If they turn and run, we'll have the cavalry mop them up."

The Major nodded. "I agree, but you only have fifty men on horseback. I think we should have at least one hundred men in the rear, just to make sure that none of them can escape."

"I tell you what, Major, I agree and think we should have a separate command. I want you to take ninety of my men, to join your 10, and then you train them. You will be in charge of the rear command."

"But Clint, I don't know your men. How will I pick them?"

"You won't. Come with me, Major, and let's go see the men."

They mounted up and rode down to the training area, where Clint called the lieutenant over, asking him to call formation.

The lieutenant gave the order and they lined up in sixteen squads, consisting of thirty men, three deep and ten across. It was an impressive sight, seeing the five hundred men all together. The officer and senior NCO stood up in front of the troops.

There were eight squads on each side. Clint and the Major rode into the middle. Clint wanted to be above the men to introduce the Major.

"Men, this is Major Charles Windham and he wants to take over command. I will leave it up to you men. If you choose the Major to be in charge, I will step down."

The Major began squirming in his saddle, not sure what Clint was doing.

There was dead silence and you could have heard a pin drop. The men started looking around at each other in confusion.

The lieutenant spoke up first. "General, I can't speak for anyone but myself, but I joined because of you and would prefer to be under your command."

A sergeant spoke up next. "I am behind you, General."

More and more began to speak out and then the group began to chant, "With Clint. With Clint we stand."

Clint held up his hand until everyone quieted down and then began to speak, "Okay, now the Major has military training. I want to assign him ninety men that will be trained under his command." Clint sized up the assembly and then said, "Out of the eight squads on the left, I want the 3rd, 6th, and 9th man in all three rows to step forward. You will be under Major Windham's command. First squad on the right, do the same."

He turned to the major and said, "There are your ninety men. Have your sergeant see the quartermaster for supplies and then ride back with me."

Clint then looked at the lieutenant and gave the order, "Back to training."

As they rode back, the Major asked, "What was that all about? You already said I was going to be in command of one hundred men."

Clint slowed his horse and said, "Major, in order for the men to follow and respect you, I wanted them to see you as an important person. I was also setting you up as second in command. While Colonel Knight is in charge of the cavalry, and he is a good choice, he is a rash and hard man. He doesn't have the disposition of a good leader. Let me give you a piece of advice. Drop the military spit and polish and make them fighting men we can be proud of going into battle with. Teach them how to be fighting men."

The Major turned his head slightly sideways and said, "I underestimated you, General. You are one of the rare men that are natural leaders."

Clint laughed and said, "Thank you, but to tell you the truth I was hoping they wanted you. It's much easier to be a Special Forces type guy, giving an enemy a hard time than to be a General." As they rode on, Clint said, "I'll show you where I want you to set up camp. Now you only have a few days to pull these men together because time is short, so use it wisely."

* * * * *

The embedded assassin was happy. Being in the group that was there during the announcement about the Major, he finally knew what Clint looked like. Seeing the troops stand behind the man was powerful. He understood his mission and it was even more important now. He would have to make a plan soon and pull it together before they left for battle. He was going to kill him as soon as the chance came up.

* * * * *

A few days later, Junior took Robbie out on a field trip. As they headed back to the beaver pond, Robbie said, "Junior, I'm sorry about Dean."

Junior looked at him and said, "Me too, kiddo, but I really don't want to talk about that right now."

"Okay, so tell me what we are going to do."

"Well, because we haven't had much fresh meat, I thought I would show you how to catch summer food. Later, in the fall, I'll teach you how to trap and snare."

Robbie was a little hurt by that and said, "But I've brought all kinds of fish home."

"That's true and you did a great job. We are all proud of you."

Robbie beamed like a flashlight. "I told Mom you would be proud of me."

"Okay, but you're walking right past other food."

Robbie quickly looked around. "Really? Like what?"

Junior said, "Snakes, frogs, turtles and crayfish."

Robbie made a face and said, "Snakes, yuck. Are you teasing me? You don't really eat snakes, do you?"

"Of course. They taste just like chicken." Junior chuckled. He went on, saying, "All of those critters I mentioned are good protein. When we talk about catching and eating turtles, there are important things you need to learn. The first thing is that eastern wood turtles can eat poisonous mushrooms and while it doesn't hurt the turtle, the toxins accumulate in its body. If you do decide to eat it, those toxins would quickly kill you."

Robbie made a gagging face and said, "Okay, what do wood turtles look like?"

Junior liked that Robbie was inquisitive and said, "They are small, like a painted turtle, but they have different colors and shapes. So, to play it safe, any turtle with a shell under 10-inches is too small to eat. Or if it has yellow and red coloring, as those are nature's way of telling us that they could be poisonous. We want snapping turtles. They never have bright colors and are mean as bulls in a china shop."

Robbie, keeping up with the questions, asked, "Okay, and how big do they get?"

Junior held out his hands to make the approximate size and said, "They can reach up to one hundred pounds, but most of the ones we'll catch are in the twelve-twenty five pound range."

Robbie's eyes got big and he said, "Wow, a hundred pounds! That is bigger than I am!"

Junior smiled at his comparison and said, "Yes, and they are incredible strong. There are several ways to catch the snapping turtle. One is to swim up behind them and grab their tail, but you have to remember to keep them away from you, or they can bite you. A good rule of thumb is to keep them half their shell length away from you. That is about how far they can stretch their neck out to strike."

Robbie was engrossed in the information and asked, "How strong are they?"

Junior said, "Well, a twelve pound snapping turtle can catch and hold a twenty pound pike."

"Wow, that is strong, but there's no pike in these ponds." Robbie said, a little confused.

"Well Robbie, they eat all kinds of fish and that was just an example."

Robbie had a look of sudden understanding and said, "Oh. Okay, I get it."

"All right Robbie, so the first thing we need to do is get some bait for the traps."

"What are we going to use for bait?"

Junior patted his rifle and said, "Chipmunks. That's why I brought the pellet rifle."

"Oh, I know where a whole bunch of chipmunks are. Follow me." They walked a few hundred yards further and

Robbie whispered, "This is my deer lookout spot. Just sit down and wait a few minutes and the chipmunks will be running all over."

Junior nodded and they sat down to wait. Less than two minutes later a chipmunk came by and Junior shot and killed it. Picking it up, he said, "Okay, now it's off to the beaver pond."

When they got to the pond, Junior cut the chipmunk in half and stuck one half on the trigger of a 220-body gripper trap. He set the trap and walked out into the water, placing it in about two feet of water, near the bottom, using a couple of sticks to stabilize the trap. He had already tied 550-cord to the trap and, walking back to shore, he tied it off to a strong branch.

He explained to Robbie, "Now the turtle will try to get a free lunch and get caught in the trap. If there isn't one around right now, we can leave the trap set and should have him in the morning."

Robbie said, "I don't understand. I can't see the trap."

"That's right and neither can anyone else. So here is your first test. Tomorrow morning you have to lead us back to this trap. So look around real good and make sure you can find it."

"Okay, I got it." Robbie said, "It's right past the first fallen log on Wood Duck pond."

"Wood Duck pond?"

"Oh yeah, I forgot to tell you that when you were gone I named the beaver ponds. I saw a wood duck on this pond, which is how I picked the name. Pretty cool right?"

"Very cool. Okay, let's walk down to the other pond. They walked down and, once they reached it, Junior picked up a two-inch diameter beaver stick that was about three feet long. He sat down on a log and pulled out some fishing line. "This is thirty-pound test fishing line and we tie this off to the stick and it has one small treble hook." He buried the piece of bait on the hook. "When the turtle swallows the bait, he is hooked and we pull him in. But again, we set this out in the mud and push the stick under water, out of sight, so you have to remember where this one is too."

"Okay Junior, this is Beaver Slapping pond."

Junior laughed and said, "I know how you picked that name."

"Yeah, there was this big fat beaver and I was trying to fish and he scared all the fish away by slapping his tail at me."

Junior laughed again and then asked, "Okay, are you about ready for lunch?"

Robbie nodded vigorously and said, "Yes, but we didn't bring anything to eat."

Junior said, "Look around you. You are surrounded by food. You can't say there is nothing to eat."

Robbie looked around. "I don't see any food."

"Yes, you don't see any food because you have untrained eyes."

Robbie wrinkled his nose and said, "I don't understand."

"Okay, first you walked by a water snake sleeping on a log, not fifty yards from here. But because you have learned how to walk quietly in the woods, he is still sunning himself."

Robbie made a face. "Yuck. Do we really have to eat a snake?"

"Yes. It's all part of training you. Besides, they don't taste bad at all. Let me show you."

They walked down closer to the snake, with Junior in the lead, slowly stalking his prey as carefully as if he was stalking a buck. He was carrying a six-foot long sapling tipped with a treble hook. He careful lay down for the last few feet and crawled up, reaching out with the sapling; he quickly hooked the snake and flipped him on shore. A quick, deadly blow to the head and the snake was dead.

"Now Robbie, even poisonous snakes are food, as long as you cut the head off. He is easy to clean," showing the boy, he cut off the head and peeled the skin off, "like this. Now gut them and wash them off, cut them into hot dog length sizes and place them on branches for roasting."

He quickly made a fire and they each roasted two pieces. When they were finished, Robbie waited and Junior ate, explaining to be careful around the bones.

Finally, after Robbie made several weird faces, he tried a tiny little piece. "Oh, that's good."

Junior laughed. "Now you can tell your mom we had wild hot dogs for lunch."

Robbie was laughing hard at that one. "Can you see her face? She is going to be mad at you." He finished and said, "I am still hungry."

Junior looked around and then said, "How about some dessert then?"

Robbie's eyes got big and he excitedly said, "Okay. What?"

"You walked right past a wild blueberry bush."

"Yum, I really I love blueberries."

"Well these are wild blueberries and quite a bit smaller than store bought ones, but I think they taste better." Junior walked over and showed him what the bushes looked like. They gathered them by the handful and ate until they were full.

Robbie turned to Junior and said, "Thank you for teaching me this stuff. My mom doesn't know any of this and Clint is always gone, you know."

"They both have very important jobs and I wouldn't be here today if your mother hadn't found me and saved my life with her medical skills. We might all be dead if Clint had not taught us how to fight. We are all part of a group and everyone is very important."

Robbie thought about what Junior said.

Junior then said, "These blueberries are delicious. I think we should pick about a quart of them to take home for everyone to enjoy. What do you say?"

"Sounds good to me, but what do we put them in?"

"We can make a birch bark container of course." He walked over to a downed birch tree and pulled his knife out, cutting a piece about twelve by twelve inches. He rolled it into a cone and folded the bottom. Then he cut a strip about half an inch wide, by twelve inches long and wrapped it around the cone, tying it off. "Here you go, Robbie. Go start filling this up."

"Wow Junior, That was cool." Within thirty minutes it was full and they walked back to the cabin.

Chapter 18

The Assassin's plan

The assassin was trying his best to get assigned guard duty in the evening, but it was tough because the guards were split up on four hour shifts; Midnight to 4 a.m., 4 to 8, then 8-12 and so on around the day. The only problem was that Clint didn't hold a set schedule. Sometimes he left at 6 or 7, while other times he left at 9 or 10 p.m. The assassin had to get approved to switch to a different guard duty shift, like the outer guard, between 4-8 shifts and 8 to midnight shifts.

He kept to himself, but told everyone that his brother had been killed and he had joined for revenge. It was always best to stay as close to the truth as possible. He omitted the fact of who killed his brother.

The next step was to kill Clint. The timing had to be perfect. If he could catch him alone, it would be over in a minute. A knife thrown to the back, or a slice across his throat and he'd be gone in a flash, riding away on the General's horse. He had switched to the 8-12 watch so he could kill him in the dark, but just his luck, Clint left around six that day.

* * * * *

Robbie and Junior made it back to the cabin as Katlin was walking up and Robbie ran up to her. "Mom, mom, look what we brought you. Fresh blueberries. Isn't that great?"

Katlin looked in the birch bark cone and smiled. "Yes Robbie. Good job. Why don't you go show Gayle?" He ran into the cabin and was yelling, "Gayle look what we have. Fresh blueberries."

Robbie got a different reaction from Gayle than he expected. She had finally got little Dean to sleep on the couch and Robbie's yelling woke him up and he began crying. Gayle roughly said, "Robbie, why did you do that? I have been trying to get him asleep for hours and look what you did." She picked the baby up and told Robbie, "You have to learn to be quiet when you come in." She yelled.

Katlin had just come in and yelled at Gayle, "Don't you yell at my son. He was just sharing his excitement with you. He hasn't been around babies and doesn't know any better."

Gayle was exhausted and little Dean was wailing. She handed him to Junior and said, "Here daddy, do your job and rock him to sleep."

Junior said, "What? Why don't you rock him to sleep?"

She was almost in tears and yelled, "Because he is your son too and you need to help me. I'm exhausted and need to go to bed." She looked at Katlin saying, "You need to talk to your son and explain about babies."

Katlin was about to lay into her when Clint walked in.

The baby was wailing and everyone was arguing. He whistled loudly and shouted, "Okay everyone, time out. The war is out there," he said pointing outside. "This is a place of comfort and peace, so let's treat it that way."

Gayle, almost on the verge of collapse, said, "Everything was peaceful and quiet until Robbie ran in yelling, waking the baby up."

Clint held up his hands. "Hold up before anymore is said and remember that we are all friends and there is a new baby in the house. We all have to adjust. Robbie, say you are sorry for waking up the baby."

Robbie had tears in his eyes from being yelled at. "Gayle, I'm sorry. I didn't mean to wake up little Dean. I didn't know he was asleep."

Gayle sighed and said, "It's okay Robbie, but just please be a little quieter around him, okay?"

"Okay. Sorry."

Junior was rocking the baby and he was quiet, so the tension in the room began to calm down.

Clint said, "Okay, good, now Robbie take those into the kitchen and wash them up."

* * * * *

The assassin practiced with his knife all watch. Over and over again he would throw the knife, sticking it the same spot on the tree. He would only have one chance at this. If he failed, a security team would surely be assigned to protect Clint after that and he would have a hard time getting to him.

He paced the road, picking his spot out. Should he try a frontal assault? No, the horse might shy or jump. On the side, the target becomes smaller and harder to hit, especially at night. Nope he had to hit him in the back; it was the only way to do it.

Assassins had changed the course of history many times. This was going to be one of those times. The loss of Clint would paralyze the ability for this ragtag army to make war. He must be careful not to enrage the men with an obscene killing. If it was too brutal, Clint would be hailed as a martyr and that could backfire on their cause.

Once his plan was in motion, he dared not hesitate. Hesitation would be doom for him. He remembered his training and how Clint might try to escape his attack. He could hide near the road until Clint was just past him, but what if he heard him? The safest was of course not to be heard. He practiced sneaking out on the road, going through the motion of throwing the knife and straining his ears to see if there was anything to warn Clint.

He wished he had more time to prepare. His need for revenge and desire for Clint to suffer at his hand were clouding his judgment. A true assassin must never allow emotions to take over. After he was relieved from watch, he meditated. Sleep could wait a few minutes longer. He needed to clear his mind and focus on the mission to kill Clint, and then quickly and quietly escape into the night.

Maybe he should just shoot him instead. When he was on guard duty, he was armed. He could get his revenge by standing in front of Clint and telling him why he was going to die. The thought did bring him satisfaction, but the other guards would quickly be on him. If he was killed, the word would never reach his own command. No, to break the spirit of this army, he had to kill him silently and disappear into the night. It would be hours before anyone figured out what had happened. That would be a powerful psychological defeat for the men. The great General Clint Bolan killed within hearing distance of his own army. His own doubt was putting uncertainty in his mind. Clint was a large man and he would not die easily. What if he called out? What if he was only wounded? He could shoot and killed the assassin.

He had to clear his mind and focus on the 6-inch blade of the knife penetrating deep into the General's lung. That would prevent Clint from calling out. The plan was going to work. He drifted off to sleep.

* * * * *

The next morning, after helping Gayle with the baby, Robbie and Junior headed out to check the traps.

Robbie was shuffling slowly just behind Junior and said, "Junior, I'm sorry for starting that big fight yesterday."

Junior stopped and looked at him. "It's wasn't your fault little buddy. This baby is a whole new experience for all of us. For such a little thing, he sure can scream loud, can't he?" He laughed.

"He sure can. I think he was the loudest until Clint whistled."

"Okay, from now on just remember that Gayle is tired from taking care of little Dean and she will be on edge, so just tip-toe in the cabin and be as quiet as you can. Now let's focus on our job."

"Okay Junior. What's the lesson for today?"

"Well, I'm assuming we have a couple of snappers in the traps, so remember what I said. Snapping turtles are

233

vicious and can hurt you quickly. I remember watching a You Tube video when a guy was showing off to his friend with a big snapper. He put his hands close to his head, telling his friend it was safe, and then OOOOOOUUUUUCCCCHHHH. The snapper bit him."

Robbie's eyes got big and he asked, "Wow, what happened? Did the snapper bite his fingers off?"

"No, but it was funny as heck listening to him cuss and scream in pain. He finally got the snapper to let go and the video ended."

"So how do I not get bitten?"

"You have to be careful and listen to me, doing exactly as I say."

"I will Junior, I promise."

"Even in the trap, he is still going to be alive. We'll take him out of the trap and put him in this old pillow case and then he is safe to carry home."

"Can't he bite through the bag?"

"No, it works great. You'll see, maybe today. Sometimes it takes the turtles a couple of days to find the bait."

Junior made Robbie lead the way, finding the right pond and then the trap. They approached the trap and Junior said, "You stay here while I wade out and check." He waded out and reached down, checking the spring to see if it had been sprung. Nothing. It was still set. He pulled the trap up and checked the bait. Still on there. "Okay, off to the next set."

"Nothing? Darn." Robbie was disappointed.

"That's trapping, Robbie. You don't always get lucky." They walked down to the next pond. Feigning forgetfulness, Junior said, "Okay, where did I make this set? I forgot."

Robbie said, "I'll show you." He walked confidently right to the spot and said, "Remember? Straight out from here." He pointed into the pond.

"Good job, Robbie. I would have never found it without your help." Robbie was beaming as Junior waded out and pulled the stake out. He pulled on the line and felt the weight. Excited he said, "Yes, it worked. We got one, little buddy."

Robbie almost ran out into the water, but stopped just short, saying, "Really? I want to see."

"Okay, but first I have to get him off the bottom." On the first pull of the line he saw that it was wrapped around a branch. He waded over to it and carefully unwrapped it. He pulled straight up and a moss covered shell broke the surface and started thrashing. The turtle was fighting like mad, using its powerful legs to swim to deeper water. Junior reached down and grabbed his tail, pulling him out of the water. Turning to Robbie he said, "Now that's the way you do it. He is about eighteen pounds."

He waded to shore and, quickly cutting the line about three feet away, he tossed the turtle up on land. He wrapped the line around the stick and said, "Tomorrow we will tie a new hook on it, bait it and try a new pond."

The turtle was up and walking for the pond. "Robbie go grab his tail and stop him, but be careful, like I told you."

Robbie ran over behind it and tried to grab the tail, but he was scared and missed. Junior walked over and stepped on the back half of the shell to prevent it from escaping and the snapper whipped his head out and back, trying to bite him. He was hissing mad. Robbie stepped back and his eyes were big as he said, "He is really mad."

"Like I told you yesterday, they have no sense of humor. Now grab his tail." Robbie got a hold of the tail and Junior removed his foot. The turtle dug his powerful front claws in and start pulling Robbie toward the pond.

Junior began laughing and said, "Hold him, and don't let him get away."

Robbie was trying to dig his feet in, but they were just slipping on the wet soil. "I am trying but he's too strong."

Junior pulled the pillow case out of his pack. The turtle's back claws scraped Robbie's hand and he let go. "Ouch." He yelled.

Junior grabbed the tail and picked him off the ground, tossing him back further on shore. He turned to Robbie and asked, "You okay?"

"Yeah, he just scratched me. They sure are strong."

"I did warn you. Now get a stick to hold the bag open and I will put him in." Grabbing the turtle again, he tossed him in the bag. He spun the bag around in a circle and tied it off, putting it in his pack.

"Wow that was exciting. Now what do we do with him?

"We'll take him back and stick him in a clean garbage can with some fresh water for a couple of days. That way it will help clean out his intestines."

* * * * *

Clint was hard at work when one of the farmers came to see him. "General, here's your chicken shit gun powder."

"Thank you, sir. How much did you make up?"

"Not exactly sure, maybe about twenty pounds I would guess."

"Great job. Thank you."

"Just doing my part for the war effort, General."

Clint shook his hand. "I can't thank you enough. This will help change the course of the battle, I am sure of it."

"My pleasure. Any way I can help, just let me know."

The day flew by and before Clint knew it, it was 9 p.m. Good time to head home he thought. He looked at the bag of gun powder and realized he'd have to drop it off in the morning to the bomb making boys. He put the powder in his pack and walked out to his horse.

Before he could mount, a voice called out, "General, I need a word."

He turned to see the Lieutenant approaching. "Lieutenant, what can I do for you?"

"Sir, we are hearing humors that the Rainbow Warriors are going to attack from Duluth."

"Oh really? Any hard facts to back that up, or just rumors?"

"Actually just rumors, sir."

"Okay Lieutenant, to play it safe I want a ten man team set up for briefing in the morning. We'll send out scouts and find out what's going on."

"Yes sir. See you in the morning."

Clint mounted up and started heading for home. God what a long day it had been.

* * * * *

The assassin's time had come. This was it. Clint had not passed by yet, but should shortly. He told himself to clear his mind and focus. Get ready, the time to strike had come. Tonight the war would be forever changed. The great unstoppable Clint Bolan would be lying at his feet, begging for mercy.

A sadistic, evil grin crossed his face. The excitement was building. He had trained for almost a year for this one moment in time. What would he say to Clint before he sliced his throat wide open and left him to bleed alone on the road like a dog?

Payback is a bitch. This is for killing my brother. He decided that sounded the best. It was short and sweet. Oh revenge was so sweet.

He was coming. Get ready. The time to strike was almost here.

He was off in the brush and out of sight. As Clint rode by, he stepped out, throwing the knife with deadly precision. Even in the dark he could tell it was a direct hit.

Clint felt the knife hit and puncture his back He fell forward on the horse, turning the horse to the left. Something had hit him, was it an arrow? He heard footsteps running for him. How many? He thought.

Chapter 19

The Assassin's Attack

Gayle was in the bedroom with little Dean; Robbie was reading by the light of the lantern, while Junior and Katlin were sitting in the living room, when suddenly there was a banging on the door of the cabin. Through the door, someone yelled, "Doc, we need you right now. Clint has been attacked."

Katlin's head jerked up. "Junior, Clint is in trouble. Grab your gear and let's go."

Junior was dozing after dinner and half asleep. "What? What's going on?" He rubbed his eyes, wondering what was happening.

Katlin called out through the door, hoping this wasn't some trick. "What's happened?"

"I can't explain. Let's go. All I was told is that he's hurt and I needed to fetch you as fast as I can. Come on, the wagon is waiting."

She got up in a flash, grabbed her high-point carbine and medical bag. "Come on Junior, let's get a move on."

Call it women's intuition, but she knew something was really wrong. She yelled out, "Robbie bolt the outer metal door once we are gone." Gayle had come out with little Dean to investigate all the noise. Katlin told her, "Gayle, lock and load, something is wrong and this might be an early attack."

Junior was up and had the 12-gauge in his hand, tossing a twenty five round bandolier across his chest; he was heading towards the door. "Let's go Doc."

They were out the door and into the wagon in a few seconds, racing to where Clint was.

Katlin yelled above the noise of the horses on the pavement, "Now tell me what's going on."

The driver was focused on keeping the wagon on the road at the speed they were going, but managed to say, "I told you, I don't know. He was attacked is all I was told, and to bring you quick."

She thought, *Gunshot wound? Oh God not again.*

The driver turned his head towards her and yelled, "I heard three gun shots."

She strained to process what he said and then asked, "Is this an attack? Are troops moving in on us right now?"

"I told you, I don't know. I have no idea, but patrols have been sent out. The whole camp is on alert."

"Tell me where Clint is. Why didn't you bring him in the wagon?"

Still pushing the horses, he replied, "Because the medic told them to take him to the medic tent."

She turned to Junior and said, "Oh God, he must be hurt bad and they are afraid to move him any further than necessary."

Junior shouted out, "There are horses coming up behind us."

The driver urged the horses on, snapping the reins to make them go faster. Junior called out, "They are gaining on us."

"Almost there." The driver yelled, "Are they friendlies?"

Junior was holding on to keep from being thrown from the wagon and said, "I can't tell. It's too dark."

As they rounded a curve, they pulled into sight of the camp. It was totally blacked out.

The driver called out, "Doctor on board." The gate swung open and the patrol caught up. Hearing the correct signal, they raced further down the road, looking for any threats.

As the wagon slowed, Junior called out, "They were friendlies."

The wagon pulled up and stopped about a 100 feet short of the medic tent. A solid line of soldiers was blocking the way. One of them said, "You have to be checked and approved before you can go any farther."

A voice called out, "ID yourselves quickly."

"Dr. Katlin and Junior. Let us through." A space opened up, allowing the two of them to race into the medic tent. Her mind was racing, wondering how bad he was this time.

Seeing Clint lying on his stomach, she could see the blood on his back and panicked, thinking he was shot in the back. He was still wearing his pack and the knife handle was still sticking out of the pack on his back.

He saw her coming and said, "Katlin, would you pull this damn knife out and patch me up already. These damn fools are scared to death to do it without you being here."

"Clint, shut up and don't move. A wrong twist and you could cut nerves, possibly putting you in a wheel chair forever."

He made a snorting noise and said, "Stop with the melodrama already. The knife is barely in me, certainly no more than an inch."

She had no patience for an unruly patient and said, "Shut up already." Katlin examined the wound and the position of the knife. "Okay, hand me the scissors. Clint, I am going to cut along your shirt and carefully lift it up, so don't move." He put his head down, knowing she was in charge. She slowly cut around the knife blade and lifted the shirt away from the wound. "Good. Bare skin and no blood pumping out." She said.

Cutting the straps off the pack, Katlin told Junior to lift his side of the pack straight up, while she would do the same on her side. They lifted the pack free of his back, lifting the knife out as they did so. The knife had pierced the center of the pack. If he had not been wearing it, the blade could have gone into his heart. She cleaned and irrigated the wound, patching the puncture. He was lucky, but any puncture wound had the serious danger of infection, so she would have to keep a close watch on it. She asked, "Clint what happened? Who did this?"

She helped him sit up and he said, "One of our own men. He was standing guard duty."

"Where is he now?"

"Well, unless I'm mistaken, unfortunately I killed him."

Katlin was applying a gauze strip, wrapping it around him to hold the gauze pad in place. The Lieutenant had been patiently waiting and now asked Clint, "What should we do now, sir?"

"Well Lieutenant, what have the patrols reported?"

"Three have reported back and they found nothing, General."

"Well, that's good. Put a third of the men on alert and get the rest to bed. Tell the men I am fine."

"Yes sir, General." He saluted and turned to carry out the order.

Junior was full of questions, but had waited until Clint was patched up. He now asked, "What the hell happened?"

"Well, I had just left the office and was riding home when I felt a stabbing pain in my back. I fell forward and turned my horse to the left, while drawing my pistol. The man ran up with a second knife in his hand, ready to finish me off. He said *'this is payback time'* just as I shot him in the right shoulder. He was knocked back a couple of steps, but he switched hands and came at me again, with the knife now in his left hand. I double tapped him in the center of the chest and he dropped like a rock."

"Why did you shoot him in the shoulder, Clint? I don't understand." Katlin said.

"I wanted to wound him so we could interrogate him and find out who sent him." Clint said.

"He must have been in great shape to recover so quickly from being shot." Junior said. "Or maybe he was on drugs."

"I don't think so. I think it's worse. He was a zealot."

Junior raised his eyebrows and asked, "For who? The Rainbow Warriors? The Chinese?"

Clint shook his head saying, "We might never know for sure. All he said was, 'this is payback time'."

"It has to be the Rainbow Warriors. Who else would be looking for payback?"

"I'm not sure Junior. Okay Doc, can we go home now?"

Katlin wrapped a blanket around his shoulders and said, "Yes, you're good, but you are staying home tomorrow." Clint started to argue, but she continued, "Chinese, in America? And now an assassin tries to kill you. What the hell is going on, Clint? Something big is going on and we don't have a clue?"

"Yes we do. Come on, let's go and I'll try to fill you in."

******

The next day Junior was hanging around the cabin, making Clint nervous, and he finally said, "Don't you have something to do?"

Junior replied, "Yes, we have a trap to set and one to check."

"Then what the hell are you doing here? I'm fine, so take Robbie and get going already."

Junior was wringing his hands and said, "But Clint, they could be attacking today. I should hang around."

"No, you should go. If they were going to attack, it would have happened last night or at first light. Besides, none of the patrols have reported anything. He was a lone assassin and now he's dead."

Junior thought about Clint's comments and said, "Okay, you're the boss." And after a short pause, he asked, "Are you sure?"

"Get out of here already." Clint made a kicking motion, like he was kicking him out. "Katlin, what are you doing here? You should be working with the medics. We have to be ready." Clint said.

"I am hanging around here to take care of you."

"Damn it, woman, I'm going to work. This is ridiculous."

Katlin got that determined look on her face and said, "Look Mister, you are taking a day off. Doctor's orders, and that's final."

"No. I'm going to work. I promise nothing is going to happen. I won't lift anything heavy, I promise."

"Just like a damn stubborn man, but I'm going on record that I don't like it one bit."

*****

Clint went outside and there were men everywhere. He saw the sergeant and said, "What's going on here?"

"Sir, we are your security detail. We have eight men all the way around the cabin, plus the colonel sent ten horsemen to patrol the immediate area. We have your wagon set up." He pointed towards the road. Clint walked out to the road and saw a covered wagon. This was getting crazy.

Clint turned back towards the sergeant and gave an order. "Get me a horse." He then turned to the wagon and said, "You two men in the wagon, get going and don't come back here with that again. You should be hauling supplies to the camp. Report back for your regular duties."

The sergeant protested, "But General, the Colonel told us to be here and stay, no matter what you say." He cringed as he finished his sentence, expecting the wrath of the leader to come down on him.

"Well did he now? I'll take care of the Colonel, you get back to your normal duties, understand?" Just as Clint had dismissed the sergeant and his men, the Colonel came riding up with all of his men. Before he could bring his horse to a full stop, Clint lit into him. "For Christ's sake, Colonel, this is ridiculous."

The Colonel said, "While you were incapacitated, I took charge and made a decision to keep you protected at all costs."

Clint responded, "Well thank you, but it isn't necessary. I only have a flesh wound and I'm going back to work now." He turned to the sergeant, who had been waiting to see what the outcome of this conversation was, and said, "Get me my horse."

The sergeant ordered one of his men to double time and get the horse. He returned and handed Clint the reins.

Clint mounted and then turned to the Colonel and said, "Ride with me."

When they were both out of earshot of the others, Bert said, "Clint, we are going to protect you. End of story."

Clint turned towards him and said, "Look, a four man security team is all I need. The rest of this is a waste of manpower. Now tell me what all the patrols said."

"Nothing, nada, zero. It was quiet everywhere."

"Good. That means my guess that he was a lone assassin is probably correct. Okay, let's get back to training, but keep the patrols out there."

Bert, trying to bring a little humor to the situation, asked, "So what do we call you from now on? Superman? You can stop speeding bullets, you're stronger than an assassin's knife and you can be back at work the next day." He laughed as he finished.

"Colonel, I got lucky and was wearing a pack, so the knife barely got me. If it wasn't for the pack, I might be dead and you would be in charge."

A worried look crossed his face. "In charge? Take your place? Ahhh, right."

Clint looked at Bert and said, "I told the Major he should be second in command, but was going to talk to you first. You just confirmed the question I had."

"What do you mean? What question?"

"On whether or not you should lead the men."

"And you don't think I could?"

"No offense, but you are a wild and ruthless type that the men admire. You're quick to action and, while those are all good traits, you don't have the patience for long term planning. But you will be third in command, so if both of us die, it will be your show."

"Good, then nothing to worry about."

Clint frowned and asked, "Why is that?"

"Because you are Superman." He said with a laugh.

"Knock that off already. I bleed like any other man."

"Sorry, but no Clint. You're not like any other man and you know it. You're one of those lucky ones that isn't going to die in battle."

"What are you talking about?"

"Throughout history some men seem to be protected, blessed if you will. I don't know what you call it, but they never die in battle."

Clint nodded his understanding. "Yes, I have read about things like that. Have you ever studied the Boer wars?"

"No. Weren't the Boer wars in Africa?"

"Yes and it's a pretty amazing story. The Battle of Majuba Hill is one that every single officer should understand."

"Why is that, Clint?"

"Because it teaches us a lesson. The Brits had four hundred and five men, while the Boers had four hundred and fifty men. After the battle was over, it was clear who the superior officers were. The Brits had ninety two dead, one hundred and thirty four wounded and fifty nine captured. The Boers had one dead and only five wounded."

"Wow that must have been one hell of fighting army the Boers had. Who were the Boers?"

"The word Boers comes from the Dutch and Afrikaans word for farmer. They were the descendants of the Dutch-speaking settlers of the Eastern Cape frontier in Southern Africa. They were like Americans, in the sense that they were trying to escape the British rule. They had formed an independent country and the British tried to annex them, so they fought back, much like our war with England."

Clint went on. "The most shocking part of the whole battle was that most of the Boers were simple farm boys armed with rifles, going up against trained British troops. But they used a tactic called fire and movement. They broke up into teams; one team advanced, then offered covering fire for the second team. This was a leap-frog approach if you will, but the enemy is always under gun fire. The Boers also refused to commit to hand-to-hand combat, instead picking the enemy off at a distance. They were a militia in every sense of the word, defending their land."

He continued. "This is what I am planning. In order to defend against an attack, you have to have a moment to think and plan, and our job is not to allow our enemy that time to think. They step into our trap and they receive a hard pounding until they are all dead."

Clint made eye contact with the Colonel and said, "Your part in the attack is to do the opposite. When I give you the command, you and your troops will rush them, slaughtering all of them before they can recover.

"Are you sure Clint?"

"Yes. I am going to employ fire and movement at a larger level. We must have a total victory in this first battle, or it's all over for us. We desperately need their supplies. I want your best men in the front with you. You must put them down and spread that fear as you ride into them."

"I understand. When are we moving out?"

"I'm not sure yet. I am waiting on a report of what's going on and where they are now. I expect to be moving out in a few days."

The colonel whistled and said, "Farm boys defeating the British Army. That kind of sounds like our revolutionary war."

"Yes, but the lesson is protecting your men. If we only lose one man, I would be grateful."

Bert winked at Clint and said with a chuckle, "With Superman leading us, that shouldn't be a problem."

"Would you knock it off with that already?"

"Okay Clint, I am off. Are you sure you're safe to ride without us?" He laughed and he raced off on his horse, calling for his men to follow.

Clint reached his office and told the sergeant, "Do not disturb me unless it is an emergency." Something had triggered a memory as he told Bert the story. Before the Boer wars there were the Zulu wars. He had been collecting all kind of war books and found the one he had been looking for.

He looked it up. The battle of Blood River. Fierce Zulu warriors numbering 30,000 men surrounded a wagon train of Boers, numbering four hundred and seventy men, so they were outnumbered sixty to one. Their only weapons were two cannons and single shot muskets, but the Zulu Army had split up, with only half of them attacking. It was a full frontal assault. With the wagons formed in a circle and their back against the river, they felt safe.

What a sight that must have been. Zulu warriors all around them, a true desperate fight to the end. Did that make the Boers a better shot, or was it simply because there were so many they could not miss?

From Jan Gerritze Bantjes' journal of the campaign.

Their rapid approach (though terrifying to witness due to

their great numbers) was an impressive sight. The battle now began and the cannons unleashed from each gate, such that the battle was fierce and noisy, even the discharging of small arms fire from our marksmen on all sides was like thunder.

The battle raged for three hours, until the Zulu retreated across the river with their wounded, turning the river red with blood. Thus that battle was named Blood River. Zulu losses were three thousand brave men. The Boers suffered only three wounded and no dead.

What was it about the Boers that made them such an impressive fighting force? They were basically just Dutch farmers. It was said that buckshot was heavily used and that would account for the high number of wounded, along with the fact that the Zulus only had short spears.

Clint was feeling the strain. This was different and every man fighting was here because they believed in him, not because they were forced to by their government. These men could quit and walk away any time they wanted. He could not afford to make any mistakes. This attack had to be perfect and with a minimum loss of life on their side. Too heavily a casualty rate, even if they won, would cause a loss of morale. How did he pull this together?

* * * * *

Robbie and Junior were heading back to the ponds again. Robbie asked, "Junior, is Clint going to be okay?"

"Yes, it looks like he is going to be fine; at least that's what your mother said."

"So why did someone try to kill him?"

"I'm not sure little buddy, but the important thing to remember is he lived, so let's be thankful for that. Now I want you to take the pellet gun and shoot us a chipmunk or a red squirrel for bait. I'll go check the trap and we will move down and set another trap with fresh bait. Okay?"

"Sure Junior. I can do this. Trust me."

Junior smiled. "Okay, meet you at Wood Duck pond."

"I will be there really quick."

Junior got to the pond and waded out. He noticed the sticks that were holding the trap were gone. He reached down and found the 550-cord and pulled on it. It had a good solid weight on it. He pulled in the snapper and had another nice one, about fifteen-pounds, caught around the neck. He hauled him to shore.

As he stepped on shore, he heard the click-click of the hammer on a gun being cocked. He froze. His 12-gauge was sitting on his shoulder, but whoever it was had the drop on him. A voice called out, "We'll be taking that turtle, if you don't mind."

Without turning around, he replied, "What if I do mind? Are you going to kill me over a smelly turtle?"

A man stepped out from the trees and lowered his gun. "No, I would not. I'm sorry, it's just that my son and I are half starved and haven't eaten in days. Heck I don't even know how to clean a turtle to begin with." As Junior focused on the man, he could see that his clothes were dirty, tattered and worn out. His 30-30 rifle was scratched up and the old bluing had worn off around the receiver. His beard was scraggy looking and the man looked like a walking skeleton.

The man asked, "Do you have any food to spare?"

Junior kept his eyes on the man and asked, "Where's your son?"

The man turned to the heavily treed area and said, "Jake, come on out here."

A boy about Robbie's age walked out of the woods. He was dirty and skinny as a rail. His dirty face, torn clothes and sunken face told of his malnourishment. His eyes were dull and tired looking. Junior immediately felt sorry for them. "I'll feed you."

"The turtle?" the man asked hopefully.

Junior looked at the turtle and said, "No that would take too long. Here, help me get the turtle in this sack so I can tie him up."

The man handed his rifle to his son and walked over. Junior handed him the sack. He set one spring on the 220-

body gripper trap. "Here's the plan, I'm going to lift him up while you get the bag under him and pull it up to the trap, and I will squeeze the spring to release him. If it works right, he'll fall into the sack. When you feel the weight and the trap is clear, spin the sack in a circle and tie it off."

The man did as Junior said and it worked like a champ. Junior said, "Good, now we can get you some food."

No sooner had they finished bagging the snapper, than Robbie came running in holding a red squirrel. "Junior, who are these people?"

He turned towards Robbie and pointed to the boy, "His name is Jake," and then, turning to the man, he said, "and I didn't catch your name."

"The name's Trevor, and yours?"

Robbie jumped in. "I am Robbie and this is Junior. You look hungry. We can help you find food, right Junior? You are surrounded by food out here."

Junior smiled and said, "Yes Robbie, we are going to help them out."

"Trevor," Junior said, "do you know how to clean a squirrel?"

He answered, "Yes, I think I can manage."

"Good. Robbie give him the squirrel. After you skin and clean it, you can cook it up while Robbie and I go and shoot some more. You can make a fire, right?" Junior asked.

"Yes, we sure can. God bless you."

"Thanks and you're welcome. We'll be back in hour or so and you can wait here."

They walked away. "Robbie, can you show me the best red squirrel spot you know that is close by? Then I want you to pick those blueberries as I hunt the squirrels."

"Sure Junior, I can do that."

They returned a little over an hour later with three more squirrels. "Here's a few more to clean and cook, plus Robbie picked you about a quart of wild blueberries. We need to make you a stew and juice, so it's easier for your body to digest the nutrients you need."

Robbie handed Jake the blueberries in the birch bark cone he had made and Junior said, "Robbie, run back to the cabin and get a cooking pot and some rice. Tell Gayle we have starving people that need our help and then run back here as fast as you can. Bring a couple of metal cups too." Robbie nodded and began running back to the cabin.

Trevor said, "I can't thank you enough for helping us, Junior, but I got to ask you why you are helping us after I pointed a gun at you?"

"Because I have a son too and understand what you were thinking. Tell me what happened to you."

Trevor sat on a log and started telling his story. "We were living in the middle of the state when it happened. You might say my wife was kind of a coupon buyer, so we were well stocked up on food. There was a pond a couple of

258

blocks from the house for water and I had a propane camp stove we cooked on for a couple of months. When we ran out of fuel, we used the fireplace for cooking."

Between the two of them, they had the squirrels skinned and cleaned. Trevor continued. "We fought off some looters, but come March the food was running out. My wife got really sick because she had not been eating and was giving her food to Jake. She came down with pneumonia and died April 10th."

Junior said, "I'm sorry for your loss. That must have been rough."

"Thank you, it was." Looking over at his son, he said, "I think it was harder on Jake than me." He went on. "I use to hunt up here years ago, so Jake and I came here hoping to find enough food to survive. We did okay for a few months, but we lost the fish hooks we had and ran out of ammunition. We have not eaten anything for three days now."

Chapter 20

The Strangers

Clint kept studying the tactics of the Boers. In the second Boer Wars, 1899 to 1902, the British troops numbered 250,000 men, fighting just 20,000 Boers. The only way the British won was by imprisoning the women and children in concentration camps and burning all the farmhouses down. That still didn't explain what made the Boer effective fighters. What was their secret?"

The Boer soldiers used a Mauser five shot, bolt-action rifle. In the hands of the Boers, it was incredibly accurate to a thousand yards, and those thousand yards were using open sights. There were units called KOMMANDO that were a militia force of men from the ages of sixteen to sixty. Each man was required to have a horse, with a saddle, a battle rifle and at least thirty rounds of ammunition. Seven days worth of food was required to be carried by each man, as well as blankets and a bedroll. The food they carried was called Biltong, a thicker type of beef jerky, along with dried biscuits, coffee and sugar. The idea was to keep the men light for a fast mobile unit. There were no foot soldiers, only horseback, and everyone rode.

The British were amazed at the accuracy the Boers had and the ability to shoot them out of the saddle on top of running horses, even from the side. But the Boers were legendary hunters. From years of shooting at running antelope to feed their families, they understood the correct lead.

On up close and personal attacks, galloping in on horseback and shooting the Broomhandle Mauser pistol, they were just as deadly. The Boer were incredible freedom fighters and the only way the British won was by sheer force, greater numbers and more money. After all, the Boer were poor farmers.

The British, in their arrogance, used outdated methods and tried a cavalry charge, using 5000 men with lances and swords, against 1000 Boers armed with Mausers. They charged and the Boer shot them to pieces, so they broke off the first charge. The British, stubborn to the end, formed up and tried a second charge, but again were cut to ribbons. It was the last time in history that the British ever employed the Lance Charge against an enemy. The Brits might be pompous, but they were not stupid; they learned their lesson.

The Boers took no prisoners; in fact they would strip their captured enemy of food, boots, rifle, ammo and pants and then they were immediately set free. This had a very negative effect on the British fighting force. If they thought they had a chance of losing, soldiers would surrender in an instant. They feared the deadly accurate Boer riflemen that much.

In fact, the General in charge of the Boer units complained he once captured the same British soldier three times in one day, but the good news was that the man had been fully outfitted each time.

Clint was fascinated with their strategy and thought it was brilliant to take the fight out of the other side. Reading this account, he understood why the British soldiers so feared the Boer. The British had to call in troops from Australia and New Zealand, and it almost turned into a World War, just to stop 20,000 Boers.

The Boer knew how to live off of the land and made a terrifying guerrilla force, which was the worst kind for an organized army to go up against.

Clint wondered about the term dried biscuits, a kind of hard tack, so he checked the book's appendix and found what they used was called Rusk - a hard, double-baked bread. It was first baked as regular bread and then cut to long chunks and baked a second time to make it hard. This was to preserve and keep it together on the long hard rides. It was often dunked in coffee or tea to soften it. Clint laughed at that part. He'd be willing to bet some of it was as hard as a hockey puck.

Clint thought about that. The British had to spend a small fortune to defeat simple farmers. It took a quarter of a million men to defeat 20,000 farmers, not professional soldiers.

If only they had the ammunition to practice, he thought. Men were being trained with paint ball and BB guns. It wasn't good enough.

Independence brought men together. The Boers were not paid as soldiers. That was their secret, independence and freedom.

Fred stopped in and brought some sniper scouts with him. "What is this I heard, someone tried to kill you?" Fred asked.

"Yes, it appears I have enemies." Clint smiled. "Get me an update."

Fred passed on information about the main force of the Rainbow Warriors. Pointing to a map, Fred said, "We stopped them here and took out a bridge here, but they found a different route around. It cost them much time and they lost quite a few men when we blew the bridge."

Clint nodded. "I want sniper teams set up to harass them all the way back. And Fred, I want to talk to you after we're finished."

He laid out the plan for the snipers, telling them to hit and run, and then dismissed those men. With just the two of them, Clint said, "I want you to capture or disable their cannon. Do whatever you have to do, but take them out. Most importantly, only the most trustworthy men can be assigned that duty. We've already had one spy amongst us. If you get rid of that cannon, we are going to win for sure."

Fred nodded and said, "We'll do our best."

"I know you will, thank you."

Clint walked him out to the door and, turning to his sergeant, he said, "Get me the man in charge of all the cooks."

The sergeant nodded and got up to retrieve the man Clint wanted.

In a matter of minutes, the man appeared before Clint.

"Yes General, what can I do for you? A special dish to be served?"

Clint looked at the man and said, "In a way. I want you to bake hard biscuits. Make beef jerky and ground corn. Make enough to last seven days for each man."

The cook looked at Clint, trying to figure out why he wanted this. "That's a tall order, General. When do you want this by?"

"In five days. Can you do it?"

"We'll have to be cooking twenty four hours a day, but I think we can do it. Sir, does this mean we are not going to the front lines?"

"Yes, that's what it means. I want our men to be able to move fast and light."

"Of course, General. What should I tell the men?"

"Tell them you are developing a new ration to be tested."

"Yes sir. I trust you want me to keep the actual troop movement under my hat."

"Yes, that's exactly what I want."

Clint walked the man out of his office and sent him on his way.

The trader came in next. "Clint, you're never going to believe what I came up with."

"I'm tired and don't have time for guessing. What is it?"

"Six giant water balloon slingshots, you know those great big ones that take three men to shoot."

"Hell man, I want to kill the enemy, not give them a cold shower." Clint said.

"Ah, but you're missing the obvious. They are also great for lobbing homemade hand grenades too."

Like a light bulb going off, Clint got a big smile on his face and said, "Oh! That's brilliant."

Beaming, he responded, "Thank you sir."

"Sergeant," he called out.

The sergeant entered his office saying, "Yes sir."

"Take this man to see the lieutenant. I want three men assigned to each slingshot. They are to practice for the next five days using fake bombs that are same size and weight as the ones we are making. They must be able to shoot every time with no mistakes. We certainly don't want our own bombs rolling around at the feet of our troops."

"Yes sir."

"Great job on the slingshots. Thank you."

"Yes sir."

Clint thought back to the Boers. Each man had only thirty rounds of ammunition, but in the hands of expert marksmen, thirty rounds meant twenty to twenty five men dead or wounded. Amazing.

The day flew by and Clint headed home with his four-man security team surrounding him. The cabin was surrounded and guarded twenty four hours a day seven days a week. No more mistakes. Not that any of this was Clint's idea, as the Colonel and Major had insisted.

* * * * *

Back at the pond, Junior told the man to split the squirrel they had already cleaned and cooked with his son and to eat it while they waited for Robbie to return. "I want to make you some stew, something that will be for today. You can save some for tomorrow too."

Jake asked, "Why are you helping us, Junior? We're not your family."

Junior smiled and answered, "Because I prefer to make friends instead of enemies. There is plenty of food here; you are surrounded by it, so I am going to show you how to feed yourselves and get you back to normal."

"Thank you."

"No problem. Have you heard the saying, 'what goes around comes around'?"

Jake answered, "No. What does that mean?

Junior told him, "It means that how you treat others will eventually come back to you."

Jake smiled. "I get it." They finished roasting the squirrel and the boy's eyes were big with hunger. "When is it going to be done, dad?"

"Soon, son. Just be patient. So Junior, tell me about you. Clean clothes, food to share and it's almost a year later."

Junior began, "Well, my dad was a prepper and we were ready when this hit."

Trevor interjected, "That's good. Are we going to meet your dad?"

"No, he was killed in the first few days when some teenagers tried to take over our camp."

"That must have been rough on you."

"Yeah. I call it the black month, the black month of pain. I slowly came back from the shock. So much has happened since then."

Robbie came running back to the pond, carrying the things Junior had asked for. Junior handed him a water filter and said, "Fill the pot up with clean water to about three quarters full please."

Robbie brought the pot back and Junior built up the fire, hanging the pot to get the water boiling. He cleaned the other squirrels and saved the hearts and livers, tossing them into the pot. He then cut the squirrels into parts and placed them in the pot. Covering the pot, he let them slow cook for about 30 minutes and then tossed in two cups of rice.

He put some clean water in each of the cups and placed a handful of blueberries in each one, smashing them with a spoon. "Let these sit for a few minutes and then drink them down. In another five minutes, check the pot to see if the rice is done and then you can eat. Save some for tomorrow. Okay, we need to get back, so we'll be leaving you for the night. We'll be back in the morning."

Trevor got up from the log and shook Junior's hand, saying, "Thank you again. You just saved our lives." As Junior and Robbie were leaving, he said, "See you in the morning."

Once they were out of sight, Robbie asked, "Why are we helping them?"

Junior smiled. "Why do we help you and your mother?"

Robbie thought for a second and then answered, "Because mom is the Doctor and I am a good worker."

Junior laughed. "We are helping them because they are starving and we have food. Looks like I will be teaching you and them at the same time."

Once back at the cabin, Katlin asked why Junior didn't bring the starving people home with them.

Junior said, "Because there is a new baby here and no room for them. Besides, I'm not sure if they have any diseases. They look really rough."

She immediately responded as a doctor and said, "I should give them a checkup as soon as possible. What are you going to do with them?"

"Well, I planned on teaching them what I'm teaching Robbie and hopefully get them back to full strength."

"Yes, but what then?"

"I don't know; maybe find a cabin for them to stay the winter in. I don't know. I haven't thought that far ahead."

Clint came home and heard just a little bit of the conversation, so he asked, "What is going on?"

Junior filled him in on the starving father and son they ran across in the woods. Clint's first reaction was to maybe add this man to his army and asked, "Is the man ready to fight? Do you think we can trust him?"

Junior shrugged his shoulders and said, "I doubt it. He is as skinny as a rail. I don't think he has the strength to fight, at least not for a few weeks. I don't know about trusting him. He seems okay."

"Oh. He's in that bad a shape? Okay, tell the men outside he is back there, just in case he comes up here for help in the middle of the night. We don't want him getting shot for no reason."

Clint then asked Junior, "You know that gun powder recipe you came up with? Well we are putting it to good use. We are making up bombs, using empty coffee cans, lead balls and fuses."

Junior asked, "They sound heavy. How can we throw them far enough to do any good?"

Clint said. "We don't need to throw them; we have giant slingshots to lob them at the enemy when they come by. We're almost ready to go."

"Do you think we are going to pull this off? Finish them off once and for all?"

"If we get lucky we can."

The next morning Junior and Robbie were back at the pond and he could smell the fire before he saw them. He immediately saw improvement in their faces.

After greeting them, he said, "You look like you have some strength back."

"We are feeling much better, thanks to you."

Junior hand Trevor a towel that was wrapped around a bar of soap. "I brought you some soap and a towel so you can get cleaned up. Our doctor is going to check you out tomorrow, but today, we're going to teach you how to find food."

Trevor said, "I know how to hunt. Do you have any 30-30 ammunition?"

Junior smiled. Trevor was still stuck in hunter mode. "No, I am talking about wild food that you can collect with your hands."

"You mean like turtles?"

"Well, that's one thing, but there are many others, like acorns to make bread with."

"Acorns? They taste horrible. We tried some last week and they made us sick to our stomach."

"That's because you didn't know how to prepare them. Before we do anything else, we need to make some birch bark containers to store them in. As you collect them, you have to check each acorn to make sure they have no small holes with black around them. If they do, they have a worm in them."

"Is that why we got sick?"

"No, they have tannic acid in them and that is what made you sick to your stomach. We need to boil some water and rinse the acorns three times to flush out the tannic acid. Then we dry them out, grind them up and you have flour. But we have to shell them first. The Native Americans used to make baskets and place them in streams to let the water wash over them for weeks."

He went on to show Trevor how to prepare them. "The water is going to turn brown the first time we boil them. We can save that water and use it as an antiseptic to clean wounds. It can also be used to wash your clothes to get the bacteria out."

He went on, "I am also going to teach you how to clean and prepare that snapper we caught yesterday."

"Why are you doing this for us? What do you want in return?"

"I'm just trying to help you out, but we do need firewood cut up, so you can pay us back that way for sure."

"Sure. We'd be glad to. You saved my son's life."

They spent most of the day collecting acorns and had about a bushel of them. Using river rocks, they cracked them open and soaked them in the pot.

Junior picked up the bag with the turtle in it and said, "Now for the turtle." He took him out of the bag and cut his head off with an axe. He hung the turtle up in a tree and all four legs were still moving like mad.

Jake asked, "What is up with that?"

Junior said, "I think the turtle's muscles are slow getting a signal from the brain. Even though the head is gone, the signal was sent to the legs to move, so they do. He will be moving for a few hours. I always said they are too stupid to know they are dead.

"Now listen to me, because this part is very important. You must bring the water to boil each time before you add the acorns and then boil them for about ten minutes. Drain the water, saving the first water for antiseptic uses, and then repeat the cycle. Do this three times. You are lucky that we have mostly white oak here, as they taste the best. After the third time, set the acorns out on a couple of clean rocks to dry and then grind them into flour for bread. It's going to be heavy, but you need that now. Any questions?" Trevor and Jake both shook their heads no. "Okay, now we're going to clean that turtle." Junior used an old nail and rock to nail one back foot on a stump. "See, he is still moving. Okay, see this line on the bottom side of the shell right here?" He pointed to it. "That's the line you'll follow once we get to removing the shell, but first we have to skin out the legs and a pair of pliers really helps."

Junior cut around the leather part of the leg and, using his Gerber multi-tool pliers, he pulled the leg and cut until he hit the last joint. "Now cut it here and pop the joint. Okay, you got it?"

Trevor nodded. "Yes. I think I can do it."

"Good." Junior handed him the knife and multi-tool. "Your turn to do the rest, while I check on the acorns." It was time to switch the water for the acorns, so he poured the hot liquid into a tin can to save. He set the acorns out on clean rock and got more water boiling. Walking back and checking on the man, he could see him struggling to skin the leg. It was hard not to laugh.

The man looked up, frustrated. "How in the world do you do this when the leg keeps moving all over the place?"

Junior smiled. "It's all in the timing, my friend. You have to slow down and cut with the motion. It just takes practice." The man kept struggling, but he didn't quit.

He finally finished the first leg. While he started on another leg, Junior added the acorns to the boiling water for the second time. It worked out that by the time the man had the last leg finished, the acorns were finished with the third boiling and were drying in the sun.

"Okay, here let me finish this up." He showed the man how to remove the bottom part of the shell and cut the legs out. Then he skinned the tail and soon there was a nice pile of meat. "Now remove the guts. See this part that looks like ribs? Well, underneath is white meat and it's very good to eat. You can have that tonight and leave the rest to simmer all night and it will be ready to eat tomorrow."

Using the pliers, he cracked the bones out and filleted the white meat. "Here you go, slice that up and fry it."

Junior used the acorn flour to make biscuits, just a small batch to make about eight. He had all of them watch him and said, "Okay, cook these up and you have your dinner for tonight."

"Tomorrow, I will bring the doctor with me. Please wash up the best you can tonight, so she can check you both out in the morning."

As Junior and Robbie got up to leave, Trevor said, "Wait, when are you going to take us to your camp so I can start working on the firewood?"

"Well, first we have to get you enough food for a week and then you can start. We have guards around the camp, so please don't try to come in or you might get shot. Better you should wait, unless it's a serious emergency."

"Oh, okay. How many people are there?"

Junior didn't give much thought to the question and just said, "Tell you the truth, I don't know. Hundreds I suppose."

"Hundreds? How in the world are you feeding them all?"

Junior smiled. "By the grace of God, luck, and one of the best traders in the world, that's how. Everyone works."

Trevor stood up and said, "We aren't looking for a free ride. I will cut your firewood and prove it to you."

"I don't doubt you. You sound like a good man. See you tomorrow."

Chapter 21

The Truth Reveal

The next morning Clint looked over his desk to see what he needed to finish up before they could move out. Oh how he wished they had horses for everyone, then they could make thirty miles a day. He checked the map to figure out how far they would have to go. He came up with sixty miles, which would be about four days of marching. He needed to see the Colonel.

He called out, "Sergeant, ride over to the Colonel and ask him to stop in to see me."

The sergeant stuck his head in Clint's office and said, "Yes sir."

Clint continued to study the maps and plan the trip. They needed stopping points for rest and spots that would have good water for them to use. He made notes, more for himself than the men, but it would save time if someone had to take over for him. The Colonel walked in and asked, "How is Superman this morning?" He sat down and inquired, "What can I do for you this morning, General?"

Acknowledging him, but not looking up from his paperwork, he said, "I want you to head out early and find us an ambush spot and get it set up. This is what need: a hill where they will have to slow down. It needs to have high banks on both sides, so we can have men on each side shooting down in to them. I want you to find a couple of mini vans and pull them up to the location, just off the road in the ditch, one on each side, and don't make them look even. Fill sand bags and make a wall in the back, so our machine nests can be protected in each one. Then you need to find a place where you and your men can stay, just over the hill and out of sight from the ambush site. Do you understand what I am looking for?" Clint had been drawing a small map of what he described and handed it to the colonel.

The Colonel nodded and said, "Yes. I have good idea. Anything else?"

"Yes, you'd better set up two or three ambush spots, roughly five miles apart. I want to make sure to hit them in the morning so the sun is in their eyes. We don't know for sure how fast they are traveling, so I want more than just one location." He pointed to the map he had drawn and said, "We'll have your cavalry up behind the hill here and the Major's hundred men down here." He pointed to each position. "We will put one hundred and seventy five men on each side and one machine gun nest on each side of the road. The signal will be the homemade bombs we lob into them. The machine gun nests will make sure no one can reach our men. Once the first bomb goes off, everyone will open up. You wait for my signal and then you come in and finish them off."

"Sounds like a good plan, Clint, but what makes you think they are going to walk right into this trap? Don't they have scouts out front?"

"If they are smart they will, but we have some silenced weapons to take care of any scouts. Okay, what are your thoughts on what can go wrong?"

The Colonel said, "Well, if they get that 105 cannon set up, they would quickly take out the machine gun nests. When we come over the hill, they could cut us to ribbons with an anti-personnel round, then turn on you and take you out."

"I agree that the cannon is our main worry. I'll have a team of snipers set up to take out their gun crew for it. What else am I missing?"

"Maybe reinforcements from somewhere else? Or they are warned of the trap and go around us."

"You're right. So make sure you tell your men nothing of the plan. Tell them they are setting up sniper positions. You need to be back in three days, can you do that?"

"That's a long ride, Clint. What are we supposed to do about food?"

"Check with the cook and tell them you are there to test the new rations. Tell him you need four days worth for 50 men."

The colonel said, "He's going to be mad with you, throwing off his schedule. What is the ration?"

"It's beef jerky, hard biscuits, ground corn meal and coffee or tea.

Bert raised his eyebrows and said, "What are we, Spartans? No real food?"

Clint responded, "I want you light, so you can move fast and quickly."

"Got it General. Hey Clint, if this doesn't work, can I make the battle plan next time?"

"Okay Bert, tell me how would you do it."

"Well, the big flaw I see is their scouts finding us first. After the trouble you've caused them before, they may have three groups of scouts moving ahead and behind the troops. If the snipers take out the first scouts, the second scouts may find us and get back to the troops to warn them. I think we should use every sniper you have, positioned in the area, and let the first scouts go on by to see if more scouts come. If my men are further down the road setting things up and we see scouts coming, we could take them out so word doesn't get back to the commander."

"I follow your thinking, but the problem is that we don't have that many snipers with silencers, so a shot would warn others and then we'd be in deep shit."

"So you're saying you don't like my plan?"

"No, I don't. The ambush is the best plan to stop them. I don't want to lose any men."

"So are you saying my plan is reckless, Clint?"

Clint was beginning to lose his patience. "Tell me Bert, have you ever been in battle with five hundred men?"

"Well, uhh, no."

"It's massive chaos at best and the gates of hell at worst. Mistakes happen. When we make mistakes, good men die. Moving five hundred men into position is a bad idea. Too much noise from even one person is a mistake that could give the other side a warning. We would have lots of casualties. I want to avoid that at all costs."

"You really care about all the men, don't you?"

"Yes I do. The way I see it, my job is to win and save as many of our men as possible. The gung ho crap of winning at all costs and losing seventy five percent of your men is bad for morale. I think a General that thinks that way considers his men as cannon fodder for his own glory. I am not in this for glory. I simply want to live free and be left alone."

The Colonel pulled on his beard and said, "You are a complicated man, Clint. Why in the world did you agree to be General of this militia army? You could have slipped out into the woods and missed all of this."

"It's because they brought the war to me, so I thought I would put my skills to the test. Afterwards people came to me and asked me to take charge. Besides, the only way we can rebuild is to clean out the vermin first."

"Vermin? Yes I guess they are. Okay Superman, see you in three or four days."

"Damn it Bert, would you stop calling me that?"

"Sorry Clint, but that's how I see you. How many times should you have been dead already? You were born lucky. Now just keep the luck going for the rest of us."

* * * * *

Junior took Katlin to the pond to see Jake and Trevor. She gave them a quick check up: checking for lice, rashes, and any signs of disease.

Trevor asked, "What's the verdict Doc?"

You're both suffering from minor malnutrition and you need to get your strength back. I want you to make sure you clean up every day. I am going to be direct with you, you have to set up a latrine and clean up every day. My God man why weren't you eating berries for vitamins?"

He was a little embarrassed and said, "I didn't know what was safe to eat."

"That's okay, Junior will teach you. I want you to start making tea to drink every night. You can get mint, raspberry and strawberry leaves and dry them out. To make tea, you just boil water, pour it over the dried leaves and let sit for a few minutes. This will give you a source of vitamins. You could have gotten scurvy. If I can, I'll check on you in a week. You are going to be fine." She gathered her medical bag and told Junior, "Okay Junior, I am off. I'll talk to you later."

Trevor turned to Junior and asked, "Okay Boss, what's the plan for today?"

"We need to collect the berry leaves first and get them drying out. Doctor's orders."

Junior was carrying the pellet rifle. It was a Benjamin Trail NP All Weather Break Barrel Air Rifle (.22) with the Nitro Piston. He was using Predator Polymag Hunting Pellets, a great round for squirrels, up to about 30 yards.

As they approach the berry patch, Junior spotted a covey of Ruffed Grouse and put his hand up to stop the others. He turned and whispered, "Stay here."

He crept up, staying as low as possible. At twenty yards he picked out one in the back of the covey. He shot it in the head and it fell over, flopping about. He quickly reloaded and the birds started to run, but one stepped out on the trail to see what the noise was and Junior shot him in the head. He fell over and the rest flew off.

Junior smiled. "Looks like you will be eating well tonight." The others walked up and Trevor said, "That was some great shooting, Junior."

"Thanks. Let's gather the leaves and I think you can handle the rest today. You have grouse to eat and you can make your acorn flour today. Make sure you drink the tea tonight."

He help them pick leaves for an hour and then walked back to camp with them. They cooked up both grouse for lunch. After lunch, Trevor said, "Junior, tell me what's really going on."

Junior responded. "What do you mean?"

"Well you have equipment, a doctor and people watching your place. What are you? Some kind of militia?"

"Militia?" Junior laughed and said. "We're just ordinary people in extraordinary times, trying to survive. I guess you could say we are militia. We are forming up to fight the enemies trying to kill us."

That got Trevor's attention and he asked, "Who's trying to kill you?"

"It's a group that call themselves the Rainbow Warriors. They want to control all the people and make everyone join their army. It's a comply or die proposition.

They brought the fight to us. We would have been happy to just be left alone to survive."

Trevor nodded. "Yeah, we heard of them. They are some kind of cult from what we heard."

"Cult? Hmmm, I guess that's a good word for them. I was captured by them and they put me through some massive brainwashing."

"You were captured? How did you escape?"

"My friend Dean and I played along with them for a few weeks and then Dean and I snuck off one night."

"Dean? Will I ever get to meet him?"

"Nope. He died on the way home. In fact we were almost here and he was shot that morning."

"By the Rainbow Warriors?"

"I don't know. I escaped into the woods and finally made it home."

"So what are you guys doing now? What's the plan for fighting them?"

Junior started to see red flags going up. Was this another spy? Another assassin? Was he being paranoid? "Why do you ask?"

"Just curious is all."

Junior was immediate on alert. Did he have a handgun? Was he in danger?

"Oh really? Okay then tell me - of all the places for you to go, you happen to end up behind my cabin? There must be hundreds of hunting camps in the area that you could have moved into."

"Come on Junior, you are just being paranoid. You know I am not a Rainbow Warrior. You've seen me eating meat. Besides, even your own doctor said we were malnourished. Come on and think about it. If we were spies, we would have our own food."

Junior wondered if was he was just being paranoid, but the more he thought about this, he knew something was wrong. He couldn't put his finger on it, but this was not adding up. He said, "You're right. I'm sorry, but being captured has made me a bit paranoid. Anyway, I have to teach Robbie how to clean a turtle today."

"Junior you're lying. We did that yesterday. What is wrong with you today? If you want us to leave, just say so and we can move on."

Junior stood up. "No, we caught a turtle the day before you showed up. But you already know that, don't you? You were watching us."

Junior leveled the pellet rifle at the man. "Who sent you here?" When he said that, the boy ran over to Junior's side, saying, "He's not even my dad. Can I come with you? Please don't leave me here with him."

"What the hell is going on here?" Junior yelled.

Trevor jumped up and anger ripped across his face, making him suddenly look very ugly. He yelled, "Jake shut up. We talked about this and now you're going to pay."

Junior leveled the pellet rifle at his face. "Shut your mouth Trevor."

He ignored Junior. "Jake, you promised to never say one word. Remember? You swore on your mother's grave."

Junior hit the man in the face with the butt of his gun, knocking him down. "You say one more word and I swear to God I am going to kill you. There is nothing in the world worse than a pedophile."

Trevor wiped blood from his lip and said, "Pedophile? Junior, you are jumping to conclusions. That boy never said anything about that."

"Get up. You are coming back with me to the camp. We have men that are going to find out what's going on here. I swear to God, if what I think is true, you won't have to worry about food anymore. Now stand up and march."

Trevor stood and started walking. "Junior listen, you are making a big mistake."

Jake said, "Don't believe him. He is working with the Rainbow Warriors."

Junior turned to look at Jake and said, "What? How many are here?"

While Junior was distracted, the man took off running into the woods. Junior started after him but Jake cried out, "Don't leave me here." Junior stopped, thinking that Jake was more important. He packed up all the gear they had in the area, including the 30-30 rifle Trevor had left. "Come on Jake, we've got to move and warn the others."

They walked back to the cabin without seeing anyone else. Junior warned the guards right away. One of the Guards said he was going to tell the General. A full alert was called around the cabin. He told Junior to get inside and lock up.

They went inside and locked themselves in the cabin. Gayle asked, "What's going on?"

As Junior checked all of the windows he said, "Seems Trevor was a spy and maybe a pedophile. Jake said he was not his real dad."

Gayle looked at Jake with horror on her face. She went to Jake and hugged him, saying, "Are you okay sweetie? We're not going to hurt you."

Robbie said. "Jake you can stay here with us."

Junior said, "Okay Jake, sit down and tell us what is going on."

Jake took a seat and began telling the story. "The Rainbow Warriors sent us to find you and work our way inside to find out what your plans are. I was supposed to make a list of the food you had and anything else. Trevor was supposed to join the army and get a full count of men and equipment and then we would run off after a few days."

Junior asked, "But how did you know where this cabin was?"

"Other spies are in your troops. They told us where to go."

"Other spies? Do you know how many?"

"No. I only saw Trevor talking with one and it was at night, so I never saw him."

Junior turned to Gayle and said, "Stay here with the children, I am going hunting."

She replied, "Junior no, wait for Clint."

He shook his head, saying, "No time. The longer we sit around waiting, that man is covering ground and we need to catch him now." He grabbed his trusty 12-gauge and loaded up with buckshot.

Gayle walked over and whispered in his ear. "Please don't go; stay here."

He looked her in the eyes. "I'm sorry Gayle, but I'm going. Don't you understand? If that intel gets back to the enemy, they will be coming here to kill all of us." He leaned down and kissed her and then whispered in her ear, "Don't trust this kid yet and be careful what you say."

She nodded her head and Junior was out the door. He walked up to the sergeant in charge and said, "I need one man to come with me - your best tracker, if you have one."

The sergeant said, "Junior, you should wait for Clint. I'm not sending anyone with you until I get orders."

"Fine sergeant, then you can explain to the General why you let me go off alone."

"Damn you Junior. Okay, George you go with Junior and protect him with your life."

George ran up and motioned to Junior to go. They took off at a trot, heading towards the pond.

George asked Junior, "What's the plan?"

"We need to track this fucker down and bring him back for questioning. He can't get away."

"Is he armed?"

"I don't think so. I took his rifle, but he might have cache. We have to be careful."

They ran all the way back to the pond. The leaves were showing their fall colors and Junior thought, *this used to be my favorite time of year.* He was filled with anger at himself for being fooled so easily. He wanted to kill the man.

They reached the camp and George asked, "Okay, which way did he go?"

Junior pointed and said, "He was heading east. I say we stay about fifty yards apart and zigzag back and forth at a trot. Maybe we can flush him out like a rabbit."

"Sounds good. Let's go." They both took off at a trot, moving back and forth, covering a lot of ground. After an hour they stopped to catch their breath.

"Nothing so far. He could be anywhere by now, Junior."

"Dammit, I should have had a real gun with me. What the hell was I thinking carrying only a stupid pellet gun?"

George said, "Don't be so hard on yourself Junior. You had no idea what was going on. You were just trying to help a family out."

"Yeah, a fake family. Dammit."

"What do you want to do?"

"I guess we should head back and talk with Clint. What else can we do?"

George said, "Maybe he'll send out some men on horseback to try and catch this guy."

They started walking back.

Chapter 22

To Catch a Spy

Clint raced back to the cabin to find that Junior had already gone. Clint complained to the sergeant, "That damn fool kid is going to get himself killed yet. I try to keep him out of danger and what good does it do? He chases after it."

The sergeant nodded and then tilted his head towards the cabin and said, "The boy is inside and says they were sent here to spy on you. He also says there is at least one spy already among the troops."

Clint said, "More like three or four would be my guess, maybe more. Okay sergeant, let me know the minute Junior is back. I'm going in to talk to the young man."

Clint walked into the cabin and nodded to Katlin, Gayle and Robbie. The boy was sitting on the couch, looking scared half out of his mind. Clint walked over and sat down next to him. "Relax son, no one is going to hurt you."

The boy nodded okay.

"My name is Clint and I just have a few questions for you, if that's all right?"

"Okay, what?"

"Do you know how the information of what you learned is passed on to the others?"

"No. Trevor did all of that. All I know is they would meet at night. Someone I couldn't see would come in and they would talk."

"Where is this person coming from?"

"I don't know."

Keeping his voice low to make Jake feel comfortable, he asked, "Do you know where he goes after he receives the information?"

"No I don't"

"Okay son, just relax. You're doing a great job. Tell me what you think is important."

"Well, all I know is that they told us to come here and learn what we could. They were going to pay us in food."

"Okay, good. How long were you supposed to stay here?"

"Two or three weeks, but no more than one month."

"Why no longer than a month?"

"I don't know."

"You're doing good. Now think really super hard. Is there anything else that you heard?"

The boy's eyes flared and he stood up. "You are all going to die next month. Now leave me alone."

"Whoa kid, sit down and relax. What do you mean we are all going to die?"

He was highly agitated now and said, "They are coming for you. They have twelve hundred men and everyone up here is going to die."

You could feel the tension in the room increase as the silence grew thick in the air. The boy must have seen the army. Clint asked, "Where did you come from?"

"Green Bay. They have food to feed thousands, maybe a million people."

"Okay, do you want to go back there and be with those people?"

"Yes, no, I don't know." He started crying.

Clint stood up, looked at Gayle and said, "I am going to take him to stay with someone else. Tell Junior when he comes back to stay home and that is an order."

He held out his hand and said, "Come on Jake. There is a nice couple that can take care of you. I'll take you there." And they walked outside.

"Sergeant, take this young man over to Mr. and Mrs. Gallagher's house." He looked at the corporal and said, "When Junior comes back, tell him he is ordered to stay in the cabin."

"Yes sir."

Clint rode off to the see the Major. He had guessed that there were spies, as they were taking in too many new people, but what was he to do? They needed the men. He had to use this intelligence to their advantage. He didn't want to bring it up to the men because it would destroy the unit's effectiveness, which they had worked so hard to build.

He found the Major in his quarters. The Major looked up and said, "Clint, what's going on?"

"Well Charles, we have a problem and I want some input from you." He explained what was going on.

Charles said, "Yes, we do have a problem. What are you thinking?"

"Well my biggest concern is how they are transferring the information back to their army. If we can find that gap and stop it, I think I have a plan that is going to work."

"Okay tell me the plan."

"I want you to pick six men that you can trust to keep their mouths shut. These men well be assigned to go out in the bush and watch all the roads coming into the area. When we find out who the spies are, we can use them to pass on false information."

"Oh devious, I like that plan, Clint. But why not kill them and stop it for good?"

"Because it has to be bigger than we know. Let's assume we have ten to twelve spies. Chances are they are going to have two, maybe three pickup spots for the information. To catch them all, we'd have to track back to each person. Better to let them think they are getting away with it, otherwise the sleeper spies would still be here."

"Sleeper spies?"

"Yeah, he's the guy watching all the other spies and if they get taken out, he is activated".

"This sound like cold war shit to me. How do you know it's not just two spies?"

"Could be you are right and maybe I'm getting paranoid, but there is only one way to find out. Get your men out in the field and find out how they are passing on the information. We need to know the who, what, where and when part of this and we need to figure it out quickly. I want two-man teams on all three roads coming in from the east and the south. Place them about three miles out."

The Major asked, "Why me? Why do you trust me, Clint?"

"Because you are an arrogant, pompous, ass, trained at West Point." He said and then broke out laughing.

Charles was taken aback at first and wasn't sure if he should be offended, but then he understood. He laughed and said, "And you're a wild ass maverick that is going to get us all killed."

"I don't think so. When the Colonel returns I want to have a sit down with just the three of us. We need to come up with a good disinformation campaign to drive the other side crazy."

"Like what?"

Clint smiled. "Like we have reinforcements of 2000 men coming from the south."

"How are you going to pull that one off?"

Clint smiled and winked. "All in good time."

He stood up to leave and the Major said, "Oh Clint, one last thing."

Clint turned and said, "Yes?"

"When are the guys watching for the spies supposed to report in?"

"They are in two-man groups, so one man should come back every three days, or sooner if there is something really important to report. Have them report to you. Work it out so no one else sees them coming or going and starts asking questions."

"Okay Clint, will do."

"And make sure you know where these men are. Bert should be back in three days and we can make our plan when he returns."

"Clint, listen to me for a minute. How do you know they are not moving on us right now?"

Clint smiled and said, "We have recon scouts watching them."

"There's a whole lot you're not telling me. How am I supposed take over if something happens to you?"

"Charles you are a West Point graduate. You could easily take over if you've been paying attention. I have already instructed certain men to report to you if anything happens to me."

"When were you going to fill me in on that detail?"

"I just did. Listen, you're a good man and the men are coming around to you. Don't worry so much."

"You do like surprising me, don't you? Have a good night."

******

Junior was a little upset that when he returned to cabin he was ordered to stay put. He had changed; he was now a warrior now and was ready to be back in the thick of battle.

When Clint returned they talked, but Clint said that for the battle he was to stay back and take care of his wife, little Dean and Robbie. Clint didn't want to explain to Gayle if anything happen to Junior.

* * * * *

Robbie and Junior were back out on survival training. Junior said, "Okay Robbie, today we going frog gigging."

Robbie wrinkled his nose. "You eat frogs too?"

Junior smiled and said, "Of course. They taste just like chicken." He laughed and went on to tell Robbie a story.

"You know the story of young Native American rites of passage in certain tribes?"

Robbie shook his head and said, "No. What are rites of passage?"

"Well, when the boys reached a certain age, they had to show that they were men and they would be sent out to prove they were ready to become warriors. They would have to travel, finding food and water for themselves, and build their own shelters. They had to survive for one month on their own, with no help from the tribe."

Robbie said, "Sounds like fun to me."

"Well, if you have the proper training and plenty of practice it might be, but if you didn't, it would be hell."

"We're doing pretty well."

"Yes we are, but you are way too young to do this on your own."

"When? Next year?"

"Maybe, but we have a lot to do first. So are there any poison frogs to look out for?"

Robbie frowned. "I don't know Junior. Are there?"

"Toads have a poisonous skin; it's a natural defensive mechanism. If any predator tries to eat them, it causes them to get sick. In fact, in South America the natives kill toads and cook them over a fire to extract the poison for their blowgun darts. They also make poison arrow tips." He went on. "The wild is full of mystery and unfortunately much of the wisdom and wood lore has been lost."

"You seem to know a lot. How do you know all of this stuff?"

"I don't know as much as I'd like to know. I've studied and researched a lot of this information and my dad taught me a lot of it. I am sure two hundred years ago a boy your age might know more than I do."

"So can we kill and extract poison from American toads?"

"I don't know any of the Native American tribes this far north that ever did and there must be a reason why. I would bet it's because the poison in the toads isn't strong enough to be effective."

They spent the morning creeping along, gigging frogs, and by lunchtime they had ten big bullfrogs. Junior showed Robbie how to clean and cook them. They were sitting next to deadfall tree that was partially in the water. Looking down under the surface, Junior could see about two dozen brook trout hiding from the sun.

"Here, let me teach you another trick. See those trout?"

Robbie looked and said, "Yes, are we going to gig them like frogs?"

"No. If you start throwing a spear in, it will spook them off. You may get one, but only if you didn't miss on the first throw."

"Okay, so what do we do?"

Junior found a branch about two-inches in diameter and broke it down to about a foot long. "You see this white silk?" He was referring to a piece of material he pulled from his pocket, "You tie a treble hook about six-inches below this. Tie the white silk on so it has two ends and kind of looks like a bow tie."

He rigged the stick as he spoke and then said, "Now here is the trick; you lay on the log so the fish can't see you. Wait a few minutes until you see the fish come back out, because they are going to hide when they feel the vibration of you on the log, but be patient. I want you to sit over here and watch how to do this. It's very important you get the action part down."

They got set up and in a few minutes the trout were swimming underneath Junior and the line in the water. He began jigging the line up and down about two to 10-inches, varying it and then letting it sink. When a trout would come up close to see it, Junior would jerk hard and snag the fish with the treble hook. He caught three trout and the rest were hiding.

"Wow that was cool, Junior. Where did you learn that trick?"

"My Dad taught me that one."

"But why do the fish come up to see the white material. I don't understand."

Junior explained, "To them, it looks like a hurt minnow and that's why I said pay attention. A wounded minnow is easier to catch than a healthy fast one."

"Oh. So the fish comes up to get an easy meal. I get it."

"Will any other colors work?"

"I have tried silver silk and that works well. Once I was fishing for bluegills and used red yarn, which caught a few. But now it's your turn. Watching me is not teaching you much; you have to do it yourself."

Robbie's eye got big and he said, "Really? That would be great."

"Listen to me closely. You are going to miss them and, when you do, don't say anything. Don't get mad and say you missed, because your voice warns the fish."

Robbie nodded. "Okay, Junior I got it."

Watching Robbie was enjoyable for Junior. He thought that in about six or seven years, he would be taking little Dean out and teaching him all of this.

Try as he might, Robbie kept missing the trout. Junior said, "Robbie, come on and let's move down to a fresh hole. I think these fish are getting too smart."

They walked down about one hundred yards and set up again. This time a large trout about thirteen inches long came up right away and Robbie caught him.

"So Robbie, what did you just learn?"

"That I caught the biggest one." He said, with a huge smile.

"Yes, but what you're missing is that if you had stayed working that first spot too long, you would have burned up energy with little pay off, so it's smarter to move."

"Oh. Okay Junior." They stayed until the sun was going down and Robbie had caught three trout.

"See, you're learning."

"Yeah, but it took you thirty minutes to catch three trout. It took me three hours to catch my three."

"Well, you are just learning and patience is important, but what is really important is that you caught three fish. Each time you do it, you will get better and better. Just think, if you were on your own, you'd be eating pretty well tonight. Come on, it's time to head back."

As they walked towards the cabin, Robbie asked, "Junior, how come you're not going to war with Clint this time?"

Junior said, "Clint wants me to stay back because of Gayle and little Dean, and to keep you out of trouble." He tousled his hair.

Chapter 23

The Spy Trap

Bert returned in a few days and he, Clint and Charles met. Clint filled Bert in on the information about the spies. Bert said, "I don't believe it's any of my troops, but I wouldn't swear to it. How about you Charles, do you have any guesses about your troops?"

The Major said, "No, but I am sure it would be hard to keep track of everyone. We have people standing guard watches, but it would be fairly easy to slip a message out late at night."

"Yes," Clint said, "and my guess is we should go on the assumption that all of our troops are spies, just to play it safe. The kid said the Rainbow Warriors are coming at us in one month and we are all going to die. He said they have twelve hundred men and that tells me they are getting resupplied from the Minnesota Rainbow Warriors."

The Colonel spoke up, "We have to take the war to them. Let's take Green Bay now, while they are at their weakest."

Clint smiled. "That's why we are going to put out disinformation saying that we are attacking Green Bay."

"Why Clint?" Bert said, "They are at their weakest numbers right now. It would be a cake walk."

"That's where you are wrong. Think man, the U.S. Army teaches that for a sure victory you want six to seven men to each defender. Even going with the low number of six, they have three hundred men. We would need eighteen hundred men and right now we are looking at about six hundred total, counting everyone."

Charles said, "If we carefully planned it, we could win."

Clint replied, "Yes we could, but at what cost in loss of men? You are forgetting gentleman; we only have enough ammo for one major battle. We don't have the supplies for a long siege, nor the time before their main battle group is back. Our best chance is to take them out while they are in the open. Oh, and some good news, the recon scout team has stolen the main battle group's cannon, but they didn't get any ammo for it. That said, the Rainbow Warriors don't know if we have ammo or could make some ourselves. I want that rumor started. Spread the word that we have enough ammo to take out Green Bay headquarters."

Bert grinned. "You are a devious son of a bitch, aren't you?"

Charles smiled. "Good plan. Psychological warfare. I like it."

Clint changed the subject and said, "Okay Bert, tell us what you learned from the area and what places you've picked for ambush sites."

He moved his chair closer to the table so he could use the map. "Alright, we made contact with the recon scouts and they showed us a few spots. Of course, there are problems. Your three spots, five miles apart, are next to impossible to find. We did find two spots that fit our needs." He pointed to the map. "Each has a hill they'll have to climb and a spot for my troops to hide. There are high banks on both sides of the road, with a clear field of fire straight down. I prefer the first spot over the second but, either way, we can set up machine gun nests at both locations."

Clint looked at where he was pointing and said, "Good. Now the important part - we have to let the spies know we've changed our plans because we captured the cannon. Then we have to catch them, but not until after they've passed the information on."

Charles asked, "Are we going to follow the rules of warfare and imprisonment for them?"

Bert laughed and said, "We are following the guerrilla rules of warfare - no prisoners."

Charles looked to Clint and asked, "Do you agree with this?"

Clint nodded his head and said, "We have no choice, Charles. What the hell are we going to do with prisoners?

You have to fed them, house them and guard them. Hell, we are struggling just to feed ourselves. War isn't nice and they brought this upon themselves."

The major shook his head. "Clint, I cannot be part of cold blooded murder. There are rules in warfare. We are not animals!"

Clint took in a deep breath. "Major, surely at West Point you studied great leaders coming up from nothing."

"Yes I have."

"Then you must remember an important lesson in all that history. When you're facing an enemy, you kill them or they come back later and kill you."

"Clint, what about the Boer way of stripping them of supplies and letting them go to take the fight out of them?"

"We could do that, Major, but these spies have to die. Throughout military history, spies are always killed."

"You're a hard, cold man Clint Bolan."

"I hate to tell you, Charles, but it's a hard and cold new world out there. We no longer have the luxury of being kind and loving to our enemies. They certainly aren't honoring the Geneva Convention and neither will we. We are moving in a few days and I want these spies identified before we move out. Bert, what else did you learn?"

"Well, our guys are harassing the hell out of them. They are wearing them out. They have no sleep or time to relax. We're always attacking them and then disappearing into the forest, not to mention stealing their cannon."

"Good. I want them worn out before we face them with our fresh troops."

* * * * *

That night the two man team of lookouts saw a lone rider come down the road and tied his horse off in the brush. One man followed him and saw the night guard pass the information off. He followed him back to his horse and the lone rider hit all three guard stations, collecting information. The lookout remembered where each guard was, so they could be identified from the duty roster in the morning.

After the man rode off, he wrote everything down and waited for daybreak to turn the information over to the Major. There were three spies for sure. He took the information and, just before morning, he walked over to the pick-up point, an old mailbox, and put the information inside. He waited and watched; guarding the box to make sure only the Major picked it up. The Major rode up and retrieved the message. The lookout man stayed concealed and watched to see if anyone was following the Major but, although he stayed there for a while, he saw no one.

* * * * *

After breakfast the Major rode over to Clint's office to pass the information on. Clint and the Colonel were already there, discussing the ambush strategy.

The Major interrupted them and said, "Okay, we have identified three spies for sure. They were all standing night guard at their camp."

Clint said, "Good. Now each of you assign your most trusted man to spy on these three. Find out who their contacts are inside our army. Major, I want you to set up your six men on the road this spy left on. Stretch each man out over ten miles, just in case he is using a trail or side road. They must have some kind of ham radio set up to pass the info on to Green Bay. We need to find out the rest of the story."

"Clint, how do you know it's a ham radio?"

"It makes sense. A lot of the old ham radios used vacuum tubes and many had battery backups, so the EMP would not have affected them. That's why we are able to listen to Crazy Larry."

"Charles said, "So they would have to have a portable one?"

"I don't know for sure, but I think so. It's just a guess, so we need to find out for sure. Once your men pick him up, instruct them to follow the spy for two miles. That should give us a 12-mile range. If he keeps going past that point, we'll need to stretch it out an additional 10 miles for the following day, starting from the last known spot. I doubt he is over 20 miles away. I would guess he is in 10-15 mile range, or less."

Bert asked, "You think he is loner?"

Clint shook his head. "I doubt it. That would be too risky. I would guess it's a three or four-man team, probably a four-man team, with twelve hour watches of two men. If they have a daytime team that is spying on us, the night team will be collecting all the info and doing a late night or early morning broadcast to Green Bay."

"With the disinformation we sent out, shouldn't we take them out now?" Bert asked.

"No. We can't show our hand yet. We need more information, gentlemen. We'll meet back here again in the morning."

Clint directed his next comment to the Major. "Make sure your six men are back out before daylight, so they can spot him coming back."

"Roger that, Clint."

Bert said, "Listen, there has already been one attempt on your life and I don't feel comfortable unless these spies are dealt with. They could easily take out all three of us."

"I know, Bert, but we need the other team caught first. I don't want to move on them until we have the full story and then we can move on all of them."

"Okay, you're in charge, but watch your back, literally."

"I will and both of you do the same."

The day flew by and Clint keep thinking about how much information had already been passed. He tried to think of what information might have leaked that could hurt them. He began doing some guessing. Supposing they knew how low the militia were on ammo and that they had an accurate count on men, supplies and supply trains, the disinformation they had put out meant they should be in good shape. The big question was if they had radio contact with the Chinese attack helicopter. That would be a game changer. They would just have to deal with that if the helicopter showed up.

He continued to play the 'what if' game. What could go wrong? They could try to ambush them. Bert was right; they had to take out the spies and the relay team. They had to cut the snake's head off the next day if they could.

* * * * *

That night the spotters watched as the lone horseman came out from a dirt road, about seven miles out.

He came out onto the road between two of the spotters. The team waited and watched. Their job was to track him on the return trip and find out where his hideout was. At least they knew which road to stake out.

That night, Clint made sure that other men were on guard duty, just to see if there were any more spies relaying information.

It didn't appear that there were more spies. When the spy saw that his contacts weren't on guard duty, he turned around and left. On the return trip, the middle scout tracked the man. He watched the man on horseback and saw the road he had turned off on. Once he was on the road, it was narrow and had lots of trees overhead, blocking out the stars. It was pitch black.

He moved quietly about a hundred yards and then stopped to listen. The horse was on the soft dirt trail and not making any sound. Should he wait? Should he risk running and maybe alert the man? He crept slowly along the road. It was too dark and risky. No one else from his team knew what road he was on. He had to pass the information on. If he were caught, the rest of his team would have to search a wide area for him, costing them valuable time. But this was too important not to take the risk. They needed to find the location. He decided to turn around and get the rest of the team.

The sergeant in charge directed one man to relay the information of the road location back to the Colonel. He directed the other five men to follow him down the road.

They traveled three miles and then came to a crossroads. Using hand signals, he called the men over and whispered, "We stay here until daylight. Get out of sight and set up in the brush."

In the early dawn light, they saw a rider coming from the right side of the crossroads. The sergeant signaled the men that they were going to stop him.

The man had a rifle slung over his back and the team stepped out of the brush when he was in the middle of them. The sergeant called out, "Freeze."

The man was clearly startled. He started to reach for his gun, but the sergeant whipped his gun to his shoulder and said, "I don't want to kill you. There are six guns on you, so don't try anything."

The man froze and said, "What do you want?" He was dressed in clean clothes and had a battle vest on. He was in his early 20's and looked like a typical college kid, except for wearing the vest and carrying an AK-47.

"Just a little chat." One of the men walked up and grabbed the reins out of the man's hands.

"Doesn't look like I have a choice."

The sergeant told the man to dismount. As the man stepped down to the ground, he said, "We are going to disarm and frisk you."

"Okay, but what's this all about?"

One of the men took the AK-47 from him and then removed the man's battle vest, which had a 9mm pistol and knife secured in it. "Any other weapons?" The sergeant asked.

"Nope, that is it."

"We are going to frisk you to be sure." The man was patted down and nothing else was found.

"Alright mister, where are you coming from and where are you going?"

The man hesitated and then said, "Ahh, I'm new to this area and was out hunting."

The sergeant smiled and said, "Sure you are. Now tell me how many people are with you?"

The man's eyes were suspicious. "Why do you ask that?"

"Listen, punk, I'm the one asking the questions here. How many people are you with and where are they now?"

"I'm by myself."

The sergeant nodded and the men standing behind him grabbed both arms and held him. The move surprised the man and he yelled, "Hey! What the hell is going on here?"

"Look kid, knock off the shit. I don't have time for games. I was in Afghanistan and learned a few tricks that...well, let's just say the officers would not have approved." He pulled his K-bar knife out and slowly moved it back and forth in front of the kid's eyes. The black blade looked cruel in the daylight. "I really don't want to cut you up and have to listen to you scream in pain, but I am going to leave that up to you. Just so you know, we can backtrack you easily enough and find the others, but I prefer to know what I am facing, so this is entirely up to you. Answer my questions truthfully and you don't bleed." He used the blade to shave some hair off of his arm as he said, "You see kid, I was what you'd call a 'go to' guy. Do you know what that is?"

The kid kept his eyes on the knife, clearly scared.

The sergeant continued, "You know, young officers want to get promoted and they can do that with a good sergeant. The young officers are in charge and accountable to the higher ups, so they don't like to get their hands dirty. They tell their sergeant what they want to know from a captured soldier. Then they mention they have to go and report to a senior officer and won't be back for a few hours. You know, a little CYA. They were covering their ass."

The whole time he was twisting and turning the blade in front of the kid's face. "So I get the information. I've learned over the years how to make it long and painful,

315

but I also did a little experimenting too. You know, keeping track of what makes most people talk. Let me tell you, the movies are fake. They lie about the tough guys holding out. Some men are made that way, but very few." He gave a command, "Corporal, head lock." The corporal let go of the man's arms and quickly put him in a headlock. "But I found out that the fastest way to get the vast majority of them to talk was to pluck out one eye." He stepped closer to the kid and inched the knife slowly towards his left eye. "Now don't move. I wouldn't want to accidently slice your face up."

When the point of the knife touched the man's eye he broke down. "Okay, stop, stop. I'll tell you everything. Please, just pull the knife back."

The sergeant inched the knife back, but held it ready. "That's better. Now, how many are in your group?"

The kid had wet himself and it was obvious. "There are four of us."

"Why are you here?"

"We were sent to spy on the army being built."

"Okay, you are doing well. Now the important question - where are the rest of the men?"

The kid was almost in tears as he said, "They are about two miles back that way," He motioned with his head, "There's a small cabin."

"Are there any booby traps?"

"No. We have been watching you for weeks and no one has ever come close to finding us."

"Corporal, tie him up and gag him, then get him out of sight." When the man was out of earshot, he said, "You and the corporal stay and guard that man. You," he pointed to another man, "are coming with me. Bill, I want you to get on the horse and ride back to tell the Major where we are."

They took off at a trot, as he wanted to get eyes on this cabin quickly. They stopped after fifteen minutes and the man with him said, "Sergeant, was that all bullshit or the real deal?" He was referring to him cutting eye out of prisoners.

The sergeant smiled and said, "What do you think?"

"You sure had him convinced and it seemed pretty damn convincing to me."

"Good. That's all that matters."

They kept going and saw the cabin, ducking out of sight to observe. The sergeant whispered, "Okay, I am staying here. You backtrack and let the Major know where I'm at. Have him send up a ten man team and we can take this place."

"Will do." The man was off.

The sarge watched the cabin continuously and, about two hours later, the ten man team showed up. They quickly surround the cabin. A plan had already been worked out; four men were going to be the entrance team and the rest were positioned around the outside to prevent escapes. They kicked the door in and stormed inside. The man that was awake tried for his gun, but was quickly shot down. The two that were sleeping were captured. The ham radio was undamaged and five men were left behind to guard it. The rest hauled their prisoners back to the General.

* * * * *

As soon as Clint learned that the relay team had been located, he ordered all of the spies arrested. When the three men were brought in, Clint said, "Great job, men. Stick them in the makeshift stockade. Go to your units and get your gear ready - we are moving out in the morning."

Clint called a meeting with Charles and Bert, telling them, "We cut the head of the snake off, but don't drop your guard because there still might be more spies among us. We move out in the morning."

Charles said, "What are we going to do with the prisoners?"

"After we are sure we have all of the information from them, they will be eliminated. Right now we need to get everything ready and make sure we win this battle. We need their guns and ammo the most."

"Okay Clint, you're in charge."

Chapter 24

Preparing for the Battle

The next morning, just as they were moving out, a rider from the west came racing into camp. After going through a number of people, he finally made his way to Clint. "General, we have the Duluth Rainbow Warriors heading from Superior and heading this way."

Clint frowned and said, "How many?"

He replied, "The first group are fifty to sixty men on horseback, but we think there is a main column coming behind them."

"Why do you think that? Did you actually see troop movement?"

"No sir, but why else would they be coming this way?"

Clint said, "Thank you. Get a fresh horse and get me more Intel. I need to know if there are only fifty men and where they are."

"General, this is third hand knowledge. I'm part of the relay team."

Clint nodded. "Of course. When you return, report directly to Major Windham and work out the details of where to meet."

"Yes, sir."

Turning to Charles, he said, "Major, I want you to take your hundred men and stop them. I'm sure it's a probe, or feint if you will, to see how we will react. If they can get our main army to switch and go to face them, the Rainbow Warriors on Highway 8 can make it back to Green Bay."

The Major looked a little surprised and asked, "How do you know this?"

"Because he said fifty to sixty men on horseback, with no troops behind them."

The major nodded his understanding. "How do you expect me to stop them? They are mounted men and most of us are on foot. Give me one of the machine guns, at least."

"No Major. I'm telling you, this is a fake move. Take barbed wire and twenty of the homemade bombs and set up an ambush to stop them."

"Clint, what if you're wrong and the main force is coming from Duluth?"

Clint could see the uneasiness in Charles' face and pulled out the map. Pointing to the highways, he said, "Look, if they were going to attack us on two fronts, with the main battle force on Highway 8, they would have already turned north. It would be foolish to keep on the route they have been going on."

The Major said, "Where is the last known position of the main army?"

Clint pointed at the map and said, "There are only two major highways heading directly north to us. They've already passed the first one. If they thought we would fall for this, they would have turned north to trap us on two fronts."

The Major was obviously nervous, but said, "You're right Clint, but what if a main battle force is coming from Duluth? The Green Bay main battle force could head north. Together they could take us out and win."

Before the conversation continued, another rider came racing in. The rider said, "The cavalry has left Green Bay and is heading this way."

Clint turned to Charles and asked, "What do you suggest Major, splitting up our forces?"

"No. What I would suggest is that you hold in place until we have more information."

Clint could see the Major's thought process, but shook his head. "No Major, that is what they want us to do. Look, we know the spies have fed enough information to them that they are worried about us. They think we are going to Green Bay. Think like a General - you're stuck in Green Bay with three hundred troops and you know an army is marching toward you that is five hundred strong. All you have to do is delay this force long enough for your main battle group to make it back. They are trying to play guerrilla warfare and now they are using these mounted troops to come in and hit us before we get there. Our disinformation is working."

Clint was getting irritated at the Major's inability to think out this problem and was now having doubts about him being in battle.

The Major continued his line of thought and said, "But General, what if this is a three sided attack? They hit us to see our power and then maybe all three forces are coming this way to attack us. We should dig in here."

Clint was now exasperated and said in a raised voice, "Major, I am not going to argue this further. Your orders are to stop the Duluth troops. Have your best scouts head out now and when you have eyewitness reports confirmed that the main army is coming from Duluth, then send them back to me and we will turn around. Until then, we stick to the battle plan."

"Yes Sir, but I want it on record that I was against the idea."

"Fine. Duly noted. Now get your troops and get out of here."

"I hope and pray to God you are correct."

"Charles, listen to me. If it is the main group from Duluth, then do a tactical withdrawal and hit them every five miles to slow them down so we can get back here in time."

"First smart thing you said. Okay, I am going now. Wish me luck."

"Good luck. And Major, don't be a hero. I want to see you when this is over."

"Yeah, me too." He saluted and, with that, he rode off.

Clint called in the sergeant. "Get me the Colonel for an urgent meeting."

"Yes sir."

Clint continued to study the map as he waited for the colonel. He was thinking, *what if the Major was right?* If the Rainbow Warriors sent five hundred men from Duluth and two hundred from Green Bay, swinging the troops from the south to the north, they would be trapped on three fronts.

He studied the map and realized that the Duluth troops would have to come across on Highway 2, heading east. The southern troops should have turned north on Highway 53. Why would they pass it? Then it hit Clint; they didn't know what was going on. They must be sending messages to them. That had to be it, unless they were going to hit Highway 51, but that was a poor choice, giving Clint's men plenty of time to set up ambushes along the whole route. The Green Bay army was heading north on Highway 141 to connect to Highway 8, so they had to be heading out to snipe and harass Clint's men as they attacked Green Bay, or so they think.

The Colonel rode over to headquarters to talk with Clint. "What's going on that is so urgent?"

Clint acknowledged him and then asked, "I want your thoughts. We have a report of fifty to sixty mounted cavalry heading out from Duluth and heading east on Highway 2. It is possible the rest of the troops and main battle force is behind them, but that is not confirmed. We also have a report of a hundred mounted cavalry heading north on Highway 141. I sent the Major and his men to stop the Duluth force on Highway 2, believing this is a ruse."

Bert interrupted, "Let me guess, you want to send my men to stop the Green Bay force. Why don't we just take out the main army?"

"No, I think the whole thing is just a feint to lure us off and give their main battle force time to get back to defend Green Bay. Look, we told the troops we were heading to Green Bay, right? We would march down Highway 51, with our troops thinking we are going to turn east once we hit Highway 8."

"The Colonel interrupted, "Right, but the two ambush spots are west of the Highway 8 intersection."

Clint continued his thought and said, "Only, once we are there, we fill the men in on the change of plans."

"There is one thing you are missing, Clint. What if the Green Bay force is a raider force instead?"

"Yes I thought of that too. If they go north at Highway 8, instead of west, then they are raiders. If they head west, then they're carrying orders for the main battle group. How quickly could they reach us?"

"If they have really good horses, three to four days."

"Great. It's going to take us three days to get into position. What are your thoughts?"

"I say we stick to the battle plan. My men and I can get to the intersection in two days. I can send out scouts to the east. By the time you reach the intersection, I will have updated information for you and we can decide if these hundred horsemen are in the fight or not."

"Sounds good to me, but what if they turn north instead?"

Bert smiled and said, "Well General, that's why you're getting paid the big bucks to make this call. What did the Major say?"

"I'm having some doubts about him on the battle field. He said we should dig in here and fight. I sent him off to stop the troops coming from Duluth. I think this a fake to protect the main battle group while we dig in, which would give the main battle group time to slip by and return to Green Bay."

"Not sure, Clint?"

"Okay, put yourself in the enemy's shoes. What would you do?"

The Colonel was pointing to the map as he said, "Well we are going to have to assume a few things. Let's say we know what the spies were sending out to both Green Bay and Duluth, but no one is heading south, as far as we know. I think the main force in the south has no clue of our strength or plans. Therefore, if I was in Green Bay, I would send the troops out to get the main battle group to change to overnight forced march to reach Green Bay and hit us from behind."

Clint had been following his idea on the map. "That makes sense, but what about the Duluth troops?"

"You said Junior's Intel was that they are supposed to control the city, so my guess is it's a simple ploy or probe to throw us off. It may be a raiding party, but militarily speaking, it is the Green Bay cavalry that is our main worry."

Clint nodded. "I agree, so head out with your troops and I'll see you in three days."

Doubt crept into Clint's mind and he couldn't help but wonder what if he was wrong? They would win the battle, but lose the war.

He was leaving a small detachment of men behind, just thirty five, but they could put up a hell of battle against the hundred mounted cavalry if they swung in on Highway 2, or they could back up the Major if the main force was coming from Duluth. He had another moment of doubt over whether he should have given the Major one of the machine guns, but he shook it off. As far as they know for sure, the Intel said the main battle force was to the south, so they stuck to the plan.

After covering twenty miles, they stopped for the night. Clint was proud of the men for travelling so far. He told the sentries that the minute any word came in, they were to wake him immediately.

* * * * *

The Major and his troops had moved about 20 miles west and set up an ambush site. Thank God he had brought the homemade bombs. He was talking to the head sergeant, saying, "If only we had a machine gun."

The sergeant responded, "We sort of do, sir."

The colonel was surprised and turned to face him, asking, "What do you mean?"

"Well, did you ever see those hand cranks you can put on a rifle to make them almost fully automatic?"

"Why yes, I've seen them. Why?"

"Because one of our men has one hooked up to his AR-15, with a hundred round drum magazine. He has it mounted on a swivel tripod."

The Major was obviously pleased about this new development and said, "That's perfect. Okay, in the morning I want a machine gun nest build for it. Put it in minivan, or a pickup with a camper shell, and surround it with sand bags."

The sergeant acknowledged his order as the Major went on to say, "Sergeant, I'm thinking we should make a formation like the point of the spear, like the Spartans, and we'll put the machine gun in the front. Their horses are their advantage, so we shoot the horses first and get them on an equal footing. We can place our men around vehicles for cover, but set up so that most of our soldiers can be shooting into them."

The sergeant said, "Why not use a solid wall defense and stop them?"

The Major shook his head. "Because I want to kill them all and take their weapons. I want the word to get back to Duluth - if you come east, get ready for heavy losses."

"But sir, we can't make it a perfect arrow or the trap won't work. We have to use semis and cars to make it look haphazard, setting up logs to close any gaps. They can't see anything obvious when they approach, or we'll lose the element of surprise. As soon as they are in the arrowhead, we'll cut them to ribbons."

The Major agreed and said, "Try to make it less obvious and still give us the cover we need. I want our best shots at the rear, shooting straight down into them. Hopefully this will split them up on each side."

The sergeant said, "How do we stop them from heading off into the woods?"

"We'll string barbed wire. That rusty old brown barbed wire will blend in. Once the horses see it, they will turn and give us another crack at them. We'll have the machine gun to cut off any retreat."

The sergeant asked, "Why are we having to fight so much when we should be helping people rebuild?"

The Major's face turned sad and he said, "Sergeant, if you've studied history, you have to know that there are always men that want power and they will do anything to get it. There is always a moment in history when good men have to stand up and stop these bad men. This is our moment. We were born at this moment in time to protect America and rebuild it, but before we can rebuild, we have to clean out the rabble."

He continued. "Okay, let's get back to the plans. I want you to send out scouts and get updates on the troops and how many men are with them. We need to know right away what the main force is, so we can change our plans if necessary."

* * * * *

The next morning Clint and the troops were moving out fast after a quick cup of coffee. Their breakfast consisted of chewing on beef jerky as they marched. He was pushing his men hard because he wanted to cover at least twenty five miles before night fall. If they could manage the distance, then they wouldn't have too far to go on the third day and would still have daylight to finish the ambush site.

He wondered if the Green Bay Cavalry had turned, because they could be waiting for him, but only if they got through the colonel's troops. What about the Duluth troops? He realized he'd give almost anything for a working cell phone. The more he thought, the more his plan became firm. He had to take the sure win and get the supplies. Then they would be feared by the enemy.

Reviewing the progress he had made, he felt better. That night a messenger arrived from the Colonel, saying that the Green Bay Cavalry had headed north. He got a sick knot in his stomach. Where were they going next? Into Michigan? Or would they follow Highway 2 over and converge on home base?

A hundred cavalrymen would take three days to head north and turn, more likely four days to get to their home base. Clint hadn't heard anything from the Major, but that was a good thing. All of the worry could be for nothing; they might be deserters fleeing Green Bay before Clint's men arrived. The Major was going to have to handle it.

The Major had his trap set up by the end of second day and his scouts had confirmed the report that it was only fifty men on horseback. He felt better knowing more troops weren't behind the cavalry. That night he ordered no fires. The men were to stay quiet and be ready to fight. The enemy could come in the night, or the next day sometime.

He set up watches, always keeping one third of his men awake. Now it was just a waiting game.

******

The Colonel was all set up and ready, checking the firing position. His scouts reported to him that the main battle force was coming and would be there in two days. Clint would be there tomorrow and the ambush would be complete. All that they needed now was a little patience and then they could spring the trap.

The Colonel was thinking out loud and said, "Come on, Clint, push the men and get here tomorrow. We need daylight to get your troops in place." He rode the battle ground for the tenth time, stopping and looking to make sure everything was in place. It had to be perfect and look natural. There couldn't be one single thing to warn the other side. Clint's words echoed in his head - every man you lose, you are going to blame yourself for it and think you should have pushed yourself harder.

He had worked side by side with these men and cared about them, but he could not show any weakness, only strength. This was the battleground, hallowed ground of the home of the brave. They were no longer mere words that sounded nice. Now was the time to make them true in actions. It was payback time and hell was riding with him.

Chapter 25

Surprise Attack

In the morning the Major waited, wondering if today was the day. He dared not have fires going, or it would tip off the other side, so they were on cold rations only. He walked around inside the spearhead shaped trap and talked to the men.

Everyone was tired and the stress was showing on their faces. Waiting was the hardest part. The night shift was sleeping and all was quiet on the western front. He worked his way to the rear, where his sergeant was. "What do you think?"

Looking up at the Major, he said, "I think we should deploy our sniper team out about two hundred yards on each side of the road. If they make it past the trap, have them kill the officer and cut down any spacing. Give them some of the smaller bombs; they can toss those too."

"Excellent idea, Sergeant. Tell them to make sure they are protected from our fire too. We don't want any friendly fire causalities."

"Yes sir."

The Major asked, "Where are the scouts?" The morning was ticking by and there were no reports, nothing.

In the morning, Clint told the men to push hard, saying that they were almost there. "If we get there by 4 p.m. today, we'll have enough time to finish the ambush site."

Cold rations did not make for happy men, but they understood the need for them and traveled on. He heard a few grumblings among the men about the cold food and no coffee that morning, but they would thank him tomorrow for making sure they were set up properly today.

* * * * *

The Colonel's men had dug foxholes at the top of the hills on both sides of the road. He made sure the foxholes were camouflaged correctly and had a clear field of fire. He also had a team clear the brush and make an opening for the monster sling shot, so men could lob the bombs down.

At 3 p.m. he rode down past the set up and then rode back up slowly, looking at each spot carefully and yelling instructions on what needed to be corrected to better conceal the foxholes. At 4 p.m. Clint had still not arrived. The Colonel paced, thinking come on Clint.

At the same time, the Major was now facing the enemy. His men were all set up and the cavalry was about five hundred yards out and slowly coming into his trap. As the tension built, he hoped the little bit of training they had done would pay off.

All of a sudden, the cavalry held up about two hundred yards out. Had they seen someone? What was the problem? He held his breath, waiting for them to advance. What were they waiting for?

The minutes ticked by and the sweat rolled down his face. If they turned around, it was still mission accomplished. The troops started advancing again, but only ten men. They split up, so there were five on each side of the trap. All of sudden they charged, racing down the ditches.

Under his breath he said, "Hold fire. Let them get into the trap." Once they were halfway in the trap, he yelled, "FIRE." One hundred men opened fire and the ten men were cut down. The Major, not expecting anyone to hear him, said, "Come on machine gunner, open fire and take out their horses before they escape."

The shooting stopped and the remaining enemy troops turned to flee. Finally, the machine gunner started firing and the snipers took out those they thought were the officers in charge. It was over in a few minutes. Twenty one of the enemy were dead and three wounded lay on the ground. In all, there were ten horses dead. The rest of them fled, racing back for Duluth.

The Major called out to the sergeant, "I want to make sure everyone is dead, then you can retrieve all of their gear and ammo."

"Yes, sir."

"And corporal, I want a detail of men to butcher some of the horses. We are eating steak tonight to celebrate."

He signaled the scouts over, saying, "I want you to follow them and make sure they are leaving. Give me a report back in one hour."

That was almost too easy, he thought, unless Clint was right and they were just a decoy to protect their main battle force.

Within an hour the scouts reported back that the enemy was still heading west, hauling ass back to Duluth.

All of the men were jubilant and were allowed campfires to grill the steaks that had been rationed to them. He had not lost one man. Only one man had been injured when he tried to climb up on a semi to keep shooting and fell off the top, breaking his arm. It was a miracle. Now hopefully Clint would be successful too.

As darkness fell, the men were in good spirits, eating well while a few bottles of moonshine were being passed around in celebration.

The Major kept twenty men from drinking shine, as they were on watch for the night, just to be safe.

* * * * *

Clint and the colonel waited for the scout's morning report and they double-checked everything. They had access to some of the large round hay bales and soaked them in motor oil. They were all set to light them afire and roll them into the army.

All of the men were concealed and waiting when they watched the enemy ride right into the trap. The giant slingshot lobbed the bombs right into them. The machine gunner tore them to shreds and then they lit the bales of hay and rolled them directly into the middle of the enemy. The Rainbow Warriors tried retreating, but Clint gave the signal and a red flag was waved. That was the signal for the colonel and his troops to ride over the hill and storm the remaining soldiers.

Hell itself was riding that day. Revenge and payback time rained down on the Rainbow Warriors. The battle was over quickly and Clint had his big prize, which was the ammo for the 105 mm cannon. They could finally take on Green Bay and end this stupid war. Clint made sure that the thirty four wounded men were getting proper medical care. They had lost twelve men in the battle, but now they were armed and had supplies like never before.

Without warning, a semi tractor-trailer showed up and Clint was stunned. Where on earth had it come from? It turned out they had some talented people on their side. Clint found out about the 4 x 4 truck they had gotten running. It would be used to tow the cannon to the meeting spot near Green Bay. Life was going to be much easier over the coming winter, with this kind of help around.

His sergeant came running up and said, "Sir, you are never going to believe this?"

Clint looked at the man and said, "Okay, so surprise me."

The sergeant was obviously excited and said, "The back two wagons are filled with guns and ammunition, plus what we took off the dead. We are truly supplied like a real army."

Clint was overwhelmed and said, "We can sure put that to good use."

They packed everything up and headed towards Green Bay.

As they rode out, Clint and Bert rode together. Bert said, "That was a great plan, Clint. We lost very few men. Good job."

Clint said, "I think you have that wrong, Bert. You deserve the credit here. You were the one that found and set up the location."

"That may be, but you brought us all together as an army."

"It's not over yet. We still need to take out Green Bay and then, in the spring, we'll march on Duluth before they can get resupplied by the Chinese."

Bert was surprised at this and said, "Why wait until spring?"

"Because I want a lot more details on what we are facing there before we can plan a solid attack. If they have twenty five hundred men, we are ready, that's for sure."

"What are you thinking?"

"I am thinking that now we have the 105 mm cannon, we can go over and blow the main bridges and cut off the route to get the tank."

"Yes, but they can go south until they find a working bridge and cross over. We can't take all of the bridges out." Changing the subject, he asked, "Any word on the Green Bay Calvary?"

"I was going to ask you the same thing."

"Nada. We have to finish this and just hope the Major has it under control."

"What's up with you two anyway?"

Clint paused and then spoke. "He's a West Point graduate. It's good that he has the training, but he just doesn't understand what makes men respect a leader and why they stand behind you. He is learning, but it's a slow process. I know he was more of a pencil pusher when he did his time, but he doesn't think about battle plans."

Bert ran a hand through his black beard and said, "So you're saying you respect him, but he just needs to drop the spit and polish? What about me?"

With a chuckle, he said, "You are a reckless, murdering cutthroat and I thank God you're on our side."

"No really, I'm serious. Tell me what you think."

Clint paused a while and then thoughtfully said, "Well, Colonel, you have come a long way and you are thinking more about saving the men than your own glory. Your attention to detail is paying off, but you have to find that middle ground."

"Middle ground? What are you talking about?"

"Well somewhere in the middle is where you keep your fighting edge, but don't become too cautious."

"Oh I see. You want me to be a safe, planning rebel, but not lose my cutthroat personality completely?"

"Yes, that's it perfectly." Clint laughed.

* * * * *

The morning after the battle, the Major woke and smiled, thinking of his victory as he starting a fire for his coffee. He looked out across the battlefield as he received the morning report from the scouts. It was all good news.

Clint had said to stop them and that's what they had done. Mission accomplished. Now he was contemplating whether they should head back or wait one more day. He thought they should play it safe and wait another day, just in case the Rainbow Warriors tried to get by again.

He felt much better having captured twenty four AK-47s with one hundred and fifty rounds each. These were issued out to the men who were only armed with shotguns and .22 rifles.

* * * * *

Junior was pacing around, wondering what was going on with the battle. They had been gone three days. He walked over to headquarters and men were running around. He could feel the excitement. The sergeant called him over. "Junior! You need to ride like the wind, my friend. Get to the Major and tell him he needs to rush here. The Rainbow Warriors hundred-man cavalry is on the way. They might be here by the morning, or even sometime tonight."

Junior's eyes got big and he asked, "Do you have positive confirmation of this?"

"Yes. Our scouts have confirmed it."

"What are you doing to prepare?"

"We're building a blockade. We have thirty five men, plus ten cooks, giving us forty five men to face them. If the

Major can get his men here in time, we can stop them. Take my horse."

"What about Clint?"

"He's too far away and would never make it back in time. Please get going, Junior. We don't have a minute to spare. I don't think we can hold them. We only have the leftover guns and I think we only have two semi autos in the whole group. The rest are lever action, bolt action and shotguns."

Junior nodded and said, "On my way." He mounted the horse and quickly rode to the cabin, telling Gayle what was going on. He told her to bolt the place up and not to have any fires. He said, "All of you need to stay inside until we know it's safe."

"Jesus, Junior, we could have Robbie watch the baby. I can be on the front lines with you."

"No. You stay here. I have to ride. The Major is our only hope." That being said, he was out the door.

As he pushed the horse to go faster, he was thinking of all the possibilities. The 'what if' thoughts were sometimes dangerous and he needed to focus on getting to the Major as quickly as possible. He was trying to calculate in his mind how long it would take him to get there. If it took him four hours to ride there and an hour for the Major to organize his men, it would be a total of nine hours before they returned.

He continued to have thoughts as the miles went by. He wondered why the Rainbow Warriors' cavalry would attack their home base. They had to be planning on a scorched earth policy - burn the crops and houses while the army was gone. He rode on, reaching the Major's camp a little after 2 p.m.

He rode in hard, identifying himself as he did. He hadn't even come to a complete stop as he dismounted near a startled Major, before he said, "Major, we have a serious problem."

"What's wrong, Junior?

"Get your men back to camp as fast as you can. The Green Bay Rainbow Warriors are coming to wipe it out and could be there tonight, or first thing in the morning."

He looked around and found a man near the horses. Motioning to the man, he said, "You. Come here." The man trotted over. "Get mounted up and tell the scouts to return to us and tell them we are moving back to headquarters a.s.a.p."

The sergeant barked out orders to the men, "Get packed up. We are headed back to headquarters at double time." It was to be a forced march back to camp and would be through the night.

Junior got a fresh horse and headed back to tell them they were coming. The Major ordered his ten horsemen to follow Junior back and lend support until he could get there.

*　*　*　*　*

Back at headquarters, they were trying to prepare for the attack. The sergeant in charge didn't have any sand bags, so they used a row of cars for protection, cutting trees and putting them in front of the barricade. "At least we have a solid line to defend from." He thought aloud. There were thick woods on both sides, so they could still flank them.

He decided that the best defense would be to place men with shotguns on both flanks that could stop them. He thought about what would happen if the enemy arrived in the dark. If it was a night attack, they would need light to shoot at them, so he talked it over with a few men and they came up with an idea. They would use old tires that they could light on fire. That would be bright enough for them to see the enemy.

They stacked tires in the area in front of the cars. If the wind shifted, it could put that black smoke right in their faces, but there was nothing else they could do. They needed light to kill the enemy and it wasn't like he could order in an artillery star burst so they could see. He had his men position the tires further out so they would backlight the enemy as they came into range.

Around 7 p.m. Junior rode in, ready for battle, with his AR-15 strung over his back and a fully loaded battle vest. As he dismounted, he called out, "Sergeant, there are ten more men coming up behind me and the rest are on their way. I would estimate their arrival around 2 or 3 a.m. Where do you want me?"

The sergeant nodded, acknowledging his report. "Just pick a spot."

The sergeant waited for the ten extra men to show up and then called everyone to a meeting. "Our weakest time is at night and right now we are outnumbered about 2 to 1. They have the advantage as they are on horseback, but we have the barricade set up to stop them." The sergeant reminded the men that night shooting was difficult, as it was very hard to see their targets. He said, "The average hits for shots fired is like twenty to one, so aim low is the best advice I can give you. It's going to be chaos, with men screaming in pain and the darkness. It can seem overwhelming, but, whatever you do, never allow panic to take hold and run off. That's a guaranteed slaughter if you do. Remember, they are counting on the confusion and for you to panic."

He continued with the defense plan. "As soon as they are a hundred yards out, we light up the tires so we can see to shoot. Make your shots count. You know we are low on ammo, but don't think this is impossible."

The sergeant pointed to the new arrivals. "You ten men that just arrived, I want you to be in the middle. Using your AK-47s, I want you to spread out so you can put as much lead down range as possible and stop the charge. I have assigned five men to cover our flanks in the woods. They all have shotguns and buckshot to stop any flanking action, so you will have some firefighting on your flanks. Take care not to shoot in that direction, unless you can positively identify your target as the enemy. We've placed the tires out far enough that the enemy will have the light behind them, making them a silhouette. It should make it easier to target and shoot them. One man will be in charge of each group. Hold your fire until they are in range and then cut them down. If we can hold on until morning, we are going to win. Now is the time to earn our right to be part of this army."

Nightfall was coming and they were as ready as they could be. They lit a bonfire in preparation for lighting the tires. All they had to do now was wait.

Chapter 26

Attack on Headquarters

By midnight neither the Major nor the Rainbow Warriors had shown up. The sergeant thought that was good news. Maybe they were going to get lucky after all. Half the men were sleeping, while the others stood ready. He paced along the front line wondering where the Major was. He hated being in charge of half trained troops in a night battle, especially being under supplied. What could be worse? Then he thought of the cropland and the livestock. They could really hurt them by burning everything and killing all of the livestock. If the Rainbow Warriors got past them, they would starve over the coming winter. Why hadn't Clint left him more men?

A little after one in the morning, he heard the call out, "Here they come." He looked up and saw a hundred torches advancing on them. It looked medieval, like something out of a movie, or a nightmare.

The sergeant gave the order. "Everyone up and light the tires. Get ready and hold your ground. Wait for them to get into range. No one fires until I give the command."

The night lit up in front of them as the tires burned brightly in three big piles. There was no breeze and the smoke slowly curled up into the sky.

The enemy formed up at two hundred yards and then charged forward. They were in a formation that consisted of twenty men across and five deep.

The sergeant ordered, "Hold and wait for it."

The sound of a hundred horses thundering down on them shook the very ground. "Hold it. Wait for it." When the horsemen were a hundred yards from them, he yelled, "Fire!"

They opened up, but it seemed to have little effect. A few men dropped, but the main force bore down on them. Ten men on each side of the charge broke off and headed to the flanks. The enemy started firing back and soon the night was filled with the screams of wounded men and dying horses. You could hear it; "Help, I'm hit." and then "Frank is dead" and the sound of a wounded horse screaming in pain. The sound of death and screaming filled the night air.

The men on the flanks tried to hold, but there were too many of them. They dropped a few, but seven of the enemy on the right side broke through. Two of the defenders were cut down, but the left side held and drove them back.

The enemy cavalry put intense firepower on the defenders. The seven men circled behind them and started shooting. The sergeant was standing next to Junior and was hit in the back and fell. Junior ran over to him and saw the riders bearing down on them. He yelled, "Behind us. Kill them." Enough men turned around and cut down all of the horsemen, but they had lost several men and many more were wounded. The ten men with the AK-47s kept the firepower on throughout the battle, until the enemy broke off and retreated.

Junior called out, "Everyone reload. Even if you are wounded, you have to fight if you can. Patch up the brother beside you, for tonight we stand together as one family."

A call rang out in the night. "Here they come again."

Everyone started firing, but this time the whole cavalry headed for the right side, the weakest side. They quickly killed the last three men trying to hold that position. Junior yelled out, "Retreat to me. Form up two lines, with the front line kneeling and second line standing behind them. When they break through the woods, kill the horses. I want a pile of dead horses between us and them." No sooner had he finished saying that, when they broke through the woods and headed for them. They were met with a wall of fire, dropping horses and men. Some tried jumping over the downed horses in front of them and soon the pile grew. The sounds were horrific, coming from both the wounded and dying horses and men screaming in pain. Some of the men died when horses fell on top of them, crushing them into the ground. The rest of the cavalry broke off and raced down the road.

Junior issued the order, "Grab the wounded and retreat to the woods behind us. Form up like that again." They made it to the woods with only fourteen men left standing and twelve wounded. The rest of the men were dead or dying.

A man called out, "Junior, we can't hold out much longer."

Junior responded, "I know, but we are the Alamo and have to buy time for the Major to get here. We only have to hold on a little longer."

The next charge came thundering down on the barricade and Junior called out, "Hold it, don't fire. Wait for it." The enemy continued their charge, shooting anybody they saw, dead or wounded, it didn't matter. Just as they slowed down and thought they had won, Junior yelled, "Fire." They opened up, pouring lead into the horses and men. The other side broke off and retreated.

Someone said, "I am almost out of ammo." Another man called out, "I only have four rounds left. We need to retreat and save as many men as we can, Junior."

Junior said, "No way. I'm not letting them burn our crops and kill our livestock, starving us out this winter. No, we buy the Major time to get here. Reload and get ready."

Just then, about two hundred yards down the road, a fierce firefight lit up the night. Oh thank God, the Major must have made it. They could see the flashes of gunfire breaking the darkness of the night. It was an intense firefight, up close and personal. Some was even hand-to-hand, as the Rainbow Warriors were cut down from their horses and forced into hand-to-hand combat. Soon they heard horses riding down upon them again.

Junior yelled, "Hold your fire. We don't know who it is yet."

The horsemen raced up, moving around the dead horses. Junior tried to count them, but he could only guess thirty five to forty horses before they retreated into the night.

The minutes ticked by, seeming like hours. The silence was eerie now, after the noise of the intense fighting. It was like the world was suddenly holding its breath. Junior saw men leap frogging forward and he called out, "We are friendly. Don't shoot."

A voice called out from the darkness, "Who's out there?"

"Just the last of the good guys. Are you the Major's troops?"

The reply was, "Yes. Who are you?"

"It's Junior and the last of the troops. We need a medic up here right away."

Junior walked out towards the voice and said, "We have quite a few wounded."

Out of the shadows the Major walked up to him, saying, "So do we, son. We can get some medics up here in a few minutes."

"Sergeant, I want all these bodies checked to make sure we have no live enemies among us and then get that barricade manned."

He looked around at all of the bodies and said, "Looks like you had one hell of a fight here."

Junior nodded. "Yes, we were about finished until you arrived. If they had charged one more time, I think that would have been all we could have handled."

"How many are left?"

"We have fourteen standing and twelve wounded. There may be more wounded out there." Junior said as he pointed to the barricade. An occasional shot rang out from someone finishing off a wounded enemy.

The Major motioned towards the wounded and said, "Come on, let's haul your wounded to the medical tent back at headquarters."

Stretchers were brought up and men were hauled back for treatment. War didn't seem so glorious now, listening to the wounded call out for help in pain. The blood and gore of the death and destruction seemed horrific.

"Major, what's the word on Clint?"

"I haven't heard. I was hoping you knew what was going on."

One of the men walked up to Junior and said, "Tell me where you came up with that idea to form two lines of riflemen."

"From a movie called Zulu, about the Battle of Rorke's Drift. In the movie they were fighting savages charging them with spears. I was sure we could kill their horses, making them pile up, taking away their advantage against us. It also made us appear a larger fighting force than we were."

The major patted Junior on the back and said, "Brilliant. Good job."

****

Clint and his army were getting ready for a morning fight against Green Bay headquarters. While advancing that morning he was disappointed to find out that the enemy had escaped on a freighter. Who could have guessed that one? But at least the threat was over for this state, so they packed up and headed for home.

Clint and the Colonel rode together and Clint said, "That was too easy."

The Colonel laughed and said, "Well they heard Superman was coming and they fled like scared rabbits."

Clint smiled. "What do you think, Colonel? A spring campaign on Duluth?"

"Now that we have the men and supplies, I think we should go right now and take all of them out."

Clint shook his head no. "Too risky. They outnumber us right now. We are better outfitted and with the 105 mm cannon we could put them under siege for a few days, but I don't think we could stand up to them going head on."

"What about luring them out to one of your famous ambush traps?"

"I don't think they will fall for it, especially if any of those survivors the Major's scout told us about made it back and told them what happened. Think like their General would. Why risk your men when all you have to do is hold on until spring, when you get resupplied with a tank and machine guns?"

"Why do you think the Chinese are supplying them?"

Clint said, "Simple really. They use these young people that are traitors to their own country. Why risk angering the Americans against you, when you can have great propaganda telling everyone that they are only here to help reestablish power and get America back on its feet. The fools in the Rainbow Warriors are just useful idiots to be used up and break down resistance forces. They can clear the way for the Chinese to say that they saved America to be rebuilt. They get the farms back up and running and, with ninety five percent of the American people dead, most of the food can go to China. That takes the huge weight of having to feed their own people off their shoulders. This leaves them open to be the one and only super power in the world."

"You don't think it might be for some other nefarious reason?"

Clint looked at the colonel and said, "Like what?"

"Like killing off most of us, leaving just enough slaves to run the farms?"

"Slaves? Never thought of that one."

The colonel asked, "You don't think we can rebuild and become a super power again?"

"Sadly no. Not in our lifetimes, and maybe never. Think about the rebuilding process. We have to get the electrical grid back up and running. That is going to take about ten, maybe fifteen years. In the meantime, we have to survive as dirt poor subsistence farmers. Really, some areas might take twenty years to get power back up and running."

"Okay, so what's the plan in the spring?"

"I'm thinking we will hit and run, drive them crazy and wear them down. No rest for the weary."

*****

When they finally reached home, Clint was fully briefed on all that had taken place, and then he called everyone together.

Clint was standing in the back of a wagon to address the gathering. "Men and women of the Patriots Army of America, I salute you for your bravery in the face of the enemy. We, all of us, from the ladies sewing your battle vests, to the farmers who provided the food, to the great medics and doctors giving us medical care, and to the awesome team of men we have become, all deserve the credit. Now we have another threat to face. In Duluth this spring, the Rainbow Warriors are supposed to be reinforced with a tank and machine guns from the Chinese. We have two choices - attack them now, or wait until spring."

There was loud murmur in the crowd and Clint waited for it to quiet down. "They are coming up the Great Lakes by freighter, which means they can't arrive until the ice is gone in May. I say we come back together in April and take them out before they are resupplied. I understand most of you here have things to do to get ready for the long, hard winter. We too have to do everything, from cutting firewood to gathering crops and things to take care of in maintaining our farms, so I leave it to you. What do you people say?"

While no official vote was taken, most people seemed to agree with Clint to hit them in the spring.

Clint nodded. "Okay then."

He went on to say, "If you are issued an AK-47, it's your job to properly maintain it. I want every man to keep your battle vest with one hundred and eighty rounds of ammo, ready to go at a moment's notice. You need to have seven days' worth of food and be out your door in five minutes when you are called on. Your local sergeant is going to hold monthly training to keep you in shape and informed, so don't miss those sessions. We will see you all back here on April 1st. We still need some men around to help take care of the sick and wounded, plus we need established patrols protecting us, so I'm asking for volunteers. My sergeant will set up a schedule, so you won't be expected to be here full time. There are things we must do. We must treat each other like brothers and sisters. Let's win America's freedom once more."

Chapter 27

What's Next?

Clint could see that the bloody battle had changed Junior. Some of his friends were dead or wounded. He looked older now and had the look of a young man that had seen battle and death. Clint attempted to make Junior understand that he had done a miraculous job at saving the headquarters and the death of the survivors over the long coming winter, but Junior was having none of it.

"It wasn't me that saved headquarters, but the brave men who died."

Clint nodded in agreement. "Yes, very fine men held the line against outnumbering forces. Night battles are truly hell." Clint wanted to change the subject and asked, "Did anyone ever find Trevor?"

Junior looked at the ground, feeling guilty, and shook his head. "Nope. He snuck out and no-one knows where he is."

Clint said, "Well hopefully he headed back to Green Bay and he can starve there without his friends."

"What now, Clint?"

"We set up patrols and sentries to keep our people safe and then we help people get through the winter. In the spring we will hit Duluth and finish off the Rainbow Warriors for good."

Junior looked at Clint and asked, "What do you think the Chinese want?"

"I think they might want to help us rebuild, but of course there will be strings attached, there always are. They need our farmland to feed their people."

Junior was shaking his head. "I don't understand why they don't land their army and just take America?"

"I would guess they don't want to. They know that people fight much harder against invaders. The easiest way is to use up the useful idiots like the Rainbow Warriors. Let them suffer the blame and consequences, instead of their own people. I'm sure they plan on killing them off after they have what they want."

"What about money?"

Clint asked Junior to clarify what he meant and Junior said "The money that we need to rebuild. We need a national currency."

"I've been thinking about that. The Chinese have plenty of U.S. dollars and they may ask us to accept it. Americans are used to it and probably would, but I think our best bet would be to establish a gold standard. We need something that the government can't inflate and destroy, like they have in the past."

Clint went on to make his point. "You know, I saw a video in college that outlined the reasons sperm whales were hunted. If the value of the whales were paid for in today's money, each sperm whale would be worth about 10 million dollars. That's why they were hunted almost to extinction. Whale oil was used in lamps to light people's houses. When we switched to oil, the whaling fleets switched to fishing for regular fish."

Junior was trying to follow, but had a puzzled look on his face. "I'm not following you."

Clint tried to clarify it. "It's simple really. Stop and think about what we need to get America back up and running. Take transformers, for instance. China can make them, but not for free, so we are going to have to trade with them. I am thinking food, iron ore and timber."

"Okay, I get that, but I still don't follow you."

"We ask for payments in gold and silver, instead of American dollars, because our commodities, like the sperm whale, are much needed for their own people."

Junior frowned and said, "What if they tell us we have to take the U.S. dollars they have?"

"We have to form a new government. The old form of government is dead and gone. We need to rebuild under a new government, using a new currency, and that should be gold and silver. If they want our resources, which they do, then they will have to pay for them in our new currency."

"I see. That could work, but first we have to take out the threats and then sit down and see what the Chinese want and go from there."

Junior went on to ask, "How badly do you think the grid was damaged in China?"

Clint paused, giving it some thought, and then answered. "I'm sure we hit back, but I think that their grid, or part of it, must have been protected. Heck, they could lose half their population and still have about six hundred million people."

Junior asked, "What do you think America is down to now? Twenty or thirty million people?"

"I'm guessing that more than ninety-five percent were wiped out, bringing us down to around sixteen million."

Junior let out a low whistle. "Wow. That's hard to believe."

Clint continued, "I am also guessing that they are about finished using the Rainbow Warriors."

"What are you saying? That they aren't going to supply them with a tank and machine guns in the spring?"

"Maybe. They want to take us out because we are becoming a pain to them, which is good and bad at the same time."

Junior frowned at that statement. "Why is that? I'm not following you."

"Well, the good part is that the Chinese know we have a powerful fighting force and may want to set up negotiations. The bad part is that they may want to wipe us out."

"I see. So what do we do?"

"First, we'll take out the Rainbow Warriors in Duluth and that will force the Chinese to negotiate with us."

Junior smiled. "I like it."

"Plus, with communities figuring out how to get wood vapors to power generators, trucks and cars, we can actually have one heck of a fighting force. Think about hit and run tactics - they are chasing us on horses and we simply drive off faster than their horses can run. Thanks to you providing us with the chicken manure gunpowder formula, we can have a small fighting force drive in, bomb them and then drive off."

"Wow, you're right. We can take out any patrols they send out."

"Right. They will really only have two choices; either they come and face us head on, or hold up. Either way they lose."

"What if they bring their full forces against us? Can they win that way? We know they far outnumber us."

"Not with running vehicles and the cannon. We can hit them all the time and drive off. We just wear them out and thin them down. We can set up ambushes that they can't survive. You don't understand how important making gunpowder is for us. Even if that powder gives off a cloud of smoke, it may not be the best, but it sure beats the heck out of throwing rocks."

"Why did these young guys ever agree to be part of Rainbow Warriors?"

"Brain washing and slick propaganda. When you were in college, did you ever read the deep ecology books?"

Junior shook his head. "No, I've never heard of them."

"Well let's say you are an academic communist. In your mind, everything that is wrong with the world is because of humans, especially capitalist. Less humans would mean more wildlife, more free space, less pollution and so forth. Therefore, the best thing to happen would be to deindustrialize America. But this plan was too slow in the making and taking too long. You take these young minds that are eager to change the world and you fill their heads full of fear mongering propaganda, telling them that mankind is killing the earth. You make Mother Gaia the religion of the group. You form little cliques that believe in this nonsense. Carefully select those people out and you build your army. They actually think they are doing good to save Mother Gaia, because they were brainwashed under the lies that humans are a cancer."

Junior's eyes got bigger and he said, "I see. Like a willful ignorance, they are trapped in a mental prison."

Clint nodded. "Now you're getting it. With ninety five percent of Americans dead, they should be doing good for mankind. Instead they are slaves to their ideology."

As Clint was finishing that statement, a rider came charging into the yard. "General, have you heard the news?"

"No. What's going on?"

"The new army is in the southern part of Wisconsin. It's thousands strong, maybe three thousands strong."

Clint frowned. "Who are they fighting?"

The man said, "They are taking over everything. It is being run by some warlord."

Clint was gritting his teeth and said, "Great. Just what we need, another army of power hungry evil idiots."

Warning: Gun Powder is dangerous.

All of the contents of this book are provided to the reader without any warranties. The survival techniques and information described in this book are for informational purposes only and are not intended for the reader to attempt to make gun powder or reload primers on their own. Gun powder and primers are extremely dangerous and flammable; by design, they are intended to burn rapidly and vigorously when ignited.

The reader bears all responsibility associated with the use of the information contained in this book, including those risks associated with reliance of the accuracy, thoroughness or appropriateness of the information for any situation represented.

The authors and publishers specifically disclaim all responsibility from any prosecution or proceedings brought or instituted against any person or body for any liability, loss, or risk, personal or otherwise, which is incurred as a consequence of the use or misuse and application of any of the contents of this book.

Reference Page for Perceptions of Reality, Volume 2 Part 2

Chapter 2

Sugardine – Page 7
http://www.tngun.com/how-to-make-sugardine-antiseptic/

http://www.peoplespharmacy.com/2007/09/17/sugar-speeds-wo/

Betadine – Page 7
http://www.betadine.com/

Fish antibiotics – Page 9
http://www.preparednesspro.com/fish-antibiotics

http://www.fishmoxfishflex.com/index.php/fish-antibiotics.html

Chapter 7

Chinese WZ-10 Armed Helicopter – Page 46
http://en.wikipedia.org/wiki/CAIC_WZ-10

Opening a can without a can opener – Page 52
http://off-grid.info/blog/how-to-open-a-can-without-a-can-opener-amazing/
http://www.youtube.com/watch?v=oH2NahLjx-Y

Chapter 8
Battle of Gaugamela – Page 62
http://en.wikipedia.org/wiki/Battle_of_Gaugamela

Chapter 9

AR-7 Survival Rifle – Page 66
http://henryrepeating.com/rifle-survival-ar7.cfm

Chapter 11

Wolf's Nose – Page 79
http://sweetwatervisions.com/Pages/isleroyale.html

Lensatic Compass – Page 83
https://www.benmeadows.com/store/assets/support_documents/102023MANUAL.pdf

Gordon Lightfoot's song, The Wreck Of The Edmund Fitzgerald, Lyrics – Page 87
http://www.azlyrics.com/lyrics/gordonlightfoot/thewreckoftheedmundfitzgerald.html

Chapter 12

1881 Gatling gun – Page 88
http://en.wikipedia.org/wiki/Gatling_gun

.45-70 Government catridge – Page 88
http://en.wikipedia.org/wiki/.45-70

Homemade primers – Page 89

Using caps –
http://www.thehighroad.org/archive/index.php/t-113826.html Scroll down to June 4th, CD Miller entry

Using matches – videos on YouTube by Ammosmith
http://www.youtube.com/watch?v=x0jxpLH8FtYpart 1
http://www.youtube.com/watch?v=9p1Xv6eDFjopart 2

Niall Ferguson's book *Civilization: The West and the Rest* –
Page 91
http://en.wikipedia.org/wiki/Niall_Ferguson

The Lost Battalion – Page 91
http://en.wikipedia.org/wiki/Lost_Battalion_(World_War_I)

Battle of El Bruc – Page 94
http://en.wikipedia.org/wiki/Combat_of_El_Bruch

Chapter 13

Gunpowder from chicken waste – Page 103
http://www.backwoodsmanmag.com/Article%20Index%20files/Article_Title_Search_Nov_2013_3.php?Title=making+black+powder+from+chicken

Chapter 14

Lt. Col. Dave Grossman's book, *On Killing: The Psychological Cost of Learning to Kill in War and Society* –
Page 111
http://www.lwcbooks.com/books/onkilling.html

Sheepdogs - Meet Our Nation's Warriors – Page 111
http://www.killology.com/books.htm

Article, On Sheep, Wolves and Sheepdogs. – Page 111
http://mwkworks.com/onsheepwolvesandsheepdogs.html

Chapter 18

Boer War
Battle of Majuba Hill – Page 151
http://en.wikipedia.org/wiki/Battle_of_Majuba_Hill

Zulu War
Battle of Blood River – Page 153
http://en.wikipedia.org/wiki/Battle_of_Blood_River

Chapter 19

Second Boer Wars – Page 158
http://en.wikipedia.org/wiki/Second_Boer_War

Biltong – Page 158
http://en.wikipedia.org/wiki/Biltong

Rusk – Page 159
http://en.wikipedia.org/wiki/Rusk

Lance Charge – Page 159
http://wiki.mabinogiworld.com/view/Lance_Charge

Chapter 20

Benjamin Trail NP All Weather Break Barrel Air Rifle (.22)
– Page 172
http://www.crosman.com/airguns/rifles/break-barrel/BT9M22SNP

Made in the USA
Lexington, KY
11 September 2014